W.W.W. Spacelink Books . COM.

1. Barnes Nobels
2 Waldon:
3. Amazon Con

Internet

Planet Keepers

Soma Vira

• • • • • • • • • • •

Book 1 . . .
. . . Checkmating Aliens

Also by Dr. Soma Vira...

Little Bit India, Little Bit U.S.A.
 Poetry collection. Vantage Press, New York, 1981

Transparencies Lean On
 Poetry collection. Hartwick Electronic Press, 1994

Earth Trap: Rings Around the World
 Novel. National Publishing House, New Delhi, 1992
 Electronic version. Bibliofile Books on Computer, New Jersey, 1994
 U.S. Edition. Space Link Books

Kuru Trap: The Forbidden Blood (forthcoming)

Twin Trap: Operation Space Sword (forthcoming)

Angel Trails: Double Life
 Space Link Books, New York, 1996

Angel Trails: Electra Undercover
 Space Link Books *(forthcoming)*

Planet Keepers I: Checkmating Aliens
 Space Link Books, 1996

Planet Keepers II: Good Bye Alien God
 Space Link Books, 1996

Planet Keepers III: Nikita's Shadows
 Space Link Books, 1996. Also Hartwick E.P., 1994

Planet Keepers IV: Lord Kito's Revenge
 Space Links Books, 1996. Also Hartwick E.P., 1994
 Originally published in India

Tinni
 Novel. Kitab Mahal, Allahabad, India

Dharati Ki Beti
 Short story collection. Alma Ram & Sons, New Delhi

Parchaiyon Ke Prashn
 Short story collection. National Publishing House, New Delhi

Do Aankhon Vale Chehre
 Short story collection. National Publishing House, New Delhi

Saathi Hath Badhana
 Radio and stage play collection. Alma Ram & Sons, New Delhi

Planet Keepers

Soma Vira

• • • • • • • • • • •

Book 1 . . .
. . . Checkmating Aliens

Space Link Books
77 W. 55th Street
New York, NY 10019

ISBN 0-9646057-1-6

First edition.
Printed in the United States of America.

10 9 8 7 6 5 4 3 2 1

Page Design and Typography, Elizabeth Strauss

Produced and distributed by . . .
BookWorld Services, Inc.
1933 Whitfield Park Loop
Sarasota, FL 34243
. . . *24-hour order lines:* 800/444-2524
. . . *Fax:* 800/777-2525

TO:

Shashi-Ashoka, Janak, and Chitra

sisterspillars of my Earth life.

Our freedom is our sword.
It ensures human being's
most valuable property--our
planet's honor.

. . . Jayarath Rao Agashe,
Chief Executive Editor,
New Space News, Editorial,
December 31, 2199.

. . .

Some Dreams Never Die.
They Become Part Of Our Legend

. . . Admiral Daniel O' Shaughnessy Shostakovich
December 25, 2199.

Contents . . .

. . *Author's Note*

*T*he time is New Year's Eve, 2199, and Earth is getting ready to celebrate with unprecedented gusto. It's also 23 E.D. (the twenty-third anniversary of Earth Unity Day). As the world is about to shut down for the seven-day holiday, the galaxy's most renowned theater-movie star, Bakul, is murdered on the stage during the last performance of the most-successful play in history.

Only the stage manager and the heroine's understudy, Maya, know that the casualty was not Bakul but his understudy. SpacePol hides this fact from public because they suspect an underground group called JALANGA (Join And Laugh At Noah's Great Ark). They don't know that the Caretaker of Jalanga Island, Jal-O, is an alien, from the planet Mandal Loka, nor that he was sent to Earth to reverse the effects of ozone depletion, using LDM, a land development machine.

Lokans don't know that an underground, subversive group has seduced Jal-O to set in motion their clandestine scheme. By the time they learn about it, driven by his own secret ambition, Jal-O has used the LDM to drown critical land area in an attempt force United Earth Council to accept him as Earth's Supreme Ruler.

On this background, plot, and counterplot stand the characters in this suspense-mystery—JR Agashe, Editor, New Space News; his assistants, Sonal and Pavan; the leaders of NOPE (Never One Penny Ever); the NYM (Nameless Monks); the Vishnu Temple priests; and, Ketki, the replacement officer sent by Lokans.

The situation is complicated because Earth's geographic, sociological, and economic patterns are experiencing critical changes. To create additional space, Earth scientists have developed man-made islands. JALANGA has grabbed a monopoly to manufacture them, and is promoting their use for specific purposes, such as rearing surrogate children, and segregating the sick, and the troubled. Marriage is becoming replaced by legal bonding. And administrative units are getting global to service the inter-linked production sectors.

There are seven teenagers, exceptionally gifted, who were hidden on a Surrogate Island when they were babies. SpacePol has information only about two, Pavan and Sonal, because data about the others was lost when the island's director was murdered. They are frantically trying to identify the others.

Pavan, Sonal, and Maya are secretly contacted by life-forms of blue skin and green-gold eyes. They wonder if the visitors are from the Blue Island that emerges from the depths of the ocean when Jal-O launches the LDM. But the strangers are determined not to reveal their identity.

One special child, not known to SpacePol, is Kumiko. Kumiko was fostered by NYM, who have been ordered by her unknown protectors to celebrate her eighteenth birthday on a gigantic scale. This sect is unique, not only because they forecast certain events, but also because they have secretly bio-engineered parrots with computerized minds.

Kumiko's boyfriend, Pushpak, is a direct descendant of an ancient Indian tribe. His grandmother can foresee his future, and wants to change its direction.

These plots and counter-plots need more time and space than one novel can provide. Therefore, the story continues in it sequels.

1

. . . Hunters Ring No Bells

True hope is swift, and flies with swallow's wings;
Kings it makes gods, and meaner creatures kings.
—Shakespeare: *Richard III*

. . .

The great question which, in all ages has disturbed mankind,
and brought on them the greatest part of those mischiefs which
have ruined cities, depopulated countries, and disordered the
peace of the world, has been, not whether there be power in the
world, nor whence it came, but who should have it.
—John Locke: *Treatises on Government, I*, 1690

. . .

Waiting for the com-window to open, Mandal Loka's Earth emissary, Jal-O, was scanning the sky. He had never doubted his destiny. Now, the day that would crown him Earth's first Perpetual Lokani, was rushing towards him. No one would be able to stop it.

Feeling overwhelmed, he flung both his arms towards the waiting sky. "O, Holy Unicorn," he called his guardian roaming on his planet parsecs away. "Is it really happening? Am I really getting a chance? A chance that not one in a million ever gets?" As if in reply, lightening cracked in the Eastern sky.

"What a glorious omen!" Jal-O danced a couple of jitterbug steps of the Unicorn Dance. "Of course, it is happening. The best way to tempt defeat is to doubt yourself," he chided himself. "Look at your living-at-the-mercy-of-elements little schooner. Just look at her. Is she doubting herself?"

As if to prove his point, Star Kahuna bounced, kicked the storm-goaded, midday tide and skidded towards the killer cove with redoubled force.

Howling waves thrashed her hull. Gyrating storm winds hammered against her glistening, dripping, straining body. But, churning the ocean into cushions of foam, furrowing her pre-determined path, she proudly forged ahead. It was as if she knew what her navigator planned for the alien life-forms and their land that surrounded this unbridled, blue ocean; and what part she would play in that Mandal Loka forbidden project.

He glanced at his two-for-twenty-credit suit. Soon! Soon he would be able to discard it and start dressing like the Supreme Lokani of a grateful and affluent planet should.

Wanting to concentrate upon the present, he pushed away his wavering worries. Adjusting his spacescope, he again scanned the distant quadrant of the cloud-shrouded sky. The com-window was still not visible. Unable to focus his thoughts, he sighed and glanced again towards the fast approaching mouth of the cove.

Caught in the fury of the unexpected storm, it was looking like an encircled battleground. Here ferocious, foaming waves, hungry like diabolical Medusan limbs, were leaping and clambering over each other to devour the ancient, unassailable cliffs guarding the cove. When repelled, they rebounded and struck the schooner with redoubled force.

The pungent odor of the weeds, wafting on the swirling winds, smelled like their poisonous breath. He wished he could block his nose. The stench reminded him of the previous night's nightmare—that dark, untamed jungle . . . those menacing, threatening trees marching towards him . . . those mocking, crackling birds. They had popped over his head, drenching him with that foul-smelling filth with such force that he could not breath.

Those curses . . . shrieking voices . . .

He hadn't had that nightmare since he started working on his diary. Thinking he had gotten over it, he actually had forgotten it. Why had it revisited him last night? Why on the eve of his crowning glory when he stood so firmly poised at the threshold of his new career? . . . his new life?

Was it a good omen? Or a bad one?

No, he decided, he should not insult the importance of omens by relating them to that stupid nightmare. His subconscious must have remembered it because he was finishing the last chapter of his novel, and had been thinking about Drupatti.

Thank, Paduka! That's one Lokan who would never bother him now as long as they both lived. Smiling, he rubbed his eyes, stretched, and yawned.

Noticing droplets glinting like tiny diamonds on the hull, he turned and saw sunlight pouring down through the slackening rain.

"Sun-showers!" he softly whispered. A smile lit up his brooding, brown eyes. Patting his schooner's glistening body, he softly murmured, "Kahuna, dear, they say it is a good omen. A second one. One for you, one for me. We'll win. We'll be A-OK."

Picking up his spacescope, he again turned towards the Eastern sky. The mid-day sun broke through the opening aperture. His mind peaceful, he was finally able to focus upon the distant star he had been trying to locate.

A smile flickered in his deep-set eyes. Quickly locking the image of the star in his spacescope, he checked the controls to make sure the engines would stop as soon as Star Kahuna entered the cove. He and turned on the demagnetizing panels to deflect any snooping radar.

Taking a deep breath, he exhaled, flexed his long arms, and with unhurried steps, went down the steep ladder to his spacious cabin. Striding towards his closet, his glance fell upon its full-length mirror. His feet faltered. He stood staring at himself.

The face staring back at him was a very ordinary looking face— pale brown eyes, small nose, ears almost hidden by dull, brownish hair falling on a small, insignificant forehead—a face that did not offer anything noteworthy, nothing remarkable to be easily remembered. A face made to get lost easily even in a small crowd.

With a sigh, he pulled off his trueskin mask. The face in the mirror, staring back at him, suddenly seemed so flawed, so deformed, that he felt like resetting the mask right away.

Dismayed by that strange new feeling, using one doubting

ϡ familiar outlines—wide lips with primrose
ʾoportioned yellow teeth, an enviable nose,
﹍ center of his wide forehead. When opened,
﹍ᴐ a little larger than the other two—a sign of upper
﹍ɪκ. On his home planet, he was considered hauntingly
﹍ᴐome.

"Be honest, you, the first Earth-Lokan titled Jal-O by these
grateful humans," he whispered. "Is this a face Pia Payal would
like to kiss? Smother between her budding breasts. And love?"

The question reminded him of the work waiting to be done.

He turned towards the other door and placed his eyes upon the
three properly placed keyholes. The visionlock whirred and the
panels slid open.

From the top shelf, he picked up his cherished picture cube, and
slid his fingers in the activating grooves. The cube's surface lit up,
depicting images of a captivating young girl—playing tennis;
eating a red apple; dancing in a torch-lit Jasmine grove; sitting
quietly dangling her feet in the waters of a solitary lake as she
contemplated the full moon.

"My dear Pia," he said, touching her cheek with one finger.
"Last night when I could not sleep, I read your favorite poet,
Thomas Moore. You remember, what he sang such a long time
ago:

Tis sweet to think, that, wherever we rove,
we are sure to find something blissful and dear.
When we're far away from the lips we love,
we've but to make love to the lips we are near.

Honey, missing you, I was so overwhelmed I couldn't read any
more."

Fondly rotating the colorful images, he kissed each one
passionately, lingering.

"Moon of My Third Eye, today your image. Tomorrow, you."

Then sighing, placing a noisy kiss on the laughing eyes, he
forced himself to replace the picture cube, and pull out a
spacelink-tripod.

As he punched numbers on the panel hidden inside his closet,
three large screens rolled down on three of his cabin walls. Sliding
back the closet panels, he double-checked the controls and
energized the spacelink. He did not have to wait long. Soon a holo-
image flickered and stabilized over the tripod.

Jal-O wished the transmission was not so clear.

In the life-size holo-image, his commander's third eye, glittering like a diamond in the wide forehead of a face that looked cruelly handsome even in the holographic shadows, glared at him threateningly. "Lokopokito, we have been waiting."

Jal-O placed his right palm on his chest and bowed submissively. "Unexpected weather turbulence, My Lord. The trip took much longer than it should have. But, the report was beamed on time. It should be there soon."

"Screen all faces," the image ordered.

Jal-O hesitated. "We don't have that much time, Lord Kito. Such a lengthy visual report invites risk of detection by Earth radar."

"We still need to worry about detection?" The regal image that disdained crowns, darkly frowned. "Why?"

"No need, My Lord." Jal-O bowed again, and hastily continued, "As noted in the report I beamed, at this time all our markers are safely sequestered at the locations where we fenced them."

He pressed a switch. The central screen lit up with a three-dimensional image. "Our Ringmaster. He wears many hats. He—"

"Why?" Lord Kito interrupted. "Why does he wear many hats? Is that a custom?"

His glittering holo-eyes stared at the image of the young executive dictating to a robo-secretary. Because the human was sitting, Lord Kito found it difficult to estimate his height, but he seemed over six feet tall. As the studied man leaned forward and moved a hand, he seemed to possess the bone structure and muscles of a professional spaceball player. His thick, golden hair seemed sun-bleached. He wore it combed straight back from a wide, high forehead as if he had no time and patience for any fancy nonsense.

He projects, Lord Kito thought, a very strong, almost too-perfect image that one is virtually forced to admire, except for one curious item. A pair of small, round glasses, sporting old wire templates—as unflattering a pair as one could ever imagine—rested on the bridge of his shapely nose.

Had he chosen them deliberately to play down his striking good looks? If he had, the ploy had not succeeded. Under their thick, solid rim, looking at his world with an indifferent, mild irony, he projected an air of quiet confidence and unquestioned authority.

The nameplate facing him was plain. In unassuming letters, it simply said *J. R. AGASHE, CHIEF EXECUTIVE EDITOR*. That bridled simplicity, hiding the power that this being must be wielding on his planet, explained a lot about the human.

Jal-O was amused by Lord Kito's close scrutiny. But he had

learned long ago not to smile in his presence. Keeping his face expressionless, he quickly replied, "I did not mean he really wears them, My Lord. It is a local colloquialism. It means he is the chief honcho, wields a tremendous clout, pulling all kinds of strings, in many hidden roles. A human impossible to isolate.

"But, I succeeded. I have sent his star reporters on out-of-town vacations and his hovercraft to its repair shop. That was necessary. He is very superstitious. Never uses rented vehicles. You see, thanks to maneuvers I learned from you, I have immobilized him like a single-cell prisoner with his hands and feet cut off."

"Good," Lord Kito's eyes lost some of their unpleasantness. His trueskin moved and slipped over his third eye.

Jal-O projected another image. "Daniel O'Shaughnessy Shostakovich, Ex-Admiral, United Earth Navy." The immaculately dressed human, pondering the baroque chessboard, looked very unpretentious.

Sitting at ease, Mr. Shostakovich gave the impression of a sailor who, after crossing many stormy oceans, had achieved port, and was content to sit. He appeared to sit under the sun, doing nothing more than moving a finger now and then—to move a piece forward, to keep playing, his cherished game.

"If he is retired," Lord Kito asked, "why bother about him?"

"Because his official retirement is just a ruse to deceive the press. Behind the scenes, he is still the top Hook And Eye in Intra-Space Intelligence. For the time being, however, I have isolated him on his home island."

"The topmost Executive in Earth-Space Intelligence? Lokopokito, you are dreaming!"

"No, Sire. Just stating facts. At this time, he does not even know his communication lines have been disconnected. The first words he will hear about us will be from our spacecast."

Jal-O was beginning to feel frustrated. If introducing each human was going to take so much time, and so many questions, he would be stuck here for centuries. Could he speed it up by bringing in those humans Lord Kito knew?

"You know Andrey M. Voznesensky, our—"

"Oh, yes," Lord Kito said, smiling. "M. for master-harpist, you said last time. Very appropriate. And that handsome, lanky pole-like human near the tiger's cage? Is that his famous partner?"

"Right," Jal-O nodded, "Milan McMillan. Smashing the known world with their latest movie, *Cobra Keepers,* was not enough for them. They have planned an eye feast for the Award Dinner."

Despite his urgency, knowing the reason for Lord Kito's interest in these two, Jal-O decided to elaborate. "As soon as the dinner is over, they are coming over to our island to launch their new movie, *Kalki*. That, as you know, is based upon your story."

Lord Kito looked pleased. "Everything set up for that?"

"Everything, Your Honor."

Having succeeded in pleasing him, Jal-O felt quite safe moving to another face. "Pavan Ishikawa—only twenty-three, but speaks five languages. An expert mountain climber, sky-diver, and underwater demolition expert, he graduated with honors in Inner-Space Science, Neuro-Physics, and Bio-Engineering. But, obsessed with the idea of proving his father wrong, he is determined to work as an ordinary field reporter who is unnoticed by anyone.

"He has a logical head on his shoulders, and likes to work hard. Only problem with him is, he thinks he knows better than anyone else what kind of work is good for him. When we are ready to utilize him, we will turn this problem to our advantage. We will teach him *what is good for him*."

Without glancing towards Lord Kito's holo, Jal-O flicked on another face. "The Bird-Man. He—"

"What kind of name is that?" Lord Kito exclaimed.

"Oh! I call him that because of that colorful parrot on his shoulder. And, because it is a real chore to keep track of his changing names. He will be very useful to us, when—"

"Enough about him," Lord Kito snapped. "The next?"

Jal-O had an inspiration. He flicked on the image of a teenager, in a trendy swimsuit, sitting on a rickety bridge. The stop-and-go, red and green, bridge lights illuminating her enhanced the concentration on her face as she lit a candle for a paper boat. The previously floated boats swam ahead serenely shadowing the tranquil waters.

"Sonal Neera," he said. "Only nineteen, but—"

"I know all about her!" Lord Kito thundered. "I have told you before. No one must touch her. She must have non-stop, round-the-Earth protection. No costs spared. That's a standing order."

"Yes, My Lord, I remember," Jal-O said smugly. "She will be delivered to you unharmed."

Taking advantage of his guardian's rerouted, disturbed thoughts, Jal-O quickly restated his previous request. "My Lord, with your permission, may I remind you, I am really getting very late. I must reach Jalanga in time. My beamed report contains a detailed briefing. Can we skip the rest?"

"All right. I would just like to view the one you call Valkyrie. By the way, why do you call her that? Has someone important to us given her that name?"

"Oh, I call her that because she is such a homely person, but when she smiles, she looks heavenly."

Jal-O smiled and the screen depicted a young girl tiptoeing upon a taut rope stretching twenty feet above a splintering, cascading waterfall. Her lips seemed to be parted by some song, and her eyes were searching space. Floating there so effortlessly, she did seem like a fragile elf.

Jal-O's voice had acquired an uncharacteristic fondness. "She calls herself Kumiko. Exceptionally gifted, she is fond of Archeology, Astrology, and Space-Geology.

"But, like any seventeen-going-on-eighteen youngster, at the moment all her energies are directed toward boys." Jal-O permitted himself another brief smile. "Or, specifically, toward one—birthnamed, Powhatan. A real maverick."

The screen changed to portray a tall, broad-shouldered, frowning young man. From Jal-O's expression, it was clear this human was also one of his favorites.

"Exceptionally intelligent. Educated in critical areas." Forgetting he was getting late, Jal-O elaborated. "Astronomy, Robotics, Astro-Agronomic, Space-Engineering, etc. Like Pavan, he also does not like any job, no matter how lucrative. But, unlike him, waking and sleeping, he dreams about commanding spaceships. Sailing between stars. I have selected several like him."

"Several?"

"Yes," Jal-O offered brief comments as the images rolled on the screen. "Maya Kiran—Historian, Archeologist, and Robo-Linguist. Her only ambition is to keep on working as an understudy for the current movie-queen, Pia Payal."

His breath faltered. Hoping Lord Kito had not noticed it, he quickly continued. "Pia Payal. A Space-Olympic athlete, champion swimmer, has black belts in four martial arts. She has studied various medical sciences, including neuro-surgery. But, her life's ambition is to keep reigning as a showbiz queen. Shakila Hunter, only nineteen, but—"

"All kids!" Lord Kito protested. "Lokopokito, have you lost your Third Eye!"

"Not kids, Your Lordship. They are the unlit beacons who will rule this planet for you. Products of the *Surrogate Age,* old customs and religions do not mean anything to them.

"Remember the historical notes prepared by our advance team,"

Jal-O reminded him. "They had emphasized one item that in their *Nuclear Age*, these earth-people used to lament, *Old is dying, and the new refuses to be born.* These young ones are their gods' answers to those lamentations."

Lord Kito was dubious. "I don't like it, Lokopokito. Either impetuous kids, or . . . It seems you have forgotten the first item I tried so hard to teach you. *It is not enough to succeed. Others must fail.* The humans you have selected don't appear to be capable of brooking any failure."

"That's the reason we need them," Jal-O insisted. "They will be our most precious weapons. The passionate puppets that with careful molding . . ."

He hesitated, then continued, "You gave me the chance of studying them closely. That's how I know, Your Lordship. These life-forms are not like us. They suffer more by the conflict of contrary passions than by that of passion and reason. You yourself taught me, *The best way to quench one passion is to kindle another.* That's what we will do, Lord Kito." Jal-O added passionately. "That's what we will do."

Lord Kito did not seem convinced. But he realized it was too late. Time was gone for making changes. He shouldn't have trusted his lieutenant blindly. He should have kept an eye on his work.

Feeling terribly frustrated, he decided to close the briefing. "I've just been advised your report has arrived. Before we talk any more on this topic, I want to check it."

"Yes, My Lord." Jal-O obediently bowed.

"And, you will call me as soon as our LDM is torpedoed." It was an order, not a question.

"Of course, My Lord."

"If anything goes wrong . . ."

"Nothing can go wrong, Sire," Jal-O assumed a confident, committed demeanor. "*Nothing will go wrong.* You may not have unfailing faith in your planning, but I do. My Third Eye's Honor, with my own hands I will make you the first Perpetual Lokani of this lovely water planet. On our home planet, none of your opponents will be able to do anything about it."

Jal-O tried to assess the impact of his declaration upon the frustrated looking holo-face. Holy Unicorn! he thought. The dumb Lord! What's wrong with him today? Why is he wasting my time like he never did before?

He had been trying to rush, not because he was urgently needed at Jalanga, but because he desperately wanted to reach the Orpheum before showtime. It would be the last show of *Spider's Stratagem,* this expiring century's longest-running mystery. It was expected that tonight its heroine, Pia Payal, would out-perform herself.

He did not want to miss a micro-second of that life-supporting experience. But he also knew he had to humor Lord Kito. Without Lord Kito's support, Jal-O's tenure on this lovely water planet would be over right away, without notice of any kind. That's why, all this time, he had been pushing himself.

"This is the time more than ever," he told his image every time he stood before a mirror. "You must be patient. You must do anything and everything to humor this slippery snake—the meanest, the most conniving snake, among all the poisonous snakes ever born on any planet."

No matter what kind of speed you may have to force out of Star Kahuna, he reminded himself, *right now, one last time, humor him. The glorious day when you kill him will soon be here. You want to enjoy that precious moment, don't you? Then be patient until the right time comes. Don't rush. Humor him. No matter what it takes. Do it.*

Making up his mind, trying his best to sound most obedient, he continued. "I don't understand why you are worrying so much, Lord Kito! Everything has been done per your specs. And, your planning, as we know, is always perfect. It never misfires."

The frown in the holo-image eyes somewhat softened.

Feeling encouraged, Jal-O added, "I know, Your Honor, you are so modest, it must have never occurred to you. It is only due to the trouble you have taken so kindly, that in the coming century, these lazy humans will get the kind of life-benefits they could have never imagined in all their past centuries. How many officers in your position can spare and devote this kind of time? This kind of affection and compassion?"

Lord Kito smiled. Feeling better, Jal-O added, "You know, Your Lordship, you know what I think?"

"What, Lokopokito?" Lord Kito asked benignly.

"When these people learn what you made possible for them, they'll write poems and plays to honor you. The actors who play your role will sing words like their beloved poet, Shakespeare once wrote. *My bounty is as boundless as the sea, my love as deep; the more I give to thee, the more I have, for both are infinite . . .'*

"Finding the best actors to play your role—they always do that for their charismatic leaders—that's the kind of words they will put in your mouth. That's how they will praise you, Your Lordship."

Lord Kito's image softened. Pride and joy glistened in his velvet eyes. His trueskin moved, and his third eye opened. "You have become quite fond of their art and literature, haven't you?"

"If you experienced it, you would also enjoy it, Lord Kito."

"I would like to believe you," Lord Kito smiled. "This is your first space assignment. I would like to hope you will justify our assumptions about your competence."

"I will not disappoint you, Lord Kito."

"I hope you don't, Lokopokito/Jal-O, for your own sake. Go now. May the winds be with you."

Lord Kito's image flickered and disappeared.

2

. . . On The Edge

The hare, the partridge, and the fox must be preserved first,
in order that they may be killed afterwards.
—John Lubbock (Lord Avebury):
The Pleasures of Life, IX, 1887

.   .   .

"Wilkes," Said Lord Sandwich, "you will die either on the
gallows, or of the pox."
"That," replied Wilkes blandly, "must depend on whether I
embrace your lordship's principles or your mistress."
—Charles Chenevix-Trench: *Portrait of a Patriot*, 1962, ch.3
(H. Brougham: *Statesman of George III*, 3rd series, 1843, p. 189.)

.   .   .

*JR*Agashe's image flickered and disappeared from her visilink.
Sonal Neera hurled the pen she was holding at the blank screen, "If
you are a Victory Wheel, I am Pouring Water. You cannot stop
me. I have cut off your chains. I'll come, but . . ."
Propelled by the steam of her overpowering anger, in one

smooth motion she picked up her purse, reached her balcony, entered her sky-shuttle, and energized it. The screen was still opening when she accelerated through it. She barely missed scratching the top.

Surprisingly, the Express Lane was clear.

Down below, the crowded streets appeared like cris-crossing pageants of magically moving tableaus serenaded by dazzling, torch-garlanded parades. Mingling and parting, each one trying to outshine the others.

The view was so enchanting, she relaxed. A slowly emerging smile lit up her enchanted eyes—but not for long. The memory of her boss, cooped up in his office, again flashed in her mind.

"Don't try to stop me," she threatened a spaceship-shaped balloon crossing her path. "My new life does not begin Tuesday. It begins tonight. Your century-terminating New Year's Eve may still be two days away, but tomorrow being Saturday, my new-century-heralding holiday is already here.

"You want to stay buried in your office? Fine. Count me out. This weekend is mine. Just like it is for all these people.

"Look at them! Just look at them! This Sunday, the dawning rays of our twenty-second century will come crowning the twenty-third birthday of our Earth Unity Day. A twin holiday. It deserves the kind of fireworks that no one ever conceived before!"

Touching a button on her wristwatch, she activated her dicta-diary. "Imagine," she softly recorded. "Imagine a galaxy not many light years away, that has many planets like ours, circling each other, trading and communicating with each other. All of them eagerly watching us.

"These coming nights—our changing Century's skyrocketing nights, when all the parades would come to a halting place; when all the lighted balloons would start floating upwards and upwards towards their waiting skies, imagine their delight. '*Look!*' they would tell each other. 'Such a small planet! Such embryonic, insulated life-forms! How delicate they are! How precious!

"'They survived the holocausts that every kid civilization must face. They did not extinct themselves like so many others. They proved themselves. They are ready to join us. Why don't we take steps to contact them?'"

Saying all that in almost one breath, she stopped. Right away Pavan's handsome face flashed in her excited mind. She could see him listening to the tape, smiling, and saying, "You know, Sonu, with proper training, you could write good fiction."

"It's not fiction, Pavan," she told her absent friend. "And I am not daydreaming. At times, I get these alien thoughts because I feel them in my bones. My ancient bones!"

Visualizing the rapidly gathering frown in his captivating eyes, she smiled, "You are so fond of saying, 'Life Is Just A Pawn On The Chess Board Of Possibilities.' One of these days, I'll prove to you that . . ." Her shuttle's monitor bleeped a signal that she needed to take over the automatics.

She looked ahead and saw she was approaching the roof of Intra-Planet Publishing. She circled once and touched down. At first glance, it felt like she had entered the wrong parking area. Then she realized: It was so empty because the hundreds of sky-shuttles that occupied it day and night, were missing.

Getting out, she noticed one time-dented hovercraft reclining in a corner lot. JR's, she knew—the one that was never used. It was a kind of insurance for emergencies that never dared to materialize. She smiled.

You are really something, Chief, she thought, looking at all the empty garaging spaces. *All* of the candle-burning bosses, always buzzing in this sky-touching beehive, have taken off early today. But, not you!

Well! Soon she would be gone too. A second time. This time, never to come back.

Walking to the down elevator, she felt guilty for feeling so happy. No doubt it had never occurred to JR that she would resign. When she had placed the envelope on his desk, his eyebrows had shot up. Looking bewitching in the absence of those stupid templates he always wore, his hazel eyes had crinkled.

She thought that finally she had succeeded in cracking his armor. That was wrong. Without saying a word, he had picked up those horrid eye-covers he did not need, pushed them over his nose, entombed himself again in his files, waving her away.

True, she had given him only three hour's notice. But, how did that matter? It had not bothered him. He had not protested. Even after he had waved her away, she had stood there a few seconds. He had not looked up at her.

He did not care. That was the simple fact. As simple as any fact can be. The whole world was his worry capsule. He loved to kick around that capsule. He had no time for her. Less care.

So, after lunch, when everyone started leaving, why shouldn't she leave also?

Why had he called her back at this late hour? Because he wanted a farewell visit? Or because now, when the day's work was done, he had time to scold her? To tell her how happy he was she had quit, so that he was spared the trouble of firing her?

Soon, she would find out. Soon.

Smoothing her soft, evening dress, she finger-combed her moon-gold hair that was straying over her forehead. As the skyvator stopped, she quickly stepped out, without waiting for the door to fully slide open, and took a deep breath. Holding her nineteen-year-old, slender body tightly under control, she gracefully strode through the long, empty corridors.

Her rubber-tipped heels did not trip the silence-masking long shadows that kept moving with her, just ahead of her.

What you must remember, Sonal, she fiercely told herself, is not to exhibit even a teeny-weeny emotion. And, do not linger there. Get in. Say good-bye. And, walk out. That's all.

Turning another corner, she saw the gleaming nameplate: *JAYARATH RAO AGASHE. CHIEF EXECUTIVE EDITOR, NEW SPACE NEWS.*

The door was open a crack. She heard a voice. His—angry, like a frustrated hunter's hungry whip-lashing. "How dare you?" the storm-ridden voice was thundering. "What's wrong with your mind-fluids? When was your last bio-check?"

The ground under Sonal's feet trembled.

Waiting, she heard the robot's voice. "Sire, I do not understand! Was my action not logical? At my last bio-check, you had ordered radiesthesic enhancement of my brain circuits. If—"

"Robo-M, you expect me to argue with you!" Behind the menacing door, the deep voice darkly thundered. "Go to your quarters. Stay there until called."

Sonal Neera felt petrified. If someone had told her JR was capable of such sky-rocketing fury, she would have never believed it. What *had* the robot done that was so horrible? This was not a good omen. No! Not at all!

It would be wise to return to her shuttle; spend some time there, reading, or dictating to her diary, then return after some time. After he had time to cool down.

But . . . but suppose that, instead of cooling down, his anger kept mounting . . . and, mounting? And, seeing her, got fueled even more because she was late? Something JR hated more than anything else it was tardiness. Procrastination. No. It would be best to tackle him right now.

Tiptoeing softly, without making any noise, she neared the door and peeked in. Her feet again faltered—she was not at all prepared for what she saw. He sat slumped in his high-back chair, his broad, muscular shoulders sagging under some unseen weight. In his winsome hazel eyes, staring blankly at nothing, lurked a strange kind of weariness that she had never seen there before.

She felt as if her breath would stop.

This tiger of United Earth's most influential Daily thrived on disasters. The tougher the problem, the more it excited him. The more lethal the challenge, the more it motivated and electrified him.

What had happened today? What had his Robo-Major done that had snatched the living breath out of his body?

Or, was it something that had nothing to do with Robo-M? Was he getting rid of some other frustration, some other problem, cutting someone conveniently available?

Was it her turn next?

You dumb Funnybones! Sonal breathed hard and chided herself. What's wrong with you? Remember? You have resigned. Nothing that he does concerns you any more. Whatever happened here, it is not your problem. As you had decided, don't pay any attention to anything. Be firm and decisive. Move. Just put one foot forward, then another, and another. And, move. Move!

She knocked, and entered.

Jolted out of his concentration, JR glanced in her direction with blank eyes, but his expression changed quickly. He smiled and switched off the data screen. Steeling herself, she walked in with a firm step.

"Chief," she said tersely, "I'm sorry, I left before you read my note." No remorse lurked in her cool voice. She added, "I should not have, especially today."

"No need to apologize, R-Seven. Today is just another day for an old tugboat like me." He smiled again, and some of his salty humor crept back in his nutcracker eyes. "Have a seat." He waved towards a chair. "We've got to do some urgent planning."

"*We?*" The ground under Sonal's feet started to jelly again. Had he forgotten that she had resigned? How could he? In the envelope she had given him, she had also enclosed her nameplate, and ID. Wasn't that an absolute act? Total and undeniably final?

Her fists tightened. He had no right to deny her request. If he had any thoughts of being difficult, she would have to put her foot down. She would not allow him to destroy the new dawn of her life. A life that she had finally found the courage to unchain. No way. Preparing herself for any and all arguments, she moved towards a high stool and stood against it, barely touching its edge.

JR realized what he was up against.

She was going to be more difficult than he had anticipated. To give them time, he turned towards his overflowing table and started to look for something.

"Have some coffee," he suggested. "It's hot."

No. She did not want any coffee. Hot or cold. She urgently wanted to get back to her land-condo and finish the work she was trying to complete before going out for dinner.

She had taken a tough job. The only way tomorrow's lunch interview would succeed, would be if her guest did not suspect it was an interview. She still had to write most of the questions.

But without saying anything, JR was leisurely sifting through his piles of papers. She was silently fuming. Why was he wasting their time? Why couldn't he just say whatever it was he had to say and get done with it? What was the matter today with him anyway? He was never short for words.

He is getting old. That's why he is dithering, she decided. If she did not try to rush him, Earth knows how long she would be stuck in his galactic-map-beleaguered-office.

But he should not be able to decipher her strategy. If he did, he might delay her more, just because he was in such a bad mood. The way to do it would be, to be nice to him. Yes. Very nice.

"Chief?" She perched on the stool and crossed her legs. "Who is going to replace me?"

"Replace you?" he stared at her. "No one can replace you, R-Seven. How can you say something like *that!*"

"That you say to everyone," she smiled. "Pavan told me why."

"Why?"

"Same old tactics, Chief!" She waved an accusing finger. "Answering by asking questions? Today, it won't work."

"Fine," he nodded agreeably. "Answers you want? Answers I got. I have cooked up an exciting assignment for you."

"Nope. Not possible," she shook her head, and her hair fell over her eyes. Impatiently jerking it away, she asserted, "You know the reason. No more work for me. I quit. Resigned."

"Yes, that you have." He leaned back in his chair and fiddled with his ridiculous glasses. "As of this week. But you know, I run a seven-day week."

So he had accepted. He *would* let her go. The air suddenly seemed lighter, easier to breath. Sonal smiled.

"OK," she said amiably. "You got me for one more day. Sunday I get off like everyone else."

He opened his cabinet and started taking out a file. A small, time-yellowed sheet of paper fell from it, fluttering down. Quickly leaning forward, he caught it. "What do you know!" he exclaimed. "I didn't know I still had it!"

"What is it?"

JR glanced at her with pride. He had been right. She was a born journalist. Always curious about everything. With time and experience . . .

"A poem," he said. "My favorite. Would you like to hear it?"

Sonal looked at him, not so much with frustration as with resignation. Thirty-three and single and, he lived alone. Perhaps, the prospect of going home to a lonely land-condo was not very appealing. Especially when everyone else was out celebrating.

She remembered what Maya Kiran always said, "A cheerful face always helps." What works for lost-soul-Maya, should work for her. She smiled. "If it's your favorite, sure."

"Well, I got no voice. Not even a bathroom singer's, but I'll try." He leaned back in his chair, adjusted those preposterous, template eye-covers, and cleared his throat.

At his theatrics, this time she really smiled.

He gave her an enigmatic, brief glance. Then his clear voice rang out softly:

No. A dream it was not
When the Eagle came down to me
With words that weep,
An' tears that speak,
Hanging from his beak,
"Of all the pains the greatest pain
Is to love, but love in vain.
Time is near. Winds are here.
Come, fly with me."
"O! Time-Blasted Knight!
The day Sun shines upon me
Without you, would be the last."
Holding the Sunflower tight,
Standing against the Wind,
I whispered your name.

"NO!" She sprang towards him as if to snatch the paper from his hand. Midway she controlled herself, turned, and walked to the nearest window.

JR had expected surprise. Indignation. But not such a violent, painful reaction.

Since she had left her resignation on his desk, he had been thinking about it. After debating, weighing the various pros and cons, he had planned very carefully. In fact, every single word that he wanted to use, he had rehearsed several times.

If it had occurred to him this approach would hurt her, cause her so much pain, he would have tried some other strategy. Now, it was too late.

He looked at her rigid back. She was standing motionless, staring out at some unseen object, visible only to her dry, smarting eyes.

Jayarath Rao Agashe, renowned psychologist, Chief Executive Editor of the only inter-space daily, the person who so often, in fun, affection and awe, was called *Custodian Of Danger Signals*, sat there feeling helpless.

He wanted to get up, go near her, turn her around, and take her in his arms. But her unmoving hands, hanging deathly pale at her sides, forbade any such endeavor. He sat glued to his chair, looking at her lonely shoulders, silently scolding himself.

You cannot touch this silence, he sternly told himself—this silence that was not born just now. This silence that she has been building inside herself for such a long time.

She would have to unseal it, unlock it, herself.

Does she have the needed courage? Or would she simply walk away like a wounded lioness, to encase herself within her solitary cavern to build more walls?

Finally, her hands turned into fists. She turned, "How did you get it?" Her voice sounded tiny and neutral. The words were softly spoken, as if the pain had gone. But the ominous fists, tightly locked, spoke a different story.

And he knew, if he was not very careful, he might lose her again—this time, perhaps for ever.

"It was given to me." Groping for proper words, he said tentatively. "A very long time ago. By its author."

"Funny! Funny!" Anger burned bright in her darkly accusing eyes. "Who gave it to you? When? Where? You must tell me the truth."

"Have you ever known me to lie?" JR asked soothingly and waited. Getting no reply, he moved and stood close to her. "Okay, the truth." He tried to choose his words very carefully. "In my college days, to earn my tuition, I used to teach."

He paused for some kind of reaction. Apparently, the words had not meant anything to her. She was staring at him mutely, with ice-cold, stony eyes.

"She was one of my students," he said softly. Then added as an afterthought, "At that age, one daydreams."

Sonal could not contain herself any longer. "Why on Earth are you making up such a ridiculous story? Why can't you tell me the truth?" she shouted. "What are you so much afraid of, that you want to hide it so badly?"

He thought about it. About the difficulties involved in the answer that would satisfy her. How good he would feel, if he could tell her everything.

But he was not authorized to break the rules concerning the SpacePol cover-up. What he had so emotionally started, he would have to somehow finish without making a total fool of himself.

He came to a decision. "Would it be easier for you to accept it if I told you I was one of those who wear a teacher's mask?"

"Teacher's mask?" Sonal Neera fearfully echoed. Her flushed cheeks turned pale and her voice fluttered like a frightened child's—like a frightened child who was lost and horribly alone. "You think you can fool me? There is no such thing."

That whispered, frightened voice touched JR like a sharp arrow. Concerned, he thought she was regressing! He could not let this happen. He must bring her back to the adult world.

At this point, nothing but truth, the whole truth would do. He must tell her the truth regardless of his orders. Regardless of the unpredictable consequences.

But the truth was not his to reveal. He was duty-bound. Oath-bound. Therefore, all he could say was, "You never worked as a teacher. How would you know?"

She bristled, "I'm not that ignorant. I know. Actors are allowed masks. . . . and those who are disfigured . . . No one else."

"You forgot the third group. Those who can prove their need."

"So?"

Partial truth, he thought, that's the answer.

Modulating his expression to match his incredulous voice, he challenged her. "Do you expect teachers to advertise the fact that they fear facing the students?"

"Afraid of facing students!" she echoed. But, her mind was jolted. Sudden curiosity shadowed and overpowered her pain and anger. She could deal later with those feelings. This sounded fantastic. An item worth a terrific story. "Why?"

JR noticed the change and felt better. "Do I have to spell it out?"

He spoke in the same challenging tone. "What is one to do if one is scared of hulking bodies double the size of his own?"

Sonal glanced at JR's tall, lithe, athletic body and tried to imagine someone double his size. At the giant image that flashed across her mind, a smile tugged at her lips. "Shooting the bull, Chief? Or, testing my gray matter?"

"Neither, R-Seven." He moved back towards his desk. "You remember what Pavan is so fond of proclaiming—'*We are less convinced by what we hear, than by what we see. Thus spoke Herodotus, 430 B.C.*'"

Making himself comfortable in his tilting chair, he stretched his long legs under his desk, leaned back, and stared at the ceiling. "Who can cook up stories like that! At least, not anyone like me, who always needs someone else to write them for him."

Sonal Neera studied him silently.

Was he aware of her scrutiny? She could not decide. Very quietly, as if not even breathing, he just sat there, reclining, communing with the ceiling.

She wondered—was he telling the truth? Once upon a time, was he really her teacher? He did not seem at all like the person with whom she was so passionately in love—in whose august presence she used to feel tongue-tied, speechless, overwhelmed. For whom had she written and torn so many poems?

How long ago that was! How hard she had tried to blank out those memories! Those unforgettable days! She thought she had succeeded.

He really used to wear a mask? Was that the reason she had failed to recognize him when she joined the New Space News?

That was almost ten months ago. Why had he never said anything? Never given any indication of any kind ever before?

Why, now?

She moved to a chair. Tossing her truant hair into place, she gripped its high back with both her hands. "If I ask you," she inquired in a cool, emotionless voice, "would you return my childish limerick?"

Pulling in both his feet, he sat up, leaned towards her, and matched her tone. "That depends. . . ."

"On what?"

He got up and stood against the desk facing her, "You know me, R-Seven. I don't believe in handouts. You know my rules."

He paused. When she did not say anything, he continued, "If you wish, we can exchange it. Fair terms, I assure you."

Her immediate instinct was not to trust him in this matter. But remembering his past behavior, she silently chided herself: He has always treated you honorably, you dumbbell! Did he *ever* ask you to do anything that you could not accomplish? that was repugnant? No. Never. That's not his style. For him 'Fair Terms' are not just words. As Pavan says, "Trust is a two-sided sword." When you answer, *remember that.*

"Exchange is OK," she replied softly, "if it's equitable." Despite her bubbling misgivings, she wanted to believe in her words. Looking him straight in the eyes, she asked, "What's on your mind?"

"Your resignation. You allow me to tear it up, and," he held out his hand holding her poem, "this is yours."

She made no move to accept it.

Instead, she sidestepped. Carefully gathering herself together, she sat down in that chair that had been waiting for her for such a long time. "Sir, you know why I want to leave." It was not a question. Simply a statement.

JR looked at her. *You mean, the official reason?* he wanted to say. *But, I know the real reason. That is not a good reason. Besides, if I let you go, old Danny O' would eat me alive.* But, of course, he could not tell her that.

He simply nodded. "Yes. I know."

The look of relief in her tear-bright eyes made him feel better—he had chosen the right answer.

"Okay," he cheerfully offered. "We will compromise. You accept today's assignment. Do your best. When it's done, you can leave." He smiled, "Without saying good-bye."

At this unjust accusation, she bristled with anger. "You are the one who didn't say good-bye. Just waved me away."

"Me?" he looked genuinely surprised. "I did no such thing. You pushed an envelope on my desk. I inquired what it was. You left without—"

"You did not say anything."

"Oh, yes I did. Sure, I did. And you left without—"

"Aw! Come on! Are you going to hold that against me forever?"

"R-Seven, *forever* is *the* time unit that scares me most." He smiled and moved to his chair. "Come. It's getting late. Let's get to work." He touched a panel on his chair's arm. The screen facing them sprang to life.

"What you are about to see," he nodded towards the screen, "was videotaped just before I called you. The last performance of Spider's Stratagem."

She nodded. "At the Orpheum."

"Have you seen the play?"

Pia's face on he screen had reminded Sonal of the lunch-interview she was planning for her. Because her mind had strayed, she did not recognize his deceptively casual voice.

"Is there any living soul who hasn't?" she asked wryly.

"With your family?"

Again *that* voice that she was too distracted to notice. "I was born on a Surrogate Island," she quietly replied.

He flinched at the answer. Such a short statement! So mechanically spoken! But it was the only one that could so effectively torpedo the other questions he had planned.

Obviously, she had said it many times before.

How many times? To how many people? What kind of people? Every time it was spoken, how much did it hurt? Or, had it turned into a numbing needle, pushing on and on, into a dead nerve?

On the screen, the camera was panning towards the audience. It paused on a familiar face—Pavan Ishikawa. Intra-planet's most ubiquitous, most sought after, star reporter. The one whom someone had jokingly nicknamed, *Time-Hawk.*

Sonal Neera kept her eyes glued to the screen, her facial muscles under tight control. But the doubts and suspicions she had been trying to suppress refused to remain holed in any more. Reviewing his searching questions, belatedly recognizing his deceptively *casual* tone, they fanned out like the flame throwing tongues of a multi-headed cobra, flinging out burning probes with every new flame. Why had JR revealed his secret identity when he did not have to?

If he really was who he claimed to be, he knew she had no relatives. Why had he asked her about her *family*? Why did he use such a roundabout way to postpone her resignation? Why was he using a new tactic to waste more time? Instead of telling her what he wanted her to do, why was he forcing her to watch this video?

This afternoon, Pavan and Nicole were going to Pavan's island. What was he doing in the Orpheum? If he was there to enjoy the last performance, why was he alone? Why was Nicole not with him?

Did JR's forcing this video on her have something to do with Pavan's presence in the theater? Did he know—or suspect—about her and Pavan? If he did, how did he find out? He could not have—should not have. Because, except for her and Pavan, no one knew that time-locked secret.

At least, that's what Pavan had claimed.

Had she made a mistake? Should she have not trusted Pavan?

Pavan Ishikawa? A real charmer. So mature and dignified for his twenty-three years on Earth! How many girls swooned just thinking about his almond-eyed, oval face! As if oblivious of them, the New Space News star trainee moved around, poker-faced, as if he were the only one of his kind on this whole United Earth.

What Pavan confided in her, was that true? Or, was it simply an on-the-spot story, made-up, recited convincingly, at his demanding boss's behest? Was that how JR knew about it?

The thought was so horrifying, she shivered. What was the truth? What were the facts? Whom could she ask? She felt numb. The world was again turning into a place where there was no one she dared to trust. No one she could trust.

As if in reply, on JR's breathless screen, Pavan's waiting face wavered like a ghostly obelisk.

***

Pavan Ishikawa, Intra Planet's reluctant trainee, was occupying the best seat in the Orpheum—front row center. Anyone else in his place would have thanked his lucky stars. Without asking for it, he had been given the truly unparalleled assignment of this soon-to-be-gone-century—psychographing the last performance of *Spider's Stratagem,* the most beloved play in any living person's memory. The play that had won every possible award, in every possible category—the best hero, best heroine, best villain, best music, best story, best stage direction . . .

But Pavan was feeling sacrificed and unwanted. Blaming it all on his demanding boss, the never-sleeping Jayarath Rao Agashe. Pavan could have named scores of splendid reasons why JR should have given this job to someone else. He had wanted to remind JR he was merely a trainee; merely a field reporter. He was getting training for field work—not for reviewing a-million-times-reviewed space opera. But one did not remind JR about such mundane items.

He could have explained to his all-rounder boss that, for one reason or another, he had seen this play too many times, had heard too many opinions about it. Therefore, he was not at all qualified to do what he was ordered to do. To video-in an unbiased, late evening review, if he tried greasing his wheels, he'd merely be wasting valuable column space, but, he did not. He could not.

Caught in the deep, dark throes of his irritation, looking all around except towards the stage, questioning the wisdom of powers that be, he was silently fuming: *Why me? Great gods of sport, Jupiter, Indra, why me? Why have you allowed everyone to escape, and left me trapped in this stupid job?*

To make the matters worse, as if to annoy him purposely, someone behind him had been endlessly sneezing. In his present frame of mind, every sneeze was touching him like a touch of pepper on a bleeding cut. Someone with such a bad cold had no right to admit herself to a public place. She must have seen the play scores of times. If she could not see it one last time, so what!

In fact, the theater was not as full as it should have been. Last night or not, all those theater lovers who spent all their leisure time in this hall had other plans tonight. Only he was stuck here, because he was the only one JR could reel in. The others, by one means or another, had escaped his unrelenting hook.

Shakeela Hunter, for example, she had reservations on the Moon Shuttle. Anwar Costa? His family was hosting a Grand Reunion of its four hundred sixty-nine members. No way he could miss it. Oscar Delarente? He was the trickiest of them all. . . .

Before he could curse Oscar, an ear-shattering sneeze again pierced his dark reverie. Perhaps she is not even using a clean hanky. He made a supreme effort not to turn and glare at her.

She won't leave, and he had a job to do. *So do it, buddy. Brooding won't make it disappear. You better get on with it.* Chiding himself, he decided to concentrate, and glanced towards the stage.

He had spent so much time hammering away at his anger that the Second Act was already waltzing away towards its finishing line. The glittering Neptunian Grand Nomarch and his Earth-born heart-throb were taking the last twirls of their ring-ceremony dance. Having seen the play more than once, everyone was waiting with hushed breath for the villain "They Loved To Hate" to enter, and do the cabalistic deed he was going to enact on the stage.

The Grand Nomarch moved to pick up the ring from a floating gift basket. A fanged, masked intruder, shouting something in a hoarse, unintelligible voice, leaped on the stage. Clearly, the hero and heroine were not expecting *him*. Before they noticed him, the fiendish villain pulled a Neptunian roborang from his waistband, and threw it at the hero's chest. Once. Twice. Thrice.

From the gift basket, a feathered serpent launched itself towards the killer's throat. But, no one saw the villain, clutching his throat, falling down and thrashing upon the floor. All the eyes were riveted upon the Nomarch, who had fallen upon his would-be-bride's feet. His blood, flowing upon her bridal gown, trickling on the floor.

"How can you die? What happened to your spider's web?" behind Pavan, the sneezer angrily shouted. Her shrill voice echoed in the stunned hall.

As if not comprehending what had happened, the bride stood staring down like an unfinished marble statue. The Nomarch moaned and tried to reach for her hand. As if waking up from a bad dream, she quickly kneeled to hold his head in her trembling hands.

There was not a single sound in the hall. Not believing the scene before their eyes, the petrified, speechless, audience sat gripping their seats' armrests.

Then someone whispered, "How realistic!"

The spell was broken. Suddenly everyone was talking. Pavan's neighbor grinned and shouted, "Bravo! Better. Much, much better." He started clapping.

But he was the only one applauding. Others, talking to anyone who would listen, sounded worried and frightened. Look! It looks like real blood! . . . They changed the script! . . . For the last show? . . . Why! You think it's not closing? . . .

People in the back rows started moving. Pushing. Behind him, the sneezer was shouting, *"Excuse me! Excuse me!"*

But, his eyes looking glazed, Pavan sat glued to his seat.

Another loud sneeze, just next to him, shattered his stupor. Hastily getting up, ignoring the chaos, he started to struggle through the milling crowd towards the stage. Before he could reach it, the curtain crashed.

That made him fully aware of the problem. Forgetting decorum, he got out of the hall and ran towards the back entrance that proudly proclaimed *STARS ONLY*.

Not wasting any time, he took out his press card and offered it to the tall, fat uniform blocking the narrow door, "New Space News. I need to get in there fast!"

The guard simply looked past him—as if Pavan had not spoken. As if he did not exist.

Pavan felt inadequate. Baffled. What does a Crime Reporter say to the Guardian-Of-The-Door?

"Please, Sir," he politely insisted. "Like you, I got a job to do. You know that. Please, let me pass."

The dark statue came to life and growled. "Just an accident. Been taken care of. No reporters allowed. Get back to your seat."

Just then, rotating its red light, an air-ambulance touched down, and close behind it, two Peace Guard hovercrafts. Other Orpheum guards had also moved in. They blocked Pavan's path, "Move. Go back to your seat. Move. Move . . ."

Realizing they wouldn't let him get in, Pavan ran towards his shuttle. He must immediately call JR . . . Also, call Nicole. Tell her he might be late.

Oh Indra! Oh, Rudra! As Nicole's image crowded his mind, his breath almost stopped. He had promised her he would be at her place, at the latest by six.

Flicking his wrist, he glanced at his watch. Would he be able to make it? If he could not, she would not speak with him for the rest of his life.

As he moved faster toward the parking lot, his veins throbbed. Not from the pressure of running; he was a mountain climber and a champion runner. The mere thought of generating anger in her dark, lightning-generating eyes, panicked him.

If JR would want him to cover the hospital, or do something else on this case—if he would not release him right away—it would be impossible to explain to Nicole that her island vacation would have to be delayed—perhaps even canceled.

She had been looking forward to it. She had been planning it for months. Had mentioned it to all her friends. She would not like it. No, not at all.

Oh, Jupiter! Oh, Rudra!

Thoroughly nonplused, reaching his shuttle, Pavan quickly punched it open. Placing one foot inside, he punched in JR's office number.

She will never speak to you again, his mind warned him, as her image, waiting for him at the Sangam Lake, standing on their new yacht dressed in her new navigator suit, shadowed his mind.

3

. . . OPERATION:
Loser Take All

Who asks whether bravery or cunning beat the enemy?
—Virgil: *Aeneid, II,* 19 B.C.

. . .

The object of a good general is not to fight, but to win. He has fought enough, if he gains a victory.
—The Duke of Alva: c. 1560

. . .

People crushed by law have no hopes but from power. If laws are their enemies, they will be enemies to laws; and those, who have much to hope and nothing to lose, will always be dangerous. . . .
—Edmund Burke: *Letter to the Hon. CJ Fox,* 8 October 1777

. . .

Shadows of his Brynhild Boat seemed today dark and menacing choking the sleeping lake. Leaning over the railing, staring into dark waters, the Lokan Space Guardian was brooding, *Why did he name it* Star Kahuna*?* He shivered.

It was not cold. No one was around. The jungle birds, mynas, macaws, and parakeets, that flew over the lake playing with swans and ducklings, were still sleeping hidden inside their secret nests.

This was his favorite time. A few flying backstrokes in the cool waters, followed by jogging on the beach or exploring in the woods surrounded by the subtle scent of Kasturi blossoms, gave him energy for the whole day.

Today, however, he did not feel like leaving his boat. His whole body huddled inside his dark brown cloak, he was asking the shadows, "I'm not a politician. But, they have given me the job of running the wheels of this undeclared war. If I refuse, if I don't, would the galaxy bend to its knees and Star Kahuna win? Would the known space again become a play-field for . . ."

His watch-link bleeped. He answered it quickly. "Yes?"

"Mano Bali, my Neha is ready for you."

"Your baby unicorn? Bring her."

He had been waiting and time for waiting was now over. Action now will have to be taken. And the fate of a galaxy would depend upon what he would or would not do. He was ready.

Pressing the coordinates on his transwatch, he materialized at the edge of Unicorn Prairie. A small figure, robed like he was, in a loose brown robe, was waiting for him. She handed him the package labeled, *Jal-O/Lokopokito's Secret Diary.*

Unwrapping it, he said, "Seems OK. Call me tonight."

Nodding, Neha's owner stood near her unicorn, touched her trans-watch, and they disappeared in a glitter of tiny sparks.

Not paying them any attention, the Guardian strode towards his lab. Locking the door from inside, he moved to his chair, inserted the disk in his scanner, and switched on the reading light.

The manuscript was bulky, five hundred pages. Right now I need to scan only that portion, he thought, the part when they took that Planet Breeder's eligibility test. Flicking the scanner, he found the pages that might reveal their truant officer's sealed aptitudes.

> . . . kneeling down, ignoring her knees getting bruised by the sharp pebbles, she peeked through the prickly shrubbery. Feeling curious, he parted the bushes above her head and glimpsed down below two black uniforms sneaking upon two seven-year olds playing hide-and-seek in the hazardous, dark shadows of the dappled ravine.

He assessed the situation. The kids should not have been there. But they were, and it was his job to protect them. But shooting at the Blackguards from high up here would be useless. If he tried a rear assault—due to the thick foliage and the terrific traps these devil-may-care-chilikos must have sneaked in their plans—his strategy would not work. In fact, it might backfire. If they spotted him, they would kill him.

Quickly pulling wide leafs over the hole he pulled her hand and commanded in his I'll-stand-no-nonsense tone, "Don't expose yourself! If they see us . . ."

Struggling to get free, she mocked, "If you don't want to be seen, why don't you join the Owl Patrol?"

The undeserved insult stung him. He stared at her haughtily. "You think you are very observant? Okay, soon we will find out a lot about you, Miss Snooty-Mind."

The image projected in his mind by that thought was so amusing, it improved his mood right away. So, ignoring the insult, sounding like the pragmatist that he was, he decided to start her training.

"You need to learn the basics. First, we need to concoct a weapon that the others do not have."

"Why?"

"Because we must win. You chose me. I take it that means you do not want to be trained for menial work—seeding minerals, germinating life elements— stuff like that. We are protectors. We have to prove our superiority. A secret weapon will give us the required leverage. If you want to win, that's what we need."

Her large, expressive eyes knew how to make one feel small.

"You did not let me complete. What I meant was—"

"Stop it!" he cut her sharply. *Tria!* he thought. Saying something, meaning something else. Who can wrestle with that!

"Listen, if we had our hunting gear, we could have made roborangs. Since we do not, what do we have that we can use?"

"That's how you're going to win?" she hissed. "Breaking rules? If you *are* such an expert, how is it you do not know we are not allowed to invent any weapon?"

How dared she question his decision!

He stared at her angrily and was struck by her unorthodox beauty. Or, was it the effect of sunlight knifing through thick leaves, trying to hold on to her flushed cheeks, tiny nose, and kissable lips!

Ignoring his calibrating eyes she quietly added, "Remember, Commander? It's a test. Those of us who are selected will be facing the same hazards on that new, uncharted planet. The question is, given the same tools, who will do a better job?"

He felt amused. Now naive! Trying to down-score him using logic? . . . Logic? Suddenly a brilliant idea throbbed his mind. Would logic break down her insubordination?

"Listen," he said soothingly. "I was only testing you. Wanted to see if you can figure it out by yourself. We already have a fantastic weapon. One that no one can match. You know what it is? . . . It is our brain, junior. Brimming with our fate-endowed intelligence. They cannot stop us from using it. Can they?"

He tried to look into her eyes to assess her, as he would have one of his dull-witted students. What were her hopes? Fears? Compulsions? Was she ambitious? If she was not . . .

But she had turned and was moving away.

If she is going to act like a spoiled brat, he thought, how are we going to work together? And, his mind rebelled, wasn't this the most stupid way of composing a team? Launch together two strangers and expect them to work like one body? One mind?

Was everyone paired with a rookie, he wondered. No. That was impossible. Then why was he burdened with this novice? An upstart who wasn't merely immature and inexperienced, but who also had no desire of showing any respect for her senior officer and wanted to fight every spoken word!

Fighting his anger he glanced at her. She was testing the ground to determine how to tackle the shrouded, treacherous slope. That voluntary, unordered, activity lifted some of his anxiety.

Was he expecting too much from her? he wondered. Was she capable of taking initiative and sharing her commander's burdens? She certainly seemed like one who did not mind menial work.

"Improper behavior? Should he worry about it? Could she have learned navy protocol without being taught? Certainly not. If that were true, that ungrateful Drapatti would have been his deputy in all his work.

No. When thrown together on a treacherous planet, a commander should be able to elicit obedience. Training her, he should remember that their relationship was a tie between a commander and a novice. It was a coupling. A bonding that, once properly forged, could last forever, should last forever.

This cool meditation sprayed ice on his feverish thoughts. But deep inside, he was still feeling insecure. Nagging doubts were still resurfacing, probing, and knocking. What if she was not capable of learning? What if she wouldn't bow down?

Why won't she? His logical self argued. Remember, she knows she has inherent problems. First, she is a plebeian and totally unskilled. Secondly, no matter how hateful it must be to her, she must accept orders from a tough, demanding officer.

I had applied, he remembered, because as the galaxy turned, I was never able to forget where my destiny ultimately lies. But how many Lokans like me, working blindly, morosely, in mundane, sedate jobs, may have applied? Perhaps none. One gets used to comforts, to lethargy induced by meaningless daily routines. Chances are, among all the applicants, there was not even one like me they could have paired with me.

Let's face it. All of the volunteers scattered in this mock jungle are recent graduates. All of them are the cream of potential space cadre. Mediocrity has no room or place here. That is not all. To enter the test, passing the qualifying exam was not enough. Sponsorship by a ranking member of the Space Navy was mandatory.

Although no one would admit it, everyone laboring here would be trying to achieve the highest possible grades, not for promoting their own career, but for crowning the officers who stuck out their necks to sponsor them.

I did not know anyone. I wonder who sponsored me. On the shoulders of our uniforms, this blue badge says, *Commander Drupad.* Did he sponsor me *and* my snooty partner?

Why? Because she knew him? Because they needed a teammate for her? Does she know? If I ask her, would she tell me? Considering the question, he decided against it. If she refused to answer, that would be a space-scalding insult. Why should he risk that to find the identity of the sponsor who did not care to call, did not care to say two words of encouragement? Why think of someone who left him to fend for himself, win or lose on the basis of his own intellect?

Yes. In this test he was his own master. He could decide what was best for him. He did not need to be reckless and jeopardize his chances. If he framed his own strategy, he would win. He would be selected commander of the new volunteers.

The logic pleased him. Whatever I do, he computed, it will not be for the owner of my blue badge, that hoax-foxy Drupad. Not for the safety and better-score-ranking of my snooty mate, Miss Mocking Eyes. It will be strictly for my personal glory.

Pleased by this logical and rational strategy, he looked for her. Pruning shrubs with her hunting knife, she was cutting a narrow path to go down to the treacherous ravine. Crouching amidst all those bushes she had murdered, she looked up as he neared. Her shaded eyes seemed inscrutable.

"What's worrying you, Lokopokito?"

"You got no eyes?" he thundered. "Do I look like an officer who worries?"

"It's just a simple test, Commander," she mocked. "I've heard the impromptu battles are lots of fun. And if those zinging dye bullets touch your lips they taste delicious. No one gets hurt. You won't get hurt either. As long as you don't fall over a carnivorous plant . . ."

"Stop it!" he barked. "You are my responsibility. I

must plan to make sure you do not get hurt. And if you must know, the idea that I might get killed did not even enter my mind. I was analyzing their blind bungling. They want to select the best ones to conquer that wild planetoid. But—"

"Bravo!" she cheered. "You got it! So? Instead of brooding why don't you get going? Prove to them what you can do?"

"But," ignoring her juvenile flippancy, he continued, "But blinded by their glorious nobility, they did not do it right! They failed to weigh crucial factors."

"'What?"

"You could not figure it out?" He looked triumphant. "I thought so. Listen, they failed to compensate for unequal skills. Different aptitudes require different tools. The weapons they gave us do not equalize the basic handicaps. Their stupid bungling has created unfair odds. Very unfair. Very unbalanced."

"Really!" Her arching eyebrows puckered with surprise. 'Would they be balanced there, Commander, on that wild planet that is waiting for us? No one knows what hazards that place is hiding for us. But we cannot carry unlimited supplies. That's why," she shook a finger at him, "All of us have the same tools and supplies. Using them, we need to prove our talent for tipping the odds in our favor. That's what the testing is all about."

"No, it's not!" he thundered. "That's a stupid theory. You know why? Because all of us thrown here blindly have different skills. You know who is here? Walking encyclopedias—technomads in fields like hydro-geology, transmutative engineering, alien biology, and metagalactic speleology. Gold-winners in protected fields like Inter-species diplomacy, secret military tactics. It is unrealistic to expect candidates with such diverse education to have comparable skills. They should have—"

"You want to teach them their job!" she scorned. "Brooding about skills, did you consider who they really are? Those who love a challenge and are not afraid of venturing into the unknown. This is one test which laughs at pretenses, at all the pre-planning."

Folding her knife, she stood up and glared at him. When he did not try to trounce her, as he had been consistently doing, she added, "Since you have your thinking cap on, can you guess why?

"I'll tell you why. It's because all of the pre-planned strategies can turn totally useless there. On a raw planet, one survives by dealing death blows to each obstacle as it strikes. That's why they select only those who love to deal with the unexpected."

He stood speechless, rooted at his spot.

Feeling furious, she asked, "Weighing your odds, did you load up team work? Do you know partners have to depend upon each other? Protect each other. Selection, therefore, also depends upon how well we work together, and what tactics we use to maximize our combined talents."

The Guardian leaned back, and rubbed his eyes. Was this a diary or an effort to write a story?

If made from pickings of his experience, Jal-O had fictionalized it, the time and effort spent to bring this diary here was a total waste. On the other hand, if he had portrayed himself honestly, it might uncover some weakness that could be used to decide what should be done to salvage the Earth Shield Operation.

The Guardian glanced at his watch, tried to find a more comfortable position in his chair, flicked pages, and resumed reading:

. . . He cursed himself. How could he forget that others were not logical. Had they discovered him? Angry that she had distracted him, he scrambled for cover. Reaching the nearest bush, he dropped down on his back, sliding backwards covertly, and saw her doing the same. Compared to his clumsy movements, she was moving noiselessly. Expertly. He felt jealous.

Why? he thought with dismay. Why should I feel badly With her background she has had lots of practice. She mentioned it herself. Just a little practice and I can do much better.

Camouflaged to his satisfaction, he looked for her again and saw the gun in her hand. "Don't!" he whispered. "Don't shoot!"

"Why not?" Moving her lips almost soundlessly, she

whispered back, "They killed those children. They must be captured."

"No. Don't," he commanded. Authoritatively, as a commander should. "By playing in forbidden area, those children asked for it. Besides, they are dead. Our getting killed won't help them."

Surprisingly, she obeyed.

They waited. Pebbles started pricking his legs. He squirmed and tried not to move. Then a sneeze started scratching his nose. On top of that, an urge came to urinate. He could not understand how she could wait and watch so inertly, like a lifeless statue.

As the rustling sounds started getting closer, his blood started buzzing in his ears. Just when he felt he wouldn't be able to take it any longer, the sounds started to move away. After a breath-stopping, long eternity, they were again alone.

She stood up cautiously, and scanned the surroundings. "They are gone!" she sounded disappointed, "Lokopokito, why didn't you shoot? Tangled up in those bushes, they couldn't have escaped."

"I told you." He was annoyed. "Too many bushes to block our bullets. I won't allow any strike-happy attack. If you had studied defense strategy, so much of my time wouldn't be wasted teaching you. To win you must always remember Rule Number One—*Never underestimate your opponent.*"

"According to the text book they gave us, our Rule Number One is—*Grab obstacles. Tackle them boldly. Don't let them slip away.*"

Watching her angry eyes, he had to smile. *Tria! Wrong sex for any kind of space spanning assignment.*

Swallowing laughter trying to suffocate him, he tried to soothe her injured feelings. "Patience, Lokani. Patience! We will have lots of opportunities. There is no need to rush into reckless confrontations. No commander will allow *that!*

"First," he explained patiently. "We must tune-up tactics that'll improve our odds and guarantee our superiority. When we confront them, their bullets should not get any chance of touching us. You know why. One spot of red, and we are dead."

Her fists tightened. Fierce fires sparkled in her gold-flecked brown eyes. Or was it the effect of sunlight sneaking through holes formed by swaying, wind-swept branches glinting upon her defiant face.

"What's worrying you?" she asked. "We only need to prove our aptitude. The sooner we do that, sooner we can return."

"Return?" He shouted. "We came here to establish new records. Not to run away as soon as we have minimum points."

"I'm an Allrounder," she stated flatly. "One who does what she must. I don't want to waste time scoring points I won't need. Those of us who go there will be working together. Not fighting.

"So why," she asked pointedly, "should we waste time here? Let's get out as soon as our score cards have enough qualifying points."

"This is a test, Ketki," he snapped. "The judges need to learn *all* the facts about us. You may not care whether we get the maximum points, but I do. And you are not going to drag me down. I don't know how the other Allrounders feel. If they hold similar opinions, I'm going to recommend that next time they should arrange a separate test for everyone like you."

She bristled at his harsh, mocking tone. In the wind-furrowed shadows, he could see coldness surfacing on her face. But she did not reply. Her storm-ridden, eloquent eyes, shaded by arching brown lashes, looked away from his face.

His chest swelled with pride. Finally she had accepted the fact that he was her commander; that he held the higher rank.

He did not allow his victory to creep into his voice. Like a good teacher he smoothly lectured, "It's a good omen we found this camouflaged hill. Let's settle down here to perfect our strategy. While we are doing that, those not worth our trouble will eliminate each other. When only superior teams are left, we will move out and take the offensive."

She felt a strong revulsion. Coward! she thought. I'll bet no one else is hiding like you. This game is to prove your command skills. You want to rule that planetoid. Would you do that by sulking in your secret trenches? By the time you invent your holy strategy, everyone under your command would get killed.

But she was only a trainee Allrounder. He was a Command Volunteer. They had his chart. They knew what he was capable of. If she was ordered to choose him, could it have been for testing her ability to work with officers like him?

If that was true, she needed to behave differently. "Fine," she said politely. "I was concerned because in field maneuvers they grade us on our specialty curves. You know," she reminded him, "this is not a chiliko-trapping contest where camouflaging oneself is essential. It is a test that requires checkmating."

"Of course, it is." He was pleased by her acquiescence. "And, we will checkmate. But not right now. Later."

Having won victory over her, he decided not to push her any more. Scanning around to locate the best spot, he pointed toward it. "See that large cave inside that giant tree? Store our extra supplies there, so we won't get tired lugging them around. While you're doing that, I'll start planning our strategy—the best that any Commander can. If you follow my orders, we'll win. We *will* be selected. And honored. I guarantee that. You can count upon it.'

He beamed at her. "I told you before. In a test, one fares better if one does not forget the basic rules. Rule Number Three is *Know thy opponent. Beat him at his own game.* That means we need to discover their strategy. That would give us the tactical leverage to checkmate them."

Despite her heroic resolution not to contradict him any more, she could not hide the contempt clamoring in her mind. "Is there a time limit on your strategy-generating meditation, Commander? Or we are just going to hibernate in this good-omen-stuffed-tree and keep dreaming the impossible dream?"

He felt like stamping his foot. Threats smoldered in his third eye. Such stupid insolence? By a subordinate *plebeian*?

But this was not the time to pull rank. "You're a *tria*," he retorted. "Planning is my job. Managing supplies yours. Check what we have that we can use to make roborangs?"

Her brows crinkled. "I told you. We are not allowed—"

"Do it," he shouted. "That's an order." *. . . And don't flaunt your rule book at me all the time,* every nerve of his body snarled. That unspoken anger's missiles knifed him. Holy Paduka! Why don't you straighten her out? Take remedial action. Kick her down the slope and kill her. That'd be easier than this eternal problem of training her. Just one push and it would be over. No one would know. Then you would be able to plan unshackled. Unhampered.

He tried to control himself and retreat into meditation. Why can't I talk with her without shouting? Is it because my nerves are under gross pressure? Is it my defense mechanism? Am I shouting to scare away my apprehensions? To cool down, wouldn't it be best to escape for a while? That would also give her time to think and accept this situation which she is finding so alien.

That seemed logical. Without wasting another glance towards her, he turned and started moving down the path she had cleared. It was tough going because the plummeting slope was strewn with sharp-edged, slithery pebbles. To avoid falling, he kept grabbing ferns, leafy vines, jutting rocks—anything that he could hold on to.

The jittery, claustrophobic descent was very tiring. He had to stop and catch his breath. Leaning against a thick tree growing crookedly, he decided to meditate, closing his mind against all thoughts. But his second-self promptly confronted him, *You are blaming her for your own insecurities, disguising your outer shell in that I'm-In-Command defense? Your knock-out hustling is not convincing her. Why don't you use some other approach?*

Instead of shouting, if you explain to her nicely, she would understand the smashing odds piled up against you. Why not tell her? Explain why you must do whatever is needed to score the highest points. Tell her

*how since you were a baby this is the only thing you
have dreamed about. A space assignment has always
been the only goal of your whole blasted life.*

Rotating on this new thought-wave, his hostility
started zooming down. She seems like a sensible kid, he
mused. When I command, she does understand. Look
how slyly she moved when we were surrounded! And
despite her childish eagerness, she obeyed and did not
attack. If I could teach her that so quickly, I should be
able to get her cooperation in other areas also.

This sparked a new query in his sapient mind right
away and he shivered as if lightning had cracked
through thick, dark clouds. Could they have given him
such an unsuitable Allrounder to test his command
ability? Wasn't a commander expected to be capable of
inducing loyalty and enthusiasm in his underlings? If he
failed to do so, wouldn't that be a reflection on his skill
and competence?

That was a chilling discovery.

No, he decided. He was not doing it right. He needed
to inflate her ego. She is only a *trial!* What does she
know! She would believe anything. Somewhere out
there in the Allrounders' theory-land, there has to be a
carrot. All he had to do was to find it. When he would
dangle it before her, she would cooperate, become a
honeyball. He smiled.

The Guardian's trans-watch chimed; time to go home.

I know, he sighed. But, I do need to understand him. His ambitions
. . . his psychological patterns . . . his gambit triggers . . . what makes
him tick . . . We must move soon. Not much time left. I'll scan just a
bit more. He flicked pages:

. . . He was feeling frustrated. Why was her theory
proving right? Why weren't they using war tactics?
They were simply chasing each other like children
playing hide-and-seek. When dye bullets hit, both
victims and killers bowed elaborately, laughed, clapped
each other's backs—as if they were characters in a
space opera—and signaled rescue shuttles to pick them
up.

In fact so many teams within his vision flew away

that he stopped counting. And the same could be happening all over the test arena. In a way, that was good. He might have lost the argument, but his strategy was working; the number of the devil-may-care teams he would have to face were rapidly declining.

But, that was only half his strategy. The lesser half.

What he really needed was details about their tactics, so that when they found him, he'd be able to anticipate their moves. Disappointed by the outrageously boisterous tableau weaving wins and losses in the labyrinth-like ravine, he sat rooted inside his bushes, wondering how he could learn about the teams that must be winning. They were the teams whose tactics he needed to learn.

As the sun went down, it began to get very dark.

The planetoid the winners will occupy has no moon. And in that area of the galaxy stars are few. Therefore, the test arena had no light. If anyone ignited light now, they'd invite a sneak attack. Who'd want that? Not only that, they had spent close to eight hours here. Even pioneers, no matter how eager and tough, need sleep. So now everyone would be settling down somewhere. His spying for strategies would have to wait until sunrise.

Disappointment had eaten up his appetite. But Ketki must be hungry. As her commander, he should allow her to eat. Therefore, telling her he was not hungry, he inflated his sleeping bag, slipped in, and rolling over closed his eyes.

Morning dawned grumpily over his tall tree. He was awakened by the morning bugle bellowing in his earpatch. Surprised at having slept so soundly, he glanced towards her corner. She was not there. Quickly scrambling up, he moved towards the cave to pick up his tooth brush and saw her coming out.

"The cave is all yours. You may start meditating on your strategy." Her face looked smooth like marble. "I'm moving."

"What do you mean you are moving?" he demanded. "You cannot buzz off alone. You know we are not allowed to separate."

She did not reply. Just shouldered her supplies. Without waiting, without giving him time to have even a small sip of *paayas* from his hot thermos, she started moving towards the slope.

He felt exasperated. Holy Paduka! Spoiling his mood first thing in the morning! Yesterday's idea was right. As soon as she reaches the edge, he should push her down. But he did not get the chance. Halfway, she stopped and looked back over her shoulder.

His job was to lead, not follow. If she did not know that, it was about time she started learning. Snatching his knapsack, trampling the bushes she had squelched, he strode ahead and started clambering down furiously. By the time he reached the ravine, she caught up with him. But, not looking at her, he just kept moving.

Either she was engrossed in some world of her own, or had finished fighting him. Keeping her mouth closed, she simply trudged behind him. Time passed. Distance from his secret shelter kept increasing. But he could not find any trace of anyone. Feeling nervous, he began to wonder if the game had ended when he was sleeping. Had the rescue shuttle beeped and he hadn't heard it? If that was the case, he was marooned here for one month.

Convincing himself of this calamity, he decided to concede withdrawal from the contest and summon the Loser's Shuttle. But the Mighty Unicorn intervened again. Before he could take that wrong step, he heard voices in his earpatch. He groaned.

"Something wrong?" Sounding concerned, she hastened and kneeled near him. "Is it your foot? Let me look."

"Stop it!" He found her anxiety embarrassing. "Can't you hear them?" he asked gruffly. "Those voices in your earpatch."

"So?"

"Instead of going to bed so early, we should have also made up a code language for ourselves. Why didn't you think of it?"

"Isn't thinking of space-shattering strategies your department?" she asked sweetly.

He decided not to get riled so early in the morning. Ignoring the insult, he asked sternly, "You realize what a strategic advantage they have regimented for themselves? They can separate, hide anywhere, and still keep in touch."

"True," she agreed. "But as you said just a while ago, team members are not allowed to separate. Any forbidden strategy can roborang. They have powered up a disabling noose for themselves."

"Want to quote your rule-book again?"

"Nope! I just decoded their secrets. They did not get any sleep last night. They are tired and hungry. And they are cursing the teams that don't have the guts to come out and fight."

He beamed at her. "Good. You did not tell me you are an AGNI trainee! That settles it. You can do it. What we need is something better: AGNI-talk that they can not decode."

"Careful! Your strategies are goading you again! Remember? We are not allowed AGNI-talk."

"Wrong. We are not given OM-AGNI words. It's not forbidden to invent some for fun." He beamed at her winningly.

"Is that so?" She moved to a lop-sided, drooping tree and stood leaning against it. "And, suppose . . . just suppose, you have them, Lokopokito. What would you do with them? How would it help you in your glorious, ultra-secret strategy that you've been designing since yesterday?"

He considered it beneath his dignity to answer such an asinine question. She glared at him and continued, "If they break rules, you think it is okay for us to break them also? Even the governing rule that requires us to stay together?"

"Did they implant a text book in your mind?" forgetting his resolve not to get angry, he snarled. "Instead of quoting rules all the time why don't you think—just once—and come up with at least one clever way of doing something differently?"

"Really?" she laughed, but it did not sound amusing. "I'm quoting rules, am I? What about your Rules—One, Two, and Three? How do *they* fit in your golden strategy?"

"Holy Unicorn! Don't you know anything, you two-tongue Allrounder?" he roared. "Didn't they teach you in any lab that no matter what kind of *no win* condition confronts you, there is always a way out. You just have to find it. That's your job. Do it. Now! For a Mighty-O given reason—we *must* be selected."

There is a limit to what one can endure. His biting insults burned her like firesticks kindling a firecracker. "Are you the only one who's dying to get selected?" she snarled. "What do you think everyone else is hoping for? Why are they here?"

Her question hung in the smoldering air like a flaming candle. She waited for a reply. Not getting any, she softly asked, "What have you done to win, Commander? What's so special about you that makes you believe you can snitch highest possible grades without doing anything? You think just talking, and being so logical and creative about nothing, would do it?"

Sometimes he hated the truth. He hated her for hitting him with the facts he had been trying to pulverize. He knew his fears had been churning him so mercilessly not only due to doubts rooted in his unsinkable apprehensions. He knew that the real culpability for their coercion lay buried in the knowledge deep inside him. He had always refused to believe that he did not have a fraction more cleverness, just that extra bit of skill which, if used right, would win against any opponent in any competition.

He could not afford any mistake. He had to wait for the right time. Why couldn't she understand that?

But being the fair-minded person that he was, he decided to forgive her and drop the issue. "Time to make roborangs," he said in a conciliatory tone. "Let's gather stuff."

She decided not to remind him it was not allowed: what had the reminder achieved before? So she simply said, "You know there is nothing here that you can use."

"Talking dumb again!' he fumed. "One can try. Can't one? It does not hurt. First, we need a couple of sturdy branches."

Frustrated, she glared at him. Then, reached up to break a low-hanging branch. As she struggled with it, her knapsack slipped down from her shoulder and its contents scattered near their feet. He stared at them—

dye darts, hooks and knotted strings, emergency beacon, compass-maps, hunting knives, laser matches, and a medi-kit containing assorted healing bandages and touch-warm food-packs.

They fueled his anger. Kicking them viciously he snarled, "Be creative, they advise! Improvise, they suggest! How can one improvise without their supplying anything? I can be more creative than all of them combined. But how can I do that without having what I need? They should have given me what I need."

"If this test required anything else," gathering her stuff to save it from his needless assault, she said quietly, "they would have given it. Not just to the two of us. *To all of us.*" Her voice sounded reasonable. Much too reasonable.

Useless to remind her that her textbook platitude was making it worse. But, something else needed to be reminded. "I am the topmost Lokan specialist in robo-engineering," he asserted. "Given the right tools I can make anything. *Anything.* But without . . ."

"Constantly lamenting for what they cannot have," her eyebrows arched, "is that how commanders plan strategies? Why do you want a roborang anyway? What would you do with it?"

The question was logical. But the answer, he knew, would horrify her textbook mind. And if he tried to sidetrack, that would provoke more insulting snickers from Drupad's darling.

Before he could think of a reply, he noticed her staring at a patch of bushes at the edge of their mini non-Lokan-land. Her quiescent body language signaled intense concentration.

He felt afraid. This was the worst place to get caught. There were some skimpy, scattered bushes to their left. To reach them, they would have to cover lot of dried-brush ground. No matter how fast they ran . . .

She whispered, "Let's move."

Grabbing her half-closed knapsack, she streaked like a wild squirrel towards the bushes he had noticed. He did not ask the reason. Loping after her, he took the spot she indicated, and feeling safe, drew out his gun. As his fingers closed around it, his shoulders shook with tension.

Stop it, he silently scolded himself. It is just a game. Calm your nerves. If a mock skirmish is making you so nervous, what would you do in a real, live battle with real, live roborangs flying and hungry for action?

Ignoring the nagging signals radiating his inadequacies, he tried to look for the evil Blackguards, but found it difficult to concentrate. His mind was lashing him: Instead of worrying about her, his mind was saying, if you had remained alert, she would not have been able to prove her superiority. You would have noticed them first.

"Ready?" she whispered. "That open space is inviting our bullets. As soon as they emerge, we should kill them."

"Wait until I tell you to shoot," he commanded. But she merely touched her gun to her lips.

The arboreal bushes on the far side of their leaning tree parted, and two tall figures cautiously stepped out. They stood towering, hesitating which way to go.

"One glance at them and his heart sank. They looked like walking sleeping bags with feet and slitted eyes. He could finish all his bullets. His dye would not penetrate their armors.

He again cursed himself. If Ketki had not been distracting him, he would have figured it out first. Then these guerrillas would not have gained a upper hand. Now, because of Miss Snooty Mind, he was facing a checkmate even before he had started playing.

The Blackguards started moving. Had they seen him?

Whether or not they had, he could not wait. If he did, they would kill him, or Ketki might kill them first. Determined that Ketki should not snatch that honor, he aimed and fired right away.

The shots bloodied the twisted tree, but did not stop the killers. They moved fast, firing indiscriminately. Their determined bullets tore through his feathery foliage. Ketki dodged. But they could not frighten him. He aimed again. Before he could fire, their bullets came swishing, and the ferns near him dripped with red liquid smelling like newly shed blood.

That carnage opened his eyes. Those armored

libertines were determined to kill him. He must escape.
Turning around, he fled. Hooting and firing, the killers
pursued, trying to close the gap.

The legs encased with sleeping bags could not run
half as fast as he. He dashed to his leaning tree, hid
behind it, and fired. The killers replied right away. As
their hungry bullets swished and careened, missing their
targets, the skirmish began to feel like a chiliko hunting
tournament. Maneuvering, dodging the deadly dye,
leaping, stumbling against the frequent crags and
boulders, they skittered like uncatchable chilikos,
hoping that in the encircling bushes, some carnivorous
plant wouldn't find them.

Reaching another thick growth, he found Ketki, and
got behind her. He was not hiding. Only following the
time-honored rule that a commander should stay behind
his troops. He should not have forgotten her
determination to humiliate him. She slithered away right
away, rapidly, blindly, and stumbled. Because he was
close to her heels, he crumpled over her. Picking
himself up, he hissed, "You stupid *tria!* In a battlefield,
you must . . ."

But his chance to teach her was cut short as a
determined bullet came swishing. He ducked and stared
at the blood-red dye licking a drooping larch. He
shuddered. *Thanks to my hell-cat, just now I could have
gotten killed.*

He could not take it anymore; his neophyte was of
the wrong sex. And a real handicap. He should have
killed her. Since he did not, the next best thing was to
stop worrying about her. Leave her to her juvenile
capers and concentrate on scoring the points he needed
to win the Commander's position for that waiting
planet.

Thinking was deciding. He ran and stopped only
when he found himself surrounded by thick jungle
growth. The alien vegetation felt slimy and smelled
worse. But the tall, leafy bushes and vines provided
benevolent sanctuary. Feeling secure, he remembered
Ketki. Thank Unicorn! She was not behind him.

But had she found a suitable hide-out? If she failed
and got shot, the game would end for him also. A

teammate's death required surrender by the survivor. Holy Paduka! She was aiming for an early recall! What if she allowed them to hit her?

The query hit like a roborang. Had she been hit? Was he finished and did not even know about it? What if it had happened? What if he had lost before scoring the minimum points?

He cursed them. Not only had they failed to balance the odds, they had made teamwork necessary. The stupid rules demanded—win together or die together. You had no other choice!

Where are you, black-hole cat? his mind shrieked. If I had thrown you down the hill, you could not have argued with me eternally, distracting me, putting my life's goal in real, stark jeopardy. Why didn't you follow me?

In his mind's eyes, he saw her grinning in her red dye sucking uniform. Not able to endure the image, he took the risk of standing up and looking around. Where was she?

Not just her. Where were the Blackguards? Finding him too clever, were they trying to catch her? Had they succeeded? Was the Loser's Shuttle on its way to pick them up? Would he soon be hearing their summons in his earpatch?

Panicking, without testing the ground under his feet, unmindful of where he was stepping, he moved quickly to find her, and stumbled at a spot where the thick foliage was concealing a steep slope. Falling, slithering down upon thorny growth, he tried to latch onto something—anything—to halt his descent. But whatever he caught came torn with roots in his bleeding hands. The next instant, hearing sounds of roaring water, he looked down, and his fingers froze. Straight down below him, not very far, thundered the most horrible river one could ever imagine. O! Mighty OM! He didn't know how to swim! He would drown!

Clutching the mossy boulders, he tried to climb up. But the more he tried, the more he slipped. His foothold loosened. His fingers slipped. Air rushed past him and clawing, shrieking, he fell straight down towards the fast flowing water. A faint voice reached his ears,

"Lokopokito? Where aaaare you? Lokopokitooooo?"

Trying to keep his head above water, thrashing with all his strength, he desperately shrieked, "Help . . . Help . . ." As if by magic, Ketki suddenly appeared. Running alongside the river, she quickly threw her rope to him. "Catch. Quickly. Catch."

Twice he missed. The third time, however, he was able to grasp it. Quickly tying the other end to the trunk of a tree, she started pulling. But either the current was too strong, or she did not have enough strength. The resisting rope started to frizzle. Noticing that, he started to shriek.

"Quiet, don't move," she shouted. "You're only making it more difficult. Don't move."

Hearing sounds of running steps, she turned. The Blackguards were rapidly advancing towards them, tearing off their sleeping bags to move faster.

The Beasts! Curses crossed his mind like midnight lightning. As soon as they are close enough, they will kill her, checkmating us at our handicap! The space-cursed beasts!

Wading waist-deep in the roaring waters, they looped their knotted ropes and threw them at him. One caught his feet, another his shoulders. The rope's rough edges hurt. But, unmindful of his pain, waving away Ketki by furious gestures, pulling hard they inched back. Straining every muscle of their bodies, they pulled, and soon he was clutching the riverbank. Ketki was pulling him, and the Blackguards were removing their ropes from his body. Exhausted, breathing hard, he collapsed on the pebble strewn shore.

As his breath normalized, the silence around him bothered him. Opening his eyes, he saw Ketki building up a pile of dry twigs. No sign of red dye anywhere on her dirty uniform! And, the barbaric Blackguards were not visible!

"What are you doing?" he inquired mildly.

"Building a fire."

His whole body galvanized. Shooting straight up, he ran towards her, "Don't!"

"Why? You want to catch cold? Get recalled right away?"

He sprang forward to catch her hand, but she had already ignited the twigs. He stamped his foot. "Are you crazy? Can there be a better beacon! The other teams will find us."

"You got such a short memory?" she scorned, "They just saved your life!"

"Are they the only ones here? Aren't there others?"

"Here," she threw some wide leaves towards him. "Cover yourself while your uniform is drying. I'll be back."

"Where are you going?" he panicked.

"Call me when you're ready," she turned and disappeared.

Saved my life! Removing his clothes, he fumed. If you had stayed close to me as you are required to, I would not have tumbled in the river in the first place. First you jeopardize my life. Then you want me to shower gratitude? Disappearing all of the time . . .

When we get back, I must report her, he decided.

Hanging his wet clothes on the branches drooping over the fire, the thought crossed his mind that she had cleverly chosen the most appropriate place. In this area, this was the only place where branches drooped like this—not very high and not very low—so that clothes could be hung like this. But he shrugged away the thought. After all, she was a *tria*. It was her job to know about such things.

Accidents can happen, he thought. I almost drowned, but got saved in the nick of time. That is good omen. . . .

Jerking away his shoes, sloping them near the fire, he covered himself with leaves and lay down near the fire. The warmth felt good to his body chilled by the river's icy waters.

His lungs were protesting. Every muscle in his body was hurting. Closing his eyes, he wondered about his next moves. The Blackguards? Would they return? Were there others? How many? Where? Had the judges made this game more difficult than what waited on that planet?

When he became Commander of that planet, he would not have a teammate. What if he fell down there in a shark-infested river and no one was around to rescue him?

Startled by the thought, he sat up. Shivering. Wouldn't it be better to declare himself disqualified right now and summon the Losers Shuttle to pick him up? But what about Ketki? If he destroyed her chances, took away from her the remaining time for scoring the minimum points she needed to get selected, she *would* write the worst possible report about him. That could—would—snatch his teaching job away from him.

Staring at the dying fire, he tried to shake off his fears. If he could find time to meditate, he would be better able to wrestle with these rotten questions. Meditation would give him the needed strength and direction. But it would be dangerous to do that here. The Blackguards were scared to shoot a drowning person. But they would consider it fun to shoot one meditating in the middle of a jungle.

. . . The Space Guardian stopped reading, stared at the screen, and smiled. *Operation: Loser Take All.* It sounded a very appropriate name for what he had to do. What he must do.

Bringing the meditation-loving Lokopokito's diary here was worth the effort. All the time that was spent, all the risks that were taken, were worth much more than imagined. Just reading a few pages, he had learned quite a lot that he had not known—information that was indispensable for refining his Plan. By the time he finished it . . .

Ketki should be allowed to read it.

But would that be enough?

Because, there would still remain a wild trump in this game—*Star Kahuna!* The robo-schooner that this omen-propelled hero of *Operation: Loser Take All* had built for himself there on Earth. If there were any blueprints, they were only in his mind.

What was that robo-schooner capable of? Why had he named it *Star Kahuna?* . . .

4

. . . *The Dagger Once Drawn*

I think the Devil will not have me damned, lest the oil that is in me should set Hell on fire.
— Shakespeare: *The Merry Wives of Windsor, V*, c. 1600

. . .

Injuries accompanied with insults are never forgiven; all men on these occasions are good haters, and lay out their revenge at compound interest; they never threaten until they can strike, and smile when they cannot.

— C. C. Colton, *Lacon*, 1820

. . .

Carrying its single-minded navigator, *Star Kahuna* lifted anchor, and leaving behind its small jetty, moved out to the open ocean.

Jal-O stood alone at the helm. A small leather briefcase lay behind him on the comfortable, cushioned seat. He looked up and around. The ocean was calm. Not a whiff of clouds in the evening skies. The sun was bidding good-bye, leaving behind as a gift the most splendid aura of colors that could buffet rejuvenating life into anyone's despairing eyes.

But for Jal-O, the gloriously lit landscape was only a stage. Against its backdrop he was savoring his self-profiled image after a full day's work. A somewhat tired caretaker going home. Not a bigwig. Just an ordinary, middle-class nobody. Just a little late. Like some others who had worked late this Friday, the last working day of this rapidly folding century. He was sure no one had noticed his departure.

Today no one had any time to pay attention to anyone. This night belonged to each of them. This clear, beautiful night that heralded hopes of so many uncensored pleasures. So many kinds of amusements. The waiting multi-mega celebrations the Earth people had been planning for six months were not just for tonight but for the whole coming week. They were not just to welcome a New Year, but to celebrate the dawning of the new Space Century. They were to greet all the forecasts, all the prospects, that the new unfolding infinity was promising to drop at their waiting feet.

Feeling happy and complacent, Jal-O waited until the land dropped out of sight. Then, stopping the engine, he scanned around to make sure he was alone. Sighting no one, he took out a small recording unit from his briefcase. Having rehearsed the message several times, he saw no need to give it a second thought, and started recording, "Jal-Two was murdered earlier this evening. This throws a spanner into our scheme. Since our plans are still covert, I cannot dig too much into their private lives. If I knew he was in danger, I would have taken steps for his safety.

"Needless to say, Peace Guards did not even bother to investigate. Anxious to leave for their vacations, they marked it off as a murder-suicide perpetrated by a jealous actor gone berserk. I was expecting it. As reported several times earlier, humans are very predictable. It is very easy to anticipate their actions. Hence, it will be easy to maneuver and control them."

Pride was beginning to creep in his voice. Suppressing it, he continued, "I have taken steps to make sure Jal-Two's murder does not affect our plans. No need for you to worry. Operation Earth Shield will be triggered on time. As I assured you earlier, it will be an unqualified success. I will keep you informed."

Placing the unit at a safe distance from the suitcase, he pushed a button. The disc started rotating, whirring. Round and round. Gaining speed it dissolved into small, glittering sparks that quickly disappeared into nothingness.

He started the engine again. Then looked at his wristwatch.

Plenty of time. There was no need to rush. Stretching on the seat, he pulled cushions under his head and shoulders. Feeling comfortable and happy, he yawned and closed his eyes.

It was one of those rare times when everything had been taken care of. When he had nothing left to do.

Twice before he had found himself in such a situation, where life had taken him to the corner, where there was nothing left to do. There was no turning back and what waited around the corner was shrouded in endless veils.

But between this time and both those past times, there was a big difference. On both those occasions, he had wanted to run away or kill himself. Both past times, those mind-killing situations—his cruel humiliation and degradation—had not been due to his fault or negligence. They had been engineered by that diabolical pussyfoot, that designing, cross-patch crab stick, Drupatti.

The first time, the pain had been greater because he had not anticipated the cruel event.

His childhood had not been enviable like that of his study-mates. But he had never minded. He had never felt badly about it.

He had never been given what was reserved for those who were born in ancient, accredited families. But using his talents, he had outdone them, gotten better stepping-ladders than what they had received as their birthrights. Ignoring games and pleasures, he had concentrated on his education, had done better than most of them in the various sciences. But in one area—his chosen area—his dedication and hard work had really paid off. He had done exceptionally well in the robotic sciences.

Finally, the wait was over. On the basis of his record-shattering inventions, he was given the opportunity of competing in the Three-Day Test Festival. If his entry won one of the top ten prizes, he would join the select group of Planet Keepers and compete for the Third-Eye Transplant Honor.

He had often dreamed of this opportunity. Since his early childhood, since he could remember, he had secretly aspired for it. But despite trying to be the most optimistic about it, he had always felt they would never give him that chance. When he got it, he had felt jubilant. He had felt good about the system that overlooked one's family status and rewarded his personal and scholastic achievements.

Jal-O had worked very hard for his entry. Unlike others, who borrowed from the previous winners' ideas, he had composed an original three-day play. It contained everything—humor, mystery, sword fights, robo-rang duels, and a ballet. It had marriages, murders, semi-nude dancing, peacock parades, bull-cobra fights, unicorn races, and chiliko-hunting tournaments. It had sunny days, rainbows, cascading snows, thunder and lightning. It was a fantastic play.

He did not allow anyone's shadow to fall upon it, kept it such a secret that it became a topic at dinner tables. He wanted to amaze them. Grab their attention. He had felt confident. If he could amaze them, titillate them, and petrify them, he would definitely receive the topmost award.

He also knew that no matter how splendid his play was, it would be a flop if he did not have a heroine who could make it come alive. And he knew the fiery spirit, everybody's favorite, who could make his dream come true. Drupatti. Just the right person. She could rotate any person, of any age, on her little finger. Drupatti, the only one who could do justice to his play. Drupatti, because she was a junior completing her qualifying year, and was not in the competitions that year.

The competitors had absolute freedom to seek help from anyone. To choose anyone. There was no reason for him to hesitate. In fact, considering her age and inexperience, the chances were when the others heard about it, they'd cheer him for giving her the greatest honor a senior could offer a junior.

Pleased with his selection, he had informed her three weeks before the rehearsals were to begin. That was the time-honored convention—a senior could choose any junior and the juniors had to accept the honor and do their best. If anyone malingered, they were disqualified from all future competitions.

But the day rehearsals were to begin, Drupatti invoked an ancient rite that had been petitioned only once before during the past five centuries. She had requested a Unicorn Race over the Unicorn Mountain. If she won . . .

He wasn't worried. He could out race her any day, under any condition. He would win. She would have to accept the grueling role of his heroine. And winning the race, he would add an additional crown to his record.

But during the race on the downhill slope, his unicorn lost her shoe, stumbled, and fell. He awoke in the hospital with a bandage over his forehead. When they removed it, he asked for a mirror and saw the third eye gracing his forehead. It was beautiful. Better than what he had ever hoped for. But the operation was done without his knowledge, when he was lying unconscious due to his severe injuries.

He had felt horribly humiliated. They had given it to him not because he had won the right to have it, but because they felt sorry for him. Not only that, they had transplanted it when he was unconscious so that he had missed all the fun and celebration that always accompanied it. He was doubly-cheated.

The third dishonor came when he received the job summons, with the title, *Lokopokito*, the lowest place in the space cadre.

The level from which *Opokitos* and *Pokitos* were never chosen. He was outraged. Despite all his dreams, he had always suspected that, due to his binary rank, he'd never be given the position of an *Okito* or *Kito*. But considering his scholastic achievements, *Pokito*, or at least *Opokito*, should not have been placed out of his reach. There was only one way to let them know how they had cheated him. How cruelly they had shattered all his aspirations, all his dreams.

He went to the Unicorn Mountain; to the spot where his unicorn had lost her shoe. When they found his lifeless body there, they would know what kind of injustice they had done to him. To their guilt would be added the shock and bereavement of knowing that, with his death, they had lost all of his future inventions—everything indispensable that he could have done for them.

He opened his thermos, poured some grape juice into a small cup and, opening the cobra poison capsule, emptied it in the cup. Then bending on his knees, he closed his eyes to pray one last time.

The brief meditation gave him inner peace and strength. Feeling calm and collected, he opened his eyes and reached out a hand to pick up the cup. Just then, a baby unicorn came racing by and knocked against his hand. It then stood close, watching him with his big, round eyes.

He looked at the spilled, broken cup; then at the baby unicorn. He still had juice in his thermos, but no other cobra poison capsule. Was it some kind of an omen?

If the baby unicorn drank juice from his hands, the animal would come with him. That would be a good omen—a growth-promising omen.

He broke a big leaf from a nearby tree, folded it to make a cup, and offered the remaining juice to the waiting watcher. The round-eyed, fearless baby sniffed it, circled him once, sniffed it again, and then drank it. All of it.

Jal-O had felt elated. The Gods had accepted his prayers. They had sent a courier. His future was still in its infancy. He should not be impatient and kill it needlessly. It will grow beautifully like Their baby unicorn. He should wait. Inaugurated and graced by his third eye, his luck was waiting somewhere nearby. It would come.

Picking up the baby unicorn in his arms, Jal-O had gone back to accept the drudgery, teaching space robotics to young kids. Initially, he had felt hopelessly depressed. He could not take care of the unicorn and had to let the animal go. But the unicorn kept coming back in his dreams, telling him, *Too bad you have to wait for your second chance. But, so what! Life is long and you are young. And after waiting so many years, you can wait a while longer.*

One morning, waking from his dream, he had vowed that one day Drupatti's kids would enter his class. He would make sure they did not get any chance to qualify for any competition. Or he would motivate them to enter those competitions that were beyond their capabilities, so they would have no chance of winning. They might even get killed. He would be vindicated. That time would come. He would get his revenge.

But the Gods were watching. Before he could do anything foolish and destroy his chances, Jal-O got a second opportunity.

Swinging on his memory lane, Jal-O felt restless and stirred. When he came to Earth, feeling friendless and lonely, he had often remembered that second disaster. Then one day, scanning an ancient Earth manuscript, he had read something that impressed him. This Earth philosopher had stipulated that the best way to get rid of a deep pain was to tell it to someone. The philosopher's logic, the way he had explained it, made lot of sense. On Jal-O's own planet, he had never talked about his pain. No doubt that's why everything was bottled inside him and hurt him so much always.

Here on Earth, there wasn't anyone to whom he could tell that painful story. But he could write it and get it published. Or get a movie made. Or stage it. Or do all three. When it was done, it would make him happier than that early play that had never gotten a chance on his home planet. Because when Drupatti heard about it, as no doubt she would, she would feel humiliated.

The measure of his glory and success would depend upon how much misery it inflicted upon her. That would be his real reward for enduring the tough labor of penning it. He was enchanted by the idea.

So he had written it. He was writing it like a story—guessing others' thoughts. And he had not been kind to himself. Remembering those events, thinking about them, where it seemed he had been wrong, he had not spared any words. This novel isn't just a self-applied therapy, he had thought. Now, that I'm more mature, if I can discern some mistakes that I may have made in the past, I won't repeat them here. That would make me a better administrator.

The novel was now almost finished. He had worked so hard on it, revised it so many times, he remembered almost every word of it. It was now time for converting it into a screenplay so that it could be given to his secret partner at Twin Films on his scheduled visit. Since he had nothing to do right now, he thought it was a good time to think about the screenplay's outline.

He had begun his story at the very beginning. Like an Earth novel, it started with a preface—worded beautifully—then went on with the heart-rending story.

A new planet was ready for habitation, he had written. It was built for bipedal life that would in time join the galactic life-forms. In its first stage, the planet harbored carnivorous plants, thorny foliage, and life-sustaining plant life. Time was coming near to seed it with rudimentary life and the elements for sustaining it.

It was a coveted space assignment.

It would be tough. Life there would be a constant struggle. It wouldn't hold any perks that came even with junior-most, off-world jobs. But it was good because it did not require prior experience, was open to juniors, and would give the pioneers a chance to prove their mettle. A chance to step on the ladder on which, if one eclipsed the others, there was only one way to go—up . . . *and up!*

The selection was done by an open competition. Anyone wanting to go could apply. Volunteers were tested in the environment they would face on the raw planetoid. Their stamina and ingenuity were evaluated, and ranks depended upon the grades one received.

He filed his application. When the acceptance came he wondered who would be his partner. There was no way to find out because he knew the command volunteers had no choice. Those volunteering for lower ranks selected their senior officer. If one did not want to work with that partner, he had to opt out.

He decided not to worry about it. This was *the* second chance the unicorn had promised. No matter who chose him, it would not matter. He did not need anyone's help. Alone he could outsmart, out-perform, all the others. He wouldn't be just one of the winners. He would come out the topmost winner. The leader who would be sent to the new planet as the volunteer's commander.

They were dropped in the testing terrain that had been transformed to resemble the waiting planetoid. With his partner, he landed, knees first, on thorny bushes. Luckily, the bushes were not carnivorous. If they were, their mandibles could have penetrated their spacesuits and crushed the volunteers. A good omen. Proof that the future was theirs.

Quickly bouncing to his feet, he looked around and up. The jungle was so thick, the sunlight was barely visible. Overhead, the service shuttle was still waiting.

He wondered why. Then, he remembered. The air was breathable. They were required to move around in their uniforms. If they were bitten by thorny bushes or crawling things, they had their med-kits. The shuttle was waiting to retrieve their helmets and spacesuits. The rope conveniently dangled near his hands.

Removing his helmet, he struggled out of his spacesuit and put both in the waiting basket. Only then he noticed that the other rope carrying his partner's things had already been pulled up. *Showing off?* he thought, *that you are faster than me.* He smiled and turned around to find him.

Behind the tall, thick ferns, he glimpsed a uniform like his own peeking at him. "Hello, Pioneer. What kind of field maneuvers are your specialty?" he asked politely.

"None. I was a Food-Science School drop-out."

He was stunned. He did not hear the words, only the voice. It was soft and melodious. *My third eye!* deep inside his mind he thundered. *A tria! A partner of the wrong sex has chosen me!*

The memory of that shock jolted him. Even now. Even after so many years. Scowling, he pulled out his manuscript. But he did not have to open it. He remembered word for word what he had told her about himself, and her noxious, indigestible reply.

"I'm a teacher—a specialist in space robotics and energy-wave direction," he had told her proudly. "I have also done extensive research on the historical factors related to the emergence, growth, and decline of alien species, with emphasis upon the use of violence in their civilizations. What are your areas of interest and specialization?"

The answer had not come right away. Then she stated quietly, "Lokopokito, you did not even ask my name. As to my interests, I'm sure you know, on a new planet they don't just need specialists. They also need janitors, cooks, and cleaners. I'm all three."

The statement was so sky-splitting, at first he had not comprehended it. Surely, she was joking. But one glance at her upturned face had convinced him that she was not.

He was dumbfounded. He felt nauseous and paralyzed. Holy Unicorn! If Gods were against him, why had They given him this second chance?

The silence that fell between them was broken by her quiet voice, "I'm called Ketki. Growing up in my codilla, I've learned many survival tactics—how to slip away without being seen; how to find hideaways; how to hoodwink and tame wild animals; how to—

"You call these tactics!" he had thundered, hoping his authoritarian voice carried enough ridicule. "These juvenile pranks? What good are these dumb charades! You won't get points for them. If you could make something from the materials available here—something the others do not have—that would give us a definite edge over them. That's the kind of assistance I was expecting from my partner. Not these *Neolithic* capers!"

Now closing the manuscript, Jal-O/Lokopokito sat with his hand upon it, gazing at nothing. Would it have been better if at that point he had withdrawn from the competition?

If he had, he would have escaped all the humiliation, all the misery, insults, and pain that he had to endure. He would have done that gladly, without giving it a second thought, if he had known Ketki's malevolent destiny was so potent it would torch his Unicorn blessings. But he did not know, and when the game was over her destiny had won. His scoring record was not just dismal, it was deplorable. He had not scored even the minimum points required to get through the space-link doors.

When it was over, he had clambered up the ladder to the Loser's Shuttle ignoring Ketki. Coming up, she roosted next to him, but he had refused to look at her.

Stupid *tria!* Not understanding the depth of his aversion, she had made excuses to justify her misconduct. False excuses—when he did not answer her calls, she thought he had caught the red dye, and she must find him right away so that the shuttle wouldn't start looking for her, and he wouldn't forfeit any points for losing her.

But he knew she was lying. Why? Perhaps she was Drupatti's secret agent, that's why.

That was it! Serving Drupatti, she had also achieved her own objective. If she got him disqualified, she would never have to work under him—ever.

She was right in that respect, he scornfully conceded. He was an authority in various robo-sciences. He had no reason to demean himself. If they had invited him to participate in the second test for the service personnel—for Allrounders, as they titled themselves to glorify their role—he would have refused. With his glorious knowledge, he was entitled to a supervisory position. If he could not work as a command supervisor, he did not need to work as an Allrounder supervisor. He would prefer to remain a teacher.

Losing was humiliation enough. On top of that had come the score cards. Three points weighed heavily against him. One—he had made it impossible for his partner to score any qualifying points. Two—he had left her alone and unprotected. And, three—while the others were playing a fair game, he had cheated, misled and hoodwinked them, giving them no credit for their intelligence. On top of that, making a mockery of the time-honored rules, he had violated the Planet Keepers' first oath.

He knew if he would have had the right partner, the report would have been different. If he had the right partner, the need to find loopholes in the rules would not have risen and he'd have won.

He had asked and discovered that the officer responsible for accepting the Allrounders' partner choices was Drupatti. I should have known, he had bitterly thought. He had wanted to kill Drupatti and then himself. But of course, that was not possible.

Now reclining in his cushioned seat in the soothingly floating *Star Kahuna*, he remembered that miserable, poorly designed test. They say *What the Almighty Om does, He does for the best.* That *must* be true. If he was selected and sent to that primitive planet, he could have died there due to exposure or some other calamity. Drupatti would not have let him live. That's for sure.

By any chance, if using his ingenuity, he had managed to survive her devilish traps, her admirers would have just left him there for the rest of his life. He would not have gotten this one-in-a-million chance of coming here; of having Mighty Om's blessings for ruling this extraordinary planet. All by himself.

"Dear Diary," he said softly. "It's true, I lost that game. But nothing goes to waste. From my defeat, I learned. I had two chances of killing Ketki. Feeling sorry, wanting to be merciful, I gave up both. If I had not, if I had gotten rid of her, she would not have been there to maneuver such a ghastly defeat for me.

"*Never make a mistake twice,* that's my motto. That's why I've eliminated Jal-Two. And I did such a good job. No one would be able to pin it on me—neither the Earth Peace Guards nor Lord Kito's and Prince Drupad's spies.

"When I was saying my good-byes to come here, they had told me they had full faith—absolute trust—in my unparalleled, creative skills. They were depending on me. They knew I could handle the job alone. I did not need anyone else. That's why they were not sending anyone with me. They knew how tough my job would be because I'll be alone on a malevolently advanced planet. But . . .

"I had not believed them then. I do not believe them now.

"All that buttering and fawning. No doubt they are pining to replace me as soon as they can maneuver it. I had seen it that day in their greed-blighted eyes. They won't tell me, they won't admit it, but

I know; my Earth must be teaming with their clever spies.

"I will find them—all of their spies. And I will take care of them, just as I took care of Jal-Two. No problem. No problem at all. I'm not a timid milksop. I know how to keep my vows. I'll never trust a partner ever again. And, I will never let an enemy come anywhere near me. I'll eliminate them—all of them—before they can come close. I know what happens when one is merciful."

That thought brought alive in his mind his chilling nightmare. That dark, untamed jungle . . . those mocking birds popping over his head, drenching him with that foul-smelling filth with such force that he could not even breath . . . those curses. Shrieking voices.

Trying to shake away that corrosive terror, he opened his manuscript and turned its pages telling himself, "Don't! Don't start regressing again. Remember. Just remember that it was a God-given, benevolent lesson.

"If you have to think, try to think what words you would use to thank Drupatti for heaping so many troubles upon you when you were young, and could endure. You suffered. Sure. But you learned. You learned a lot.

"Now using that knowledge, laughing at their stupid efforts, you will make yourself Perpetual Commander of this lovely planet.

The thought rejuvenated him. Feeling peaceful, content, and confident again, he smiled. They would, no doubt, probe and try to discover the reasons for his success. But he would never let them find out. He'd plan as meticulously as he had planned Jal-Two's murder. As carefully as he had planned everything for tonight.

No, not just for tonight—for all the coming glorious days and tempting nights. Now he had nothing to do but relax, and enjoy the fruits of his hard-learned wisdom.

They'll be coming to his precious island—the remaining eleven members of the Board. Celebrating the arrival of the new century, they will gorge themselves on hard liquor, ancient wines, and the kind of food that only the Food Islands can provide. Then, when the new dawn was splashing pink in the eastern skies, heralding the arrival of the new Space Century—the new Space Age—his LDM would explode, bringing to this water planet a new-born day that'd be beyond these humans' wildest imagination.

Lord Kito had programmed all kinds of celebrations.

I insisted only on one, he thought. But, that will be the one remembered by everyone for centuries to come.

He envisioned it now—all kinds and shapes of flying vehicles. Sky-writing in all the world languages in rainbow colors:

Welcome Lokopokito. Welcome. Glory to thee, Lord Lolopokito. Long live our new guide. O' ye come all. Sing a billion cheers for our bountiful, glorious Guardian . . .

The people of this grateful Earth will then stage plays and sing songs to spread his glory. He will fully deserve all those honors. . . .

Everything will change.

Lord Kito and his stooges will then have to listen to him, and applaud him. They will need to publicly proclaim how proud they were to call him the Perpetual Lokani of this sector of the galaxy. Despite the fact that to visit here, even for a few hours, they'll need his permission. . . .

He felt restless and replaced his diary in his suitcase.

Perhaps, he thought, perhaps, I'll feel sorry for the loss of the land that will disappear with its human and animal population.

But this mourning, he assured himself, will be only mine.

Not of this grateful Earth. Because these earthlings know the value of violence.

They will understand that without their suffering this small, inevitable, selective sacrifice, their government would not have allowed me to bestow upon them the bountiful gifts I have so generously planned to shower upon them. Now, and through all the coming centuries.

Moving his eyes from the twinkling lights of the receding shore, he turned and glanced towards the approaching Jalanga Island. The sky there suddenly lit up with glittering sparks, like scores of cascading fountains adorned with multi-colored lights, sparkling gold and green, and pink, and blue . . .

A smile lit up his trueskin human face. So! The celebrations had already begun! On his home away from home, someone had already sparked the new year's festivities.

Suddenly, he needed to talk with someone. He remembered his last birthday, when he had sat alone in his cabin, lighted only by one small candle, gazing at the holocube containing Pia Payal's alluring images.

Should I call Pia Payal, he thought.

Why not? *A friend who shares one's sorrow,* they say, *is the most endearing friend. A friend in need,* they maintain, *is a friend indeed.* What better time to offer my sympathy and affection than now, when she is mourning the death of her stage partner?

Many times I have wondered how a male of this species addresses the female he adores in their privacy and seclusion? If I see her . . . when I see her . . . what would I say? She would not know me. How would I start the conversation?

Isn't this the best time to solve the problem? The best opportunity? . . . Won't this be the best way? First, I offer her my condolences. Then, to share her bereavement, I express my grief. Then I remind her about her land's ancient philosophy that I heard her singing on spacevision just last week.

When I am dead, my dearest
Sing no sad songs for me;
Plant thou no roses at my head
Nor shady cypress tree.

And then I'll ask her where and when we should meet. Surely, she'd like to meet a well-wisher who shares her likes and dislikes, who would like to share her songs and dances, her days and nights.

At this inspirational thought, Jal-O felt so happy that he sprang from his cushioned seat like a slingshot, reached his stool at the helm, and punched the combination of his cabinet.

The cabinet door slid open and, mounted on a long arm, the visiphone moved within easy reach.

5

. . . *Friends and Shadows*

When I was one-and-twenty,
I heard a wise man say,
'Give crowns and pounds and guineas,
But not your heart away;
Give pearls away and rubies,
But keep your fancy free.'
But I was one-and-twenty,
No use to talk to me.
　　　—A.E. Housman: *A Shropshire Lad* (1896)

.　.　.

If I do vow a friendship, I'll perform it to the last article.
　　　—SHAKESPEARE: *Othello, III* (1604)

.　.　.

Switching off the polychromatic visiphone, Maya Kiran stepped
out of the public booth. Her face expressed her feelings better than

a million words might have. Alarmed, the Energy Station attendant peered at her.

"Miss?" he asked anxiously. "Are you all right?"

He towered above her.

She looked up at his rugged, chiseled face and broad shoulders. His big, brown eyes reflected concern and apprehension. That touching sympathy brought tears to her eyes. Trying to push them back unshed, she found her voice getting stuck in her throat. "Someone just got killed. At the Orpheum."

"Oh! . . . Your friend?"

"No." Trying harder to hold back the tears threatening to reveal her feelings, she shook her head. "I never saw anyone die before. Blood. So much. All over." Her voice cracked.

His shoulder seemed so close. And there, under its accessible hollow, it seemed such an impregnable place where no one would be able to reach her, touch her. She felt like hiding there and having a good cry. But a total stranger?

Are you crazy, you dumb Kiwi! Mind your manners! Silently scolding herself, she started to look for a tissue in her purse.

"Poor guy!" the service-person was saying. "What a day to die!"

He wanted to remain unaffected by her sorrow, but was finding it impossible. So, he did the only thing possible for him. "No need to pay, Miss." He spoke softly as if confiding a big secret. "I'm closing up. This is on the house."

Then as an afterthought, he picked up a spare and filled it up for her. "Better keep it. For emergencies. You never know what may happen. Everything may now be closed for weeks."

She was startled, "For weeks?"

"Don't you think so? Everyone's going to need time to recover from the celebs they have been planning." He smiled a wide open, cheerful smile. "What are you planning?"

She could not help smiling.

"I bet something quite exotic."

His cheerful mood was infecting her. On an impulse, she picked up the gift package lying on her auto's back seat. "For your girlfriend," she said offering it to him. "A small memory of this never-to-come-again evening. From me to you, and her. To wish you both lots of luck and happiness in the new century."

"Oh thank you, Miss!" He looked crestfallen, but his voice retained its cheerful friendliness, "Thank you, very, very much. I'm sure she will like it."

Maya Kiran found it difficult to move away from him, but Bakul was lying in the hospital. He would ask for her. He would need her. She had to reach the hospital as soon as possible. With an effort, she turned and moved towards her auto.

As she settled on her seat, the door slid in and automatically locked. Through the open window, she waved at the stranger who had given her the courage she needed so badly. "Live long and always free, my friend."

"May the Earth be with you always," he smiled and waved back.

As she drove away, the thought crossed her mind: So! He belongs to our New Minority?

Or perhaps not. Perhaps he just knew the greeting and was returning it as a polite gesture. Perhaps it was only another kind and gracious thought, because he is such a friendly person.

Next time when she is in this area, should she stop by to thank him again for his tremendous help? Help and concern. Real and sincere. And friendliness. The warm supportive aura that was simply there. That did not ask for, or expect anything, in return.

Or perhaps not.

"If you want to grow up and live an independent life like Pia," she told her image in the dashboard mirror, "you must learn not to be swayed by whatever fate brings your way. You must learn to depend upon yourself. Only upon yourself—on no one else. A vagabond island does not need an anchor."

That's what Bakul used to say.

"Why am I thinking about him in the past tense?" she asked her mirror-image with dismay. "He was not killed. It was his understudy whose life was snuffed away on Orpheum's stage.

"When Bakul learns about it, would he feel responsible? Would he feel guilty that his talented assistant, who had so many years of sparkling, exciting life ahead of him, died because of him?

"Why should he?" She argued with herself. "It was not his fault that when the killer fired his boomerang weapon, he was not on the stage. He had put on his make-up and costume, and was waiting for his cue, when suddenly that twisting stomach pain made him double-up, and collapse, and he started thrashing on the floor."

She again remembered the scene. The stage manager was so scared. Saying it was probably his appendix, he ordered Bakul's understudy to take his place and carried Bakul in his arms to his own hovercraft to personally rush him to his hospital.

Everything had happened so suddenly, so unexpectedly, that

except for her and Pia, no one, not even the stagehands, knew that Bakul had gotten sick. No one knew it was not Bakul, but his understudy, who was on the stage performing the role of the Neptunian Grand Nomarch.

No one likes to get sick, especially not a person like Bakul. When he had walked in earlier, he was looking his usual self, a handsome prince in perfect health. Joking and laughing. Teasing Pia about her vacation plans.

No reason for him, or anyone else for that matter, to even imagine that such a life-threatening pain was about to get hold of him. And that it would twist and torment him so horribly that he would not even be able to stand on his legs.

It was just one of those things that no one can anticipate.

But honestly, who would want to kill Bakul?

No one. He never gave anyone any reason to dislike him. Theater was his whole life. He did not have any relationship with anyone outside it, and he never quarreled with anyone. No reason for him to have any enemy, not in the theater-world or outside.

In fact, it would be a lot easier to imagine someone's wanting to kill an innocent baby, than wanting to do anything to hurt a dove like Bakul.

Bakul Enrique Lopez—a guy in a million. The kind of genes they had programmed for him . . .

Her thoughts got a jolt. Her auto's automatic controls had suddenly braked, throwing her back against her seat. Surprised, she looked up. Beyond the vehicles lined ahead, a children's band was crossing the street. People standing at the crossroads were cheering and applauding. The scene was delightful.

But her smile disappeared with the quick-stepping band. As it turned the corner moving out of sight, she thought, how tragic it is! Today, the day of planet-wide celebrations, instead of living it up, one died who was not even the intended victim.

And Bakul? The intended victim? She asked herself, is he really that much better off? Right now perhaps, he is lying unconscious in surgery, barely breathing, totally unaware of the surgeon's hands tearing and mending him.

I do hope it was just his appendix. I do hope it was not anything serious.

Well! The gift intended to cheer him up is gone! And all the stores are now closed!

Bakul, my Rakhi-brother, if I am a 'Vagabond Island', you had a lot to do with it. It's your fault that your gift belongs to a stranger. When I tell you about it, I know what you will say. You will grin, pat my shoulder, and say, "Fine, Kiwi. Wonderful. I want such surprises. That's what makes you such a special sister."

Okay Bakul, if you want me to be your *special sister,* you have to get well. When the manager was carrying you to his hovercraft, I promised God Kalki, when you leave the hospital, I'll take you to His temple, even if I have to bully you and drag you. So you see, brother of mine, you've got no choice. You can't let me down. You've got to leave the hospital quickly and in perfect health.

The horn of her auto beeped softly. The engine accelerated.

Looking ahead, she noticed that the traffic had disappeared.

At the end of the solitary street loomed the stony face of the grim-looking hospital.

Switching to manual control, she hit the speedometer. "Hold on, Bakul," she whispered. "I am coming to cheer you up, brother of mine. Just hold on until I get there."

***

"My partner had promised he'd be my little brother," Andrey Voznesensky said to no one in particular. "He'd be just like my Never-Giving-Up Nikita, who was lost in space."

He was standing half-leaning against the picture window facing the ocean that was lapping leisurely against the sheer walls of Mubarak, the island, the technological marvel. He shared this marvel with his friend and business partner, Milan McMillan.

"My little brother," Andrey drawled, his deep baritone several octaves higher. "My knock-about Nikita, who knows how to make my two hands and two feet four, when I am in trouble."

He glanced at his bosom buddy, but apparently his words had just washed over that statue of despair without leaving any mark on his troubled psyche. Milan McMillan just sat there, drooping in his chair like a lightning bruised Banyan, whose keeper had given up on him and abandoned him forever.

As a movie producer, Andrey had known many writers. Experience had taught him that where ordeals of the psyche were concerned, his childhood friend towered above them all. Over the years he had learned to live with his moods. But never before had he seen him so discouraged. He was trying very hard to think how to deal with this unprecedented situation.

So far all his efforts had failed.

Andrey had a basic rule. He never wanted to be caught in a situation where he might feel unhappy. Seeing his friend crushed by such overpowering shadows was making him feel very unhappy and very uncomfortable. McMillan's tall, lean frame seemed to have shrunk. His sandy-golden hair, that was generally well combed, was horribly mussed-up. In his ocean-blue eyes a far-away look was logged, as if he were not really there, but were marooned somewhere near some uncharted, unidentifiable place. In his eyes there was no entry for anyone else, no matter how much one tried.

Andrey picked up a magazine from a nearby shelf, tore a few pages, and crumpling them into a hard ball, threw them at his friend. The paper ball struck McMillan's fingers and started falling down. Leaning automatically, McMillan grabbed it and stared at it as if he had never seen a crunched paper ball.

"Buddy, I've know you since you were that high," Andrey leaned, holding his hand a few inches above the antique Kashmiri carpet. "But I never suspected you had feet of clay."

"So!" McMillan lifted his long feet and plunked them down on a carved, ivory-inlaid side-table lying nearby. Throwing the ball back at his friend, he asserted, "You live and learn."

The paper ball flew back to hit McMillan's feet. However, this time the troubled long legs made no effort to retrieve it. Turning sad again, his eyes acquired a sort of defiant look. "Tiger-Tamer," he lashed out, "you're front-loading such a grand show of bravely holding up! Tell me, what are you going to do?"

Andrey did not allow his irritation to reflect in his voice. Moving, he pulled a chair and sat down near his friend. "Isn't it obvious?" he asked amiably. "I've turned every stone that can be turned to find her."

"You know what time it is?"

"Why? Is this precious antique of yours, chirruping every quarter hour, not keeping correct time?" Andrey pointed at the jade inlaid, ornate grandfather clock adorning the inner wall. "You know what I mean," McMillan sizzled. "We are working with a skeleton crew. Soon they'll start leaving too. Or have you forgotten," he growled, "that we are facing a world holiday? A ridiculously fantasized Earth ocean-sky holiday."

He stood up towering over his friend as if it were all his fault. "A few more hours and the trains will stop, the planes will be grounded, and all the ships and boats will drop anchor. Even robo-cabs won't be running. Tell me, if the award ceremony is not taped within the next hour, what will you tell the audience when they tune in at the scheduled time?"

Andrey Voznesensky, United Earth's renowned film producer, had lived through many disasters. One reason for it, although he did not know it, was that in his early years he had formulated a theory. One should never admit defeat. One should never give up.

He believed admitting defeat meant taking the irreversible step that kept plunging one down the bottomless slump. It meant losing right away a ninety-nine-and-a-half percent chance of success; then, or any time in future.

Therefore, he ignored his friend's hypochondriac outburst. "Have you considered this?" he asked cheerfully, "If she has been kidnapped, we have nothing to worry about."

"Why not?"

"Because the kidnapper knows if she misses the award ceremony, the whole world will be thirsting for his throat."

"And what if," McMillan found another devastating bullet, "she has decided to disappear of her own free will?"

The shot hit its mark. Andrey thought he had considered all the possibilities. This one had escaped him. Considering it, he refused to believe it. "Why would she do that?"

"How do I know? She is young. Today's young ones do things you and I do not understand. Cannot understand. Maybe she did it on a lark. Maybe she thought it would be lots of fun to disappoint everyone."

Andrey stared at his friend's night-watchman face. Yes, he thought, today's parentless youngsters were capable of horribly nasty things—to hurt people merely to have some fun. But not Pia Payal. She was not like that. She was different. He knew her.

Or did he?

He knew Pia the movie star, Pia the stage queen, Pia the perfect hostess, Pia the person who met once, one could never forget. What did he know about Pia the recluse, Bakul's shadow who never dated anyone? perhaps not even Bakul?

Nothing, he decided. And he felt panicky.

Suddenly he had an inspiration. "You know the last time I was talking with her, Pia had said something about having a lunch date, with that baby reporter—what's her name—Sonal? Yes, Sonal Neera. One thing we do know about Pia. She is particular about her appointments. If she has not been kidnapped, she'd call Sonal to confirm or cancel. I know Sonal is at home tonight."

"Now you are talking, Tiger-Tamer," McMillan's brooding blue eyes brightened up. "Let's call Sonal. You have her number, or should I call info-link?"

Without waiting for an answer, McMillan accessed info-link, got Sonal's number, and punched it.

***

Sonal's eyes were watching *Spider's Stratagem.* Her mind was elsewhere. It was re-evaluating issues she had gotten used to embracing at their face value. Like a trusting child, she had never doubted their validity, never questioned their authenticity. Now, JR's roundabout way of trying to achieve—whatever it was he had on his mind—made her wonder if what she had been led to believe was true. Or until now had they been playing Blindman's Bluff?

Was she an orphan, or not? Pavan claimed they were not. They were four. When they were born, their bickering parents had made a bet—when the kids grow up, if they find each other, their parents will reclaim them. If not, the kids will never learn their identities.

Pavan said that Pia Payal had found him and he had discovered Sonal. Now it was her turn to look for the *fourth* link.

What did this *fourth link* look like? Pavan did not know. Then how was she going to find him? Or was it her? Pavan could not say. It was her job to find the way. Okay, why this mysterious riddle-me-ree? When she finds this fourth person, how will they all find their parents? She will find out when the time comes.

She had agreed. Okay, fine. She will do it the hard way, finding everything all by herself. But now that he had told her the mind-boggling secret—that, except the three of them, no one else knew—that Pia was their sister, she would like to meet her. He should introduce them. That was the least he could do.

He had flatly refused. "Not until the fourth link is found," he had asserted firmly, decisively, trying to explain the logic behind this rule. But Sonal was not interested in his logic or rules. She was not able to understand his uncompromising attitude.

There are millions of people, she was thinking, on our United Earth, on the Moon, and on the various space-labs. Without any clue of any kind, without knowing what a person looks like, without even knowing if she was searching for a man or a woman, how could she find him or her?

For all she knew, she could be seeing this person's face somewhere every day—even working with him or her—without knowing the two of them were so closely related. What would happen if this person was determined, like Pia Payal, never to get found? Even more ridiculous. Why were they giving her the job of finding *him? Her?* Why weren't the three of them working together to find this fourth *link?* Aren't three heads better than one?

How stupid! She was silently fuming: I cannot just waylay everyone and say, "Hey! Listen, I'm trying to find someone. Let's diary talk, and determine whether you are the one I need to find." Won't they laugh at me and think I'm 'Nth percent' scatterbrained? Or that I have escaped from a Funny Farm?

When her frustration was reaching the breaking point, she had a brainstorm—why not invite Pia Payal for lunch? Tell her she has to interview her for a front-page story on her winning the Twin Film's topmost award. Then, with her subtle, news person tactics, she could dig out the basic facts from Pia's unsuspecting mind.

Surprise! Surprise! Pia Payal had accepted the lunch invitation. Had not even queried the reason.

She needed to plan her questions carefully. Because neither Pia nor Pavan should suspect or discover her looking-glass strategy. This interview needed lots and lots of thinking and meticulous planning. And, the time to do it.

But this old dragonfly—no, *Old Tug Boat*—as he called himself, was holding her prisoner. Her precious time was slipping away and he was lounging in his never-resting twenty-four-hour-chair so comfortably, there was no sign he'd soon release her.

She decided to try a time-honored tactic, "Chief, why don't we go to the revolving Virunga? On Fridays, they serve Osaka Shrimp." She modulated her voice to sound very friendly, very pleasant. "I can easily jot down details of my assignment there when waiters are bringing our order."

To forestall any chance of his saying a big NO, she continued in the same breath. "Besides Chief, if you want to give me the job of "historifying" this sexy soap opera, you really need to reconsider. You know I am not a drama critic. If I dare do it, I can see Pavan laughing at my green-toggle effort!"

The hazel eyes did not turn toward her.

JR had lit his pipe. With both his feet propped against the table, he was reclining. He looked as if, at this moment he was in his living room in his favorite chair, enjoying his favorite soap opera, with all the problems of the New Space News smoked out of his hair.

Sonal could not believe it. She knew he had heard her. Why was he behaving as if he had not?

She had no way of knowing that he was putting up a front, that this unhooked appearance was a deception he was finding very difficult to maintain. Actually he was very much aware of her voice, tones, and body movements. He had heard and understood the anxiety and impatience in her voice. But he had no choice. Like a good teacher, he had planned an outline very carefully, painstakingly. No matter how much he disliked hurting her, he had to see his plan through. Somehow he had to finish it.

"Chief," Sonal spoke more boldly, "if you are not in a mood for Virunga, we could . . ."

"Not much longer now, R-Seven," he said softly. "This is their last performance. Let's watch it. Just a few more minutes."

Sonal bristled. The coded answer was quite clear. She was a cub reporter. He was her boss. Cub reporters can't invite bosses for dinner. She had better keep her place. She squirmed in her chair. The evening was not moving along at all as she had planned.

When JR had called her, she was mystified by the summons. But then she had considered her leaving without saying a proper good-bye was reason enough.

That is why she had felt somewhat guilty. After all, he had hired her. Despite her determination not to learn, he had tried to train her. In fact, JR had thrown a kind of protective shield around her. If anyone else had produced the kind of work she had been submitting, that one would have been fired long ago. New Space News did not accept second-best. For that kindness, no matter how misplaced, didn't she owe him some time-honored courtesy?

Only a few more minutes? she thought. Okay, JR, you have me for a few more minutes. But then I'm walking out. With or without your permission.

Silently seething inside, she glanced towards the screen. The villain was darting on the stage. Lifting his arm, he shouted something, and threw a strange looking weapon at the hero's chest. Startled, Sonal leaned forward—what happened to his cabalistic, witchcraft weapon, the Spider's Web? They had changed the script. For the last show? Why?

And what a horrible change! That red dye looked like real blood. Bakul seemed mortally wounded. Looking like she was ready to faint, Pia was kneeling, stretching her arms to support his head.

"Earth Almighty!" Sonal whispered. "That's not Pia. That's not my sister."

JR was startled. But not a single muscle on his face moved. He simply lowered his feet and flicked off the screen.

He had expected Sonal's surprise. But not her statement about Pia. Especially not such an astounding declaration.

Sister? Pia? It struck him like a sharp bolt of lightning.

New questions cartwheeled in his mind—just now you had stated you were born on a Surrogate Island. Surrogates do not have sisters. How can you have one? Why did you make this statement that was so spontaneous it has to be true? . . .

When you were born, if someone had played tricks, how did you learn about it? How and when? I know you have never met Pia. Who told you? Was it Pia?

Not just Pia, are you also involved in this murder? Did you two conspire it together? Is that why she is meeting you tomorrow?

Composing his running thoughts, he turned towards her, his face expressionless. He asked softly, "Where is Pia? Where is your sister, Sonal? We need to talk with her."

Sonal Neera's face had lost all its color.

She was not supposed to tell anyone, not even Pia, that she knew Pia was her sister. What kind of a fool was she! How could she forget? How could she fail Pavan? How could she have allowed this bloodhound to extract this precious secret from her?

Why is he asking her where is Pia?

Is Pia missing? If she is, why does JR think *she* knows about it? Does he know they are sisters? Was Pavan lying when he said that, except the three of them, no one else knows this secret?

She did not know where Pia was. But if she knew, did he really believe she would tell him?

Ex-teacher or not, if he really believed that, then he really did not know her.

Her fingers again turned into fists.

"Sorry, Chief." Keeping her face emotionless, she softly said, "I do not know Pia. We have never met. Sometimes feeling lonely, I play mind games making her my sister. I mean, my Rakhi-Sister. All that blood on the screen must have shocked my alter ego terribly. That's why it blurted out like that."

Despite her best efforts, her voice quivered, "Why are you asking me about her? Is she missing?"

***

"Holy Moon-Shuttle! Is that Pia Payal?"

"Where? Gosh! You're so right. That is Pia."

"I need an autograph."

"Hold her for me. Let me call Rukma. She will never forgive me if she misses her."

The waves of excitement reached Maya Kiran. Her steps faltered. Was Pia waiting here? In the lobby? Why? Why not in Bakul's suite? Where is she? She glanced around looking for her.

The electrified nurses in their high heels and starched, white uniforms were rushing towards her.

Maya Kiran remembered—worried about Bakul, anxious to reach the hospital, while changing her blood-drenched stage costume, she had forgotten to remove Pia's mask from her face.

This was not the time for any explanation.

Hoping they would get discouraged and leave her alone if she did not pay attention to them, she pretended as if she had not heard. Walking a straight line, she strode to the inquiry window and asked pleasantly, "What is Mr. Bakul's suite number, please?"

The nurses looked surprised. They exchanged glances. Then several voices clamored. "You did not hear? . . . *You* don't know! . . . All the news stations were repeating it again and again. . . ."

"You crazy?" they started scolding each other. "Pia was rushing to be here with her hero. She had no mind to listen to news! How would she know? . . . ."

One, who was perhaps the Head Nurse, raised her hand to silence them. "You were so brave." With stars sparkling in her emotion-clouded eyes, she told Maya Kiran fondly, admiringly. "You did not shriek. You did not throw tantrums when, wounded and dying, our Bakul fell on your feet."

Maya Kiran opened her mouth to speak, but closed it without saying anything.

Why were these nurses under the impression that it was Bakul who died on the stage?

Her head hurt. Blood pumped faster in her veins. Why? She wondered. In the confusion, were the facts reported incorrectly? Or had the police, scared of the death-ridden gloom that would destroy the New Century Eve festivities, withheld the truth from the press? If he is not here, where is Bakul?

Not just the stage manager, everyone in the theater knew Pia's fixed aversion to stepping on the stage with Bakul's understudy. So, no one ever had to tell Maya Kiran. Any time Bakul's stand-in had to take his place, Maya Kiran automatically moved forward to perform Pia's role.

When Bakul had started thrashing with pain, she had seen the stage manager supporting Bakul on his fat arm and rushing towards the back door. She had heard his soothing words. "Hold on, Bakul. Hold on, Tiger. We'll take my shuttle. You know my super-shuttle. You'll reach your hospital before you can say doctor. And, Pia . . ."

Was Bakul taken somewhere else? Not brought here? Why?

Because they did not want to reveal the victim's identity? But then where was he taken?

If she called the Orpheum, would the manager tell her? No, he would not. The police must have told him to keep his mouth shut.

That means, she decided, I cannot ask the nurses anything. I cannot tell them anything.

Then how am I going to find out? she asked herself. Where is he? Was it his appendix? Was he operated on? Was the operation a success? Is he OK? Oh, Mother Earth! Oh! God Kalki! Please, guide me. Silently, inwardly she prayed.

She felt lonely, frightened, and confused. But she could not just stand there. Somehow gathering her courage, she softly asked, "Was he brought here from the theater? Is Bakul here?"

The Head Nurse sadly shook her head, "No. The ambulance took him directly to the crematorium."

"To the crematorium?" Maya Kiran echoed, horrified. But as soon as she said it, she realized the nurse was talking about Bakul's understudy who had died on the stage.

"Yes. The newscasts said it was done according to our Bakul's last will. Those were his instructions." Their eyes were tear-bright. "No crowds. No fuss. No lying-in, in any church or tempie. Simple cremation. Fast and quick."

Seeing Maya Kiran move, they remembered their duty, "Were you also hurt? You should have a check-up."

"No, thank you. I'm OK." Dodging the requests for her autograph, she politely touched a few hands, and striding firmly, quickly walked out.

So! The reporters were not given the name of the victim.

Crossing the almost empty parking lot she thought, what else were they not told? What else was not disclosed?

She felt angry. The nurses' behavior had made it quite clear that it was not just the victim's identity that was not given to the press. It was also not revealed that Pia Payal had not played her role. No one was told that her place had been taken by her understudy, Maya Kiran.

Now, believing her to be Pia Payal, would they hound her? Would they ask her all sorts of personal and painful questions that would make her feel even more miserable?

Where was Pia? The self-righteous person who always claimed she believed in nothing except the truth! Why had not she come forward to expose the government's lies? Why had she not called the press?

Despite her brave front, deep down inside herself, was Maya also afraid of the vicious reporters? Had she run away and was hiding somewhere because she was afraid of the merciless news-hounds?

If that was true, Maya Kiran realized she was in big trouble. Without Bakul's guidance, she would not know how to expose the government's lies. Believing her to be Pia Payal, the reporters would shake this United Earth to find her. They would hound her and grind her until she would break down and tell them everything.

Maya Kiran reached the parking lot. Her auto was waiting for her. Mercifully it stood alone. So far no one else was there. But this situation, Maya told herself, would change quickly.

Hoping to get their names on their hometown airways, the nurses right now would be calling the news media. As soon as the reporters learned she was at the hospital, they would follow her trail and soon catch up with her.

Yes, they would. Most certainly, they would.

Maya Kiran panicked.

have any option What could she do? Whom could she ask? Did she?

She definitely did not want to be interviewed again and again, by cruel and hard-hitting snakes who did their best, their utmost, to ferret out the tiniest detail, to turn you inside out.

Where could she hide? Hunter Island?

But no one would be there. Earlier today, Shaku had left with her parents for some undisclosed destination.

Why is that a problem? she asked herself. Many times before, in their absence, you have stayed there. Your room is always there. Always ready and waiting for you.

Peace and quiet. Books, music, and mute robots to obey all your orders quietly and efficiently. Yes. That would be the best self-therapy.

Sliding open her auto's window, she punched in the homing signal and sent it to her garage. Then she quickly walked over to the nearby visibooth and called in a robo-hovercraft.

She would need clothes and other personal items. But it would be wiser to travel in an unidentifiable vehicle than in her own.

Waiting for the hovercraft, it occurred to her that Pia might have accompanied Bakul. If she did, as soon as he got a chance Bakul would ask Pia to call her. She should leave her secret call-code on her video-corder.

The robo-hovercraft glided in and touched down near her feet. Getting in she silently prayed. Please Mother Earth, please God Kalki, please make Pia call me.

She must call me.

6

. . . *Kobra Keepers Targets*

Policy says, "Be wise as serpents. . . ."
  —Immanuel Kant: *Perpetual Peace,* Appendix I, 1795

. . .

It is not surprising that lambs should bear a grudge against birds of prey, but that is no reason for blaming birds of prey for pouncing on lambs.
 • F.W. Nietzsche: *The Genealogy of Morals,* 1, 1887

. . .

"*B*uddy, Pia has not called. Let's face it. We won't have the award ceremony tonight. Let's announce it on the evening news."

"Did I hear you right?" McMillan shook a finger at his friend. "You giving up? Noooo! Something's wrong with my ears."

"Funny! Funny!" Andrey Voznesensky snarled and slumped in his chair. "In my situation, even Sherlock Holmes. . . Before you say another word, just remember; sometimes even the best sleuths have to face a NO WIN situation."

"Then what happens? The sleuths play Bale-Fire?"

Stupid question! Andrey grimaced, roused himself and moved to his favorite window. Outside, the ocean was unusually calm, its gentle waves playing hide-and-seek with the twinkling stars. The full moon rode high surveying it all.

In the silence that ensued, McMillan drifted in a reflective mood. "Andy, you remember the day when it all started?"

Oh, yes! Andrey Voznesensky remembered. As if it were only yesterday. How could he forget! Was it already three years? On this very island?

After the decision was made, that *aut vincere aut mori* day, to produce the unconventional movie, *The Cobra Keepers,* he had serious doubts about it. Bowing down to the majority, he had hidden all his fears, all his doubts, deep inside his mind. He had silently thought, if this project fails, we'll have to sell this island, and its name, *Mubarak,* will haunt me for the rest of my life.

"You remember?" McMillan mused. "That *nil desperandum* evening? How all our fishing and aquaplaning plans had suddenly gone haywire when that thundering storm hit and we had to quickly round up our guests and nose-up the weather shields."

Andrey smiled at the memory. "And our doomed moonlight dinner, refusing wreckage, turned into that ballyhoo affair, drunk by dazzling flares of lightning. Many of our guests had never had a lightning-punctuated, thunder-dipped dinner before. They were delirious with delight."

"After the ding-dong dinner," McMillan continued, "we moved to our Jasmine Garden where torches were lit. And picking up a flute, someone started to play that gypsy song."

Andrey smiled. "Still jealous? Are you?"

"Jealous? Who, me?"

"Who else? The flute player fellow was capturing such a crowd, you couldn't stand it. Toasting your corny jokes, you started refilling glasses for everyone you could catch."

McMillan protested, "What nonsense! I was just being a good host. Ah! I know. You're saying it because you were jealous."

"Me? C'mon! I can't tell jokes. Everyone knows that."

"Is that why you got up on that high chair and started to sing that haunting sonnet that made everyone stand and clap and clap? You have a magical voice. You can't deny that."

"So! The secret's out!" Andrey grinned. "It was to snatch their straying loyalty, you dragged them down to your crummy screening room."

"That's not true! You know that. Everyone knows that. It was only your song that had given me the inspiration to make a mystery movie without a hero."

"I know it now. But I didn't that night. And I got so annoyed the movie almost didn't get made. I nastily opposed the idea. 'How gross! How weird! You want to alienate half the world?' I kept shouting. 'You want to ruin our name! Want to go down in history as a writer, who . . .'"

"Not your fault," McMillan laughed. "You had one too many of that Russian stuff you like so much."

"We were lucky our promoters did not listen to me."

"Some of them did," McMillan reminded him. "They kept following you, chanting with you, 'How gross . . . how stupid!'"

"But most of them were echoing you," Andrey reminded him.

"And hollering, 'No. Mac's right. Let's do it. It will intrigue men. And the women will come so they can butcher it. Media headlines will have fun with it. Let's do it.' And then, you had another one of your record-shattering brain waves."

"You always say that! Was it really my idea?"

"How can you forget?" Andrey sounded surprised. "Of course it was your idea. Shoot two versions of the movie—one comedy, another a tragedy. And let the audience vote. Let them tell us which one should win the Better Movie Award."

Andrey's mood sparkled, "So we all crowded in the projection room and looked at the stories in our library. After lots of debate, lots of head-shaking and shouting, finally everyone agreed upon your play, *The Cobra Keepers*."

"Having two heroines was that flute-fellow's idea," McMillan remembered. "And the promoters insisted the winner be given a two week, all-expense-paid vacation on the Moon. And now the award ceremony will be spacecasted on all space channels, and it will begin as the midnight clock ticks in the New Year of the new century."

They fell silent.

The project had succeeded beyond their imagination.

Everyone in the living world—in every township, city, and sector, had joined the fun. Both versions, comedy and tragedy, were dubbed in one hundred and ninety languages. There were official bets and unofficial bets made in bars and beauty salons.

Everyone over age ten had voted. The OMNI computer had to work round the clock to count all the ballots.

The tragedy queen, Pia Payal, was the people's choice. She had won the unique award that no one else in the history of Earth had ever won before.

And now, when the long-anticipated time of showering the accolades upon their chosen heroine was ticking in, she had disappeared . . . without any reason . . . without any trace.

If she was kidnapped, because she might have recognized the murderer, they might have killed her also.

If she was taken for ransom, they will call. Believing their demands will be instantly obeyed, they will call.

Thinking the Twin Films' owners have no choice, they will name a horrendous sum.

Neither Andrey nor McMillan would have admitted it, not even to themselves, but both of them wanted to be near the phone when that call came. That's why they had not moved from their office.

Calls came, but not the one for which they were waiting.

McMillan stared again at his mercilessly ticking clock.

Andrey rocked on his heels. Perhaps she got injured in some accident. Maybe she got sick and is lying in some hospital!

McMillan just could not take it any more, "Partner," he said, "We can't just sit here! We have to do something."

"What?" Andrey did not look at all like the *Tiger Tamer* he claimed he was. His tired eyes asked, "What can we do?"

"We have been worrying so much about this tape-on-time business, we plumb forgot something!"

Andrey simply stared at his partner-in-misery.

"We know Pia did not perform in that last show. It was her understudy. But no one noticed it. They think it was Pia who got soaked by Bakul's spurting blood."

"So? What's that got to do with anything?"

"A lot. A helluva lot." McMillan's eyes danced. Suddenly he sounded chipper, just like his old self. "Consider this—no one at Orpheum is buying that Pia was not there. In fact, the manager is insisting she was. We know better because we had a shadow-eye on her shuttle. We know it took off just before show time."

"Well, it's not her shuttle that settles it for me," Andrey said. "I think we are right because the manager got so upset. Did you notice it? His face turned so pale, and he kept insisting we should not mention it to anyone. '*ANYONE*'. He begged, 'It was nothing.

Just her temper tantrums.' And his hovercraft—"

Jumping Jehoshaphat!"

Andrey left his thoughts dangling and stared at his friend. "What?"

"I just remembered. I have both the tapes."

"What tapes?"

"I got our *The Cobra Keepers* tape, and the *Spider's Stratagems* tape celebrating its Golden Jubilee, with Pia dancing her heart out. Watching the two tapes together, we can find out just how good Pia's understudy is, the girl who no one is willing to admit was on the stage when that last curtain fell."

Andrey stared at his friend. He had known him too long not to understand the scheme being born in his nimble mind.

"Oh no, Buddy!" he shook his head vigorously. "You cannot do that. Don't even think of it. You cannot present to the whole waiting galaxy, Pia's *dame d'honneur* in *Spider's Stratagems*, as our *Cobra Keepers* winning heroine."

"Don't insult her! An understudy is *not* a *dame d'honneur!*"

"Semantics!" Andrey snarled. "I won't let you do it. People don't vote for stand-ins. They vote for the heroines. In our movie, your precious *dame d'honneur* was not a stand-in for Pia."

"In our movie," McMillan emphasized the word *movie,* "People voted for a character in a story. They voted for *Nageena,* the dancer who laughingly embraced death. Once a stand-in always a stand-in. If the hero or heroine are not available, the stand-ins must replace them. That's their job."

Andrey stared at his partner's closed face; at his adamant eyes. He knew he had lost the battle even before it had started. When Milan McMillan got in such a mood, no power on Earth could budge him. So he tossed the only clincher he could think of. "How would you find her, that *nobody* understudy? Like everyone else, she must have also gone somewhere to celebrate the New Year."

"First things first." McMillan sprang from his seat. "Let's watch the tapes. Come."

Andrey had no choice. He followed his partner.

In the projection room they inserted the tapes in two viewers, so they could watch both together. They had to admit it. If they did not know the facts, they would have sworn that the same actress was performing the role of heroine in both the tapes—the old one in which Pia had performed under their direction, and the new one in which they were convinced she had not.

"Look!" suddenly Andrey whispered.

"What?"

Andrey rewound the *Cobra Keepers* tape until he found the frame he was looking for. He froze and enlarged the image. Then he searched for a frame in the *Spider's Stratagems* tape. He froze and enlarged that image also. In that prisoned instant in time, both the tapes depicted the heroine, caught in an explosive dancing pose—both arms outstretched.

"What's so important about these, except the proof that for these dancers gravity doesn't exist?" McMillan asked impatiently.

"Look at their left arms!"

"Nice and smooth. Not crooked. You don't like them?"

Andrey smiled, "I've worked with Pia in many movies. I know her left arm. See that blue birth mark near her elbow? No one else I know has it. In this second tape, see this left arm. . . ."

He did not have to say any more. On *Spider's Stratagems* last show's tape, the gravity-defying arm that looked so much like Pia's, held no blue birthmark.

"Partner," McMillan beamed, "I knew I could depend upon you. I knew you would find a way. When I see that bastard manager, I'm going to wring his neck."

"Forget the manager," Andrey said indulgently, a satisfying smirk shining like a bloodhound's grin on his radiant face. "We got to find this girl. What's her name?"

"I don't know. The play was so popular, Orpheum stopped printing names long ago. And the employees have their own stupid code. They won't release anyone's name to an outsider."

"If I could just find her name." Like a leashed changeling, Andrey strode to his window, then strode back. "Just her name. . . ." He paced the floor, staring at the Kashmiri carpet, as if the answer were hidden somewhere in its thick fibers.

They heard the antique grandfather clock chirruping the half hour. At the sound, Andrey's eyes moved towards it and an idea struck him. "Buddy, why are we worrying? The news media believe this understudy *is* Pia Payal." He grinned. "*They* are tracking her. Let's hear the latest news bulletin."

***

The latest news bulletin is the answer, Jal-O thought.

He had been trying Pia's number. It was not out of order, but it was not answering. Her video-corder was not on, and calls were not being forwarded.

Jal-O was feeling annoyed. How could a person like Pia be so careless! When she came under his care, he would have to teach her how to take care of small, routine things—how to be responsible.

Would she listen to him? Or, like Ketki, would she fight him at every step?

What nonsense! he chided himself. Why was he remembering that knave hellcat so much? This was the time, at last, to be happy. To forget the past. To forget her for all the time to come. To totally burn her from his memory. As long as this Earth spun around its sun, she would never be able to cross his path.

Feeling somewhat happier, he turned on his wristwatch-radio. In heavy, somber tones, it softly intoned, "Ashes to ashes. Bakul's body has been cremated."

Jal-O swelled with pride at such a flawless success. A wide grin swarmed on his dark, swarthy face. "Did you hear that, dear *Kahuna?*" He fondly caressed it. "Isn't it good? Just what we needed. JOLLY GOOD, as Jal-One would say."

It will be impossible now, he thought, for anyone to find out that Bakul was the Number Two human in our jackal committee. Without any physical evidence, without any clue, no one will be able to link us. So, when the land-scooper torpedoes, my anonymity will remain intact. Perfectly undisturbed.

He glanced towards Jalanga, his home-away-from-home, the island he had secretly reconstructed and reshaped to suit his needs and requirements. It was coming closer. Soon he would be there. Soon it would become his private island—the seat of his government from where he would rule this lovely water planet.

My Jalanga is the best—the biggest—human-made island, he thought with pride. The rules, that I tricked the Board of Directors to approve, are not for my benefit. Not really. As I had explained to them, they were constituted for their comfort and protection only. They had understood and agreed.

Why wouldn't have they agreed? he thought smugly. If only the members can use the island, that keeps it safe and exclusive. If no one is allowed more than two weeks' vacation, it ensures that everyone is guaranteed a crowd-free, peaceful place to have relaxation and fun. If only robots are allowed to work, it frees the members from the drudgery of daily routine.

He picked up his binoculars—everything seemed OK. Like a huge garland, the rowboats ringed the island. He had told the Board the boats were for their pleasure. He smiled at the memory. Because he had gained their trust, it never occurred to them that their real purpose was to catch any intruder who might dare to enter the island without his prior permission.

The island had three docking bays—one for residents, one for non-resident members and their infrequent guests and one for the Board Members—the so-called Elected Twelve.

Jal-O generally used the Non-Resident Bay. It gave him visibility, which in his position was very important. But his real reason was that it gave him an opportunity to observe the visitors, without their suspecting.

This time, however, he steered *Star Kahuna* towards the Council Bay. It was guarded by his personal robots. He wouldn't be scrutinized and would pass through quickly.

He had, he realized, wasted too much time thinking about his novel, and then trying to contact Pia. He was getting very late and needed to rush.

Opening the secret closet in the visi-cabinet, he pulled out her mannequin that he always kept there. "Pia, dearest," touching its legs, its cheeks. He softly whispered, "Star of my dreams, you are my only companion, I want to make that day real when you'll be with me. Laughing, and joking, and singing your favorite poems."

Kissing the mannequin's lips, he asked her, "Would your cheeks, your lips, taste like apples? The apples that I know you like so much. For you, Apple of My Third Eye, I'm growing an orchard in my backyard, so that you can pick your choice any time you want. When you stretch your arm to reach a higher bough, I'll pick you up. When you bite into an apple, I'll bite with you, biting your lips. My darling consort, you would love that, wouldn't you?"

Kissing the mannequin's apple-red lips once again, he replaced it and locked the cubicle.

Then, maneuvering *Star Kahuna* towards the docking gates, he thought, tonight, after everyone's gone to sleep, I'll carry my Visi to the apple orchard and call Pia from there. When she answers, the sight of all those apple trees around me will stimulate her, and she will straight away express her desire to join me.

I will tell her she has nothing to fear. When she arrives, I will personally greet her. I will climb in her shuttle, kiss her, and with my own hands decorate her lovely face by the mask I have specially prepared for her. It does not look like her lovely face. So here, no one, absolutely no one, will recognize her. After she has rested a bit, I will take her to her apple orchard. I will tell her I have not named it, because I want her to give it its name. Then, when she is plucking an apple, she won't be able to reach the high branches. I will pick her up in my arms and, if she is not feeling shy, let her ride upon my shoulders.

Then, reclining against her chosen tree and munching her apple, I will light candles, and sit near her feet. The dinner that will follow, our first dinner together, I will make sure she will remember forever.

***

Pushpak Prado Powhatan sat at his dining table munching a red apple. His companion, tiny Orion, sat cushioned against his sprawled feet, tackling his evening meal.

In his grandmother's house, Pushpak would not have dared to touch the clothes he was sporting now—faded jeans, and a bright blue T-shirt that proclaimed boldly in several languages, *DON'T DROP OUT. DON'T COP OUT. DON'T BLOW-OUT. DON'T SPACE-OUT . . .*

"Tell me, Orion," picking up the earmuffs from the edge of the table, and twirling them around his fingers, Pushpak asked, "Why does everyone assume one has a girlfriend?"

Orion did not look up. As a rule, he never ignored his lord and master's conversation. But at the moment, the nine-inch Silky Terrier was interested in his long delayed dinner, not in small talk.

Pushpak persisted. "Outrageous! Isn't it? And, this chit of a girl, with big-bang tearful eyes, tops them all. First, she gives me a non-existing girlfriend. Then she bestows upon me these silly earmuffs for that nowhere person and doesn't even give me a chance to say, 'Thank you, but . . .'"

Orion had finished licking his bowl. He looked up and lifted one small paw.

"Right you are," Pushpak picked him up. Scratching softly under his ears, he combed his hair with his fingers.

When he came home, before taking his own shower, Pushpak had given his tiny toy terrier a quick bubble bath. The dog's silky body fur, blue, with tan on his head, chest and legs, looked glossy in the indirect, overhead light. And his philosophic eyes, candid and wide awake, devotedly declared that no matter what, he adored his owner.

Pushpak scratched him between his ears, then started fixing the muffs around his ears. "Orion, big buddy, the next moon shuttle is scheduled for the fifteenth. They won't let me go because they say I'm needed here. Fiddle-dee-dee! Well, I could stow away. How about you?"

Orion shifted his weight on another leg and looked fondly at his surrogate protector.

Just then the visiphone bleeped. Pushpak pressed a panel on his chair's arm and his grandmother's time-furrowed face lit up on the big screen hanging on the opposite wall.

He smiled at her frowning image. "Hello, Grandma. Hello. Are you ready to tackle the new century? Orion says hello and Long Life. Come on, Orion, wish Grandma good luck." Taking Orion's small paw in his hand he waved the terrier's hello.

"Prado, my son," Grandma was clearly not in a mood to exchange any hellos. "Listen to me. At least once in your life, listen to me. I don't want you to go out tonight."

"But Grandma, I've promised."

Pushpak loved his grandmother. In fact, there were times when he felt that, in the whole world, she was the only one who cared for him. She was all he had, and he would do anything to please her. To make her happy.

But this issue was different. It concerned duty and responsibility; elements that could not be measured on the same scale that hugged such a delicate item as love. It was Grandma who had taught him that! Then why . . .

With Grandma logic generally worked—her own logic.

Pushpak decided to try it. "You need to understand Grandma. It may be a global holiday, but all the work cannot stop. Life cannot stop. Some things have to be taken care of."

"Why are you always the one who is called to wet your shirt when no one else would?"

Pushpak felt concerned. What lurked in her intuitive eyes was not anger at his 'immature' decision. She was upset about something that really mattered to her.

"Why, Grandma," he asked trying to sound very cheerful. "What's bothering you?" Wanting to cheer her up, he alluded to their private joke. "Is someone about to clip-clop the fragile thread holding that famous Damocles's Sword over my head?"

"It may just come to something like that, Kaku." She shook her head in frustration. "When cobra keepers get ready to dance, anything can happen."

"Cobra keepers! What cobra keepers?"

"Time for you to learn. That's why I want you to come."

"I will. As soon as my shift is over. Till then . . . "

"Tonight something very bad is going to happen, son. I can feel it in my bones." Her image seemed to waiver, "I'm feeling afraid, very much afraid. I don't want you to get hurt."

Pushpak was always amused by her attempts of forecasting the future. It had never bothered him before. It did not bother him now. "Grandma." He wagged an accusing finger, "you've again been reading your beads."

"And what's wrong with that?" she bristled. "Beads don't lie. They only tell folks to be careful and avoid danger."

"I'll be careful." He nodded his shapely head. "Very, very careful. I'll avoid all danger. I promise. Rama's truth."

"Prado, my son. You think everything's fun and games." Her helplessness encased her age-creased eyes, cried in her earnest voice. "All your friends—those you bring home—have such good jobs. Why can't you settle down like they have? Find the right job?"

That's the real problem, Grandma, he wanted to say. I do not know what I really want to do. What is the right job for me? There are times I don't like anything. I don't want to do anything. Then there are times I want to do something so bad that if not allowed to do it, I'd burst up and stop breathing. But the powers that be won't let me handle it; won't let me come near it. Is it really my fault, Grandma, that I can't find a job? Is it?

But, these thoughts could be communicated only to his buddy, Orion. Not to Grandma.

"In the old days," she was saying, "Much before you were born, there used to be a governing body named *United Nations.* When political units, called *Nations,* could not mind their ways, could not keep their people under control, the United Nations used to send its armies to the infested areas to sort out matters."

She found a handkerchief and, under the pretense of blowing her nose, wiped her eyes, *Keeping the PEACE,* they called it.

Sometimes, I feel," her voice got stuck in her throat. Clearing it, she continued, "you were born at the wrong time. You would have been very happy in those days, minding everyone else's work except your own."

"Wow! Grandma," he gave an awestruck look and a winning smile. "What a big speech! I remember once you told me, they used to give colossal speeches—long and winding with big words. By any chance, were you one of them? Minding everyone else's business except your own? If that's the case, I'm your grandson. I've got your blood."

"Go on." She smiled a tearful smile. "Do your promised job. Then fly home. I want to see you tomorrow. Not on Visi—in person. Until then, you call me. Every half hour. You hear?"

"You got a deal, Grandma. UN person signing off."

He saw her smiling as she broke the connection at her end. It lifted some weight off his chest. But it did not reassure him completely.

She rarely tried to look into the future. When she did, if she got such feelings, sometimes she had nightmares all night. Very bad ones.

She needed someone near her.

Her housekeeper was on vacation. The maid had taken off to celebrate the New Year with her family. She'd be alone tonight.

Should he call the duty officer at Space Central, cancel his watch and fly home right now?

He gently placed both his palms against Orion's silky face. "Orion, old buddy, should I cancel my assignment, and go to Grandma's right now? What should I do? You know about those nightmares. You know how bad they can be."

7

... *Nightmare Lines*

A dreamer is one who can only find his way by moonlight, and his punishment is that he sees the dawn before the rest of the world.
—Oscar Wilde: *The Critic As Artist,* 1891.

. . .

Some say that gleams of a remoter world visit the soul in sleep.
P. B. Shelley: *Mont Blanc,* 1816.

. . .

Maya Kiran was having a nightmare. The same old spooky, chilling nightmare that she often had since her early childhood. Since she could remember.

As memories go, it was one of her first memories. As she grew older, the haunting malevolence, lurking in the terrifying shadows of its revolving blue wheels, got a little more comprehensible. Each time she understood its nebulous nuances a bit more. A little better.

Gradually its outlines had become so familiar that even when snared in its petrifying spell, she knew what would happen next.

Each time the nightmare came, the menace grew. Each time, the story moved ahead. The menace expanded as if someone were slowly unfolding a story. Or as if it were a living, growing thing, hiding inside her like a baneful invader, waiting for the time when it would grow to its full size and totally devour her.

. . . The revolving blue wheels move. Under their receding shadows, she senses her taut, unyielding body, covered up to her neck by a snow blanket, lying vulnerable in a vast, circular bed. . . . Under the warm snow, her hands and feet are tied with some strange kind of halyard that she cannot locate. Tied so tightly that her muscles hurt. Her bed is ringed, surrounded by garishly painted robots, yelling at her to stop breathing so that their masters can start butchering her.

. . . Craving to ignore them, thrashing helplessly, she wants to close her eyes to resume her sleep, but she cannot because, like a strange shimmering wheel, a ghostly face is floating over her. A savage, lusty, barbarous, face that is colored deep blue, and is half-hidden under a dark blue veil. Peeping through its two eye holes, trying to drink-up every drop of her blood, his cavernous eyes are sparkling gold—gold, flecked with a wild green—the glutting green that lichens at the bottoms of stormy, thrashing oceans.

. . . Suddenly, a long blue pole, ending in ghastly blue steel claws, catches her neck and starts removing her blanket. Is he going to rape her? She shrieks. And shrieks again.

And she wakes up.

There is no sound in the room. But, she does not dare to open her eyes. You dumb Kiwi, she fiercely scolds herself, there's nothing to be afraid of!

It's the same old stupid nightmare, narrowing her eyes she furiously reminds herself. Open your eyes and look. You are on Hunter Island. You are in the guest room that has always been yours—where you have so often laughed and cried, and played so many funny games with your dear friend, Shaku.

If you try to open your eyes, she advises herself, you will find the night alarm blinking red; the doors and windows closed. Your personal Robo, Neemu, is standing guard near your feet, ready to spring and attack anyone who even brushes lightly against any wall, door, or window.

You silly Kiwi, there is nothing to be afraid of.

Slowly she opened her eyes.

As if her fiendish nightmare had come true, a blue face was hovering above her. A sea-blue face, half covered by a dark blue veil. Through its eye-holes glared those spooky, eyes—pure gold, flecked with that ocean-bottom green.

She screamed and closed her eyes—her nightmare had again extended itself. A new dimension had been added to it. Hunter Island had now become a part of it. She was still asleep.

"Miss Ypsilantis, please wake up."

Yes! There could not be any doubt about it. It was some kind of a time-locked extension of her childish nightmare. No one in this part of the world, absolutely no one, knew her birth-name.

"Miss Ypsilantis, PLEASE!" The blue hand moved towards her neck.

She shrieked, sat up upright, and pulling in her feet, gathered the blanket around her, tightly clutching it. Well! Perhaps it was not a nightmare anymore. Perhaps she had awakened, and this burglar who had colored himself blue from head to toe, from fingernails to toenails, was alive and breathing . . . and, real! Why hadn't Neemu caught him?

She glanced at Neemu standing guard at his customary place, and at the night alarm blinking red. In Kalki's name, how on Earth had this obnoxious ruffian managed to bypass the security system and sneak in? How had he made the impossible, possible?

Those gold-green eyes smiled, "You are wondering why your alarm did not bleep? Why did your robo-major not try to stop me?"

. . . Not questions! Statements! And the voice! So pleasant? So husky and seductive? Hearing it, looking at those snaring eyes, she panicked. No. He is not going to rape her! He wants to seduce her! She shivered and gathering herself, clutched the blanket around her tighter.

"I would have loved to explain it to you," he said affectionately, "But right now we don't have that much time."

We've got all the time in the world, she thought. Shaku and her parents won't return for weeks. And I've got nothing to do and nowhere to go right now.

"Two robo-keepers are coming to kidnap you. They will be here any minute. I rushed to advise you that you should not ask Neemu to deactivate them. You should let yourself be kidnapped."

"This is *advice!*" Jolted by what she thought was a hellish joke, she found her voice. "What are you! Some kind of a frugging psychopath? No sane person will give another such a crazy advice. No one will accept it? Not even a Pinko."

"You are right," he nodded solemnly. "It does sound crazy, and I plead guilty for springing it upon you like that. But you are a very intelligent person. Almost a genius." He smiled a very winsome smile, "I'm sure you know when and how to heed a much-needed warning. Now, I must leave. Close your eyes."

"Funny! Funny!"

"We are not playing a game!" His expression changed. He sounded annoyed. "It's time. You must start learning to obey me, and you're going to start right now. You will let them kidnap you," he said firmly. "And, you *WILL* close your eyes. *RIGHT NOW!*"

"Why?" she demanded angrily, belligerently. "Why should I close my eyes?"

He frowned, "Because, I'm asking you." Without waiting for her reply, he lifted up one end of her blanket and wrapped it over her head.

It took her only a few minutes to struggle free, but he was gone. . . . Neemu was still standing guard at his post. . . . The night alarm had not bleeped. It was still blinking red.

She swallowed hard, moved to the edge of her bed, and put her feet in her night slippers. If she could walk and drink some water, would that mean what had happened just now was not a hellish nightmare, but was real?

Or perhaps she should throw some cold water on her eyes? Take a cold shower? . . . Would that disperse this abominable hallucination without leaving a shadow-dot on her mind?

She moved to her bathroom. In the mirror, her face was the same old Greko-Spanish face. Her eyes were still her father's dark mahogany eyes. But around her neck sparkled a gold necklace that she never had, a necklace that she had never seen. The necklace held a sparkling blue pendant that glistened, and scintillated, like the surface of a sparkling ocean.

She touched the pendant. As if by magic, the intruder's blue face appeared in the mirror, smiling at her in a friendly manner. She whirled around. There was no one behind her.

Slowly, she turned back and stared at the strange face. Her dream must have warped her mind, that face was not dictatorial at all. Having shed that hypochondriac veil, those golden eyes flecked with that sparkling green, did not look menacing. On the contrary, they seemed quite attractive.

Taking an anxious breath, she closed her eyes. When she opened them again, she found only her own face in the mirror. Full of curiosity, she touched the pendant again, and again right away, she saw that blue face, and those hypnotic eyes smiling at her.

"Wouldn't you like to join Bakul and Pia?"

Maya Kiran jumped back. She was not sure if the image in the mirror had spoken those words, or she had imagined them. If he had spoken, if he knew where they were, this time she would not let him get away without getting answers to some urgent questions. No risk was too high or too great, if she could find Bakul and Pia.

"Bakul and Pia?" Clutching the pendant in both her hands as if—if she loosened her hold even a little bit—it would fly away, she hotly demanded, "You know them? Where are they? Were they also kidnapped? By whom? That assassin's friends? Why? Are the kidnappers going to kill them too? Why? What more do they want? What—"

"Hold it! Hold it," he raised an admonishing blue hand.

"Wouldn't it be better if you get all your questions answered by the kidnappers? I believe," he smiled engagingly, "first-hand information is always more trustworthy."

If Bakul and Pia were waiting for her, wherever the robo-kidnappers were taking her, any delay she made would be a big mistake. "Okay," she quickly promised those mesmerizing eyes, "I'll allow your robots to kidnap me."

Not giving him another glance, she turned and quickiy walked back to her bedroom. Ordering Neemu to get into his closet, she deactivated him. Then with quick fingers, she reprogrammed the security alarm and the island security circuits.

"Shaku," she whispered as she settled herself inside her blanket, "I'm not dreaming all this, and I've done it right. As soon as I leave, the security system will be reactivated. It will not recognize anyone except you and your parents."

I need to consult with Bakul about lots of things. Trying to encourage herself, she meditated somberly. I'm Pia's understudy. She needs me. If they want me to join her, that's fine with me.

But her mind found a new threat. What if he was lying? What if the robots were not taking her to Bakul and Pia? Oh, God Kalki, why did you make me trust him?

It was a well-known secret. On some space stations they were trying all sorts of genetic experiments. Could this Blue Person be a product of one of those experiments? If he was, was she being taken to his space station for some devilish experimentation? Did they need blue women for their Blue Men?

But Pia was missing. Bakul was missing. She had left her secret code on their Visi. They had not returned her priority call. It had never happened before. If it was happening, it could be only because it was impossible for them to call.

Since the Blue Person had used the words, *first hand,* he must know where they are. When she'd face him again at his space-station, he would not be able to demur and hide behind clever words. He'll have to answer. Wasn't that worth taking this risk?

Or was he a NOPE agent cleverly disguised? Could it be all NOPE's deviltry? She had been told by more than one person that one method used by NOPE for recruiting new members was to kidnap them. If their sinful methods of brutal persuasion failed, they altered their victims' thought-personalities by injecting a new, secret drug in their minds.

They would not dare alter Pia's mind. No way. Bakul would make sure of that. He would also make sure nothing happens to me.

In fact, she thought, feeling somewhat cheerful, as Pia would have said, this crime would be a *blessing-in-disguise,* because it will bring us together again. Thinking together, planning together, surely we will be able to find a way to escape.

It seemed very long—or not long enough—when she heard the robo-invaders opening her door. An image of her mysterious captors, eating and drinking and dancing, and herself hanging on a wall riddled by drug-injecting needles, flashed in her mind. Then a needle softly pierced her arm and she lost consciousness.

***

Eyes like sharp needles . . . silently Sonal Neera was trying to compose a lyric. *. . . craving for my mind, probing every pore, numbing every nerve . . .*

Trying to think of a suitable word that would rhyme with *mind,* she stared at JR. Why was he trying so hard to extract all her secrets, all the hidden facts, everything that she had always hidden deep inside her mind? Had never mentioned to anyone.

Why was she so different? So tough? Why couldn't she be like the other girls who found an easy escape from such nightmares by fainting? Losing consciousness?

JR had noticed the change in her body language, but he had no choice. He was trying his best to act naturally, to do nothing by even a word, or a gesture, that would alarm her again.

Earlier when Sonal had flared up at his question concerning Pia, his robo-server had saved the situation by wheeling in their dinner. To buy time, he had told him to serve drinks. For Sonal, he had told the robot to prepare the pomegranate cocktail that he knew she loved. The robo had placed it on a high stool near her. But it was just lying there. She had not even looked at it.

JR felt his worst nightmare had come true: he did not know how to handle her. Those who thought he could handle any situation, had miscalculated. But something had to be done to salvage the situation, and the sooner, the better.

Collecting his thought, he said gently, "Where were we when our dinner walked in? Oh, yes! I asked you about Pia. She was planning to have lunch with you. I thought she might have called."

Sonal relaxed—was that all? Pavan's right. I get too suspicious! Too quickly! For no reason at all. I must try to get rid of this wretched habit.

"No," she shook her head. "I have not heard from her. But, there was no reason for her to call. The date *is* confirmed."

"You may be disappointed."

"Why? Everyone knows Pia never misses a confirmed appointment."

"I've heard that," JR nodded. "But sometimes, circumstances can be beyond one's control. What if . . . if she has been kidnapped?"

"Kidnapped? Pia?" Sonal smiled. "Everyone worships her. Even criminals. People like her don't get kidnapped." She picked up her drink. "Here's to your wild theories."

"Not so wild, R-Seven," JR sipped his wine. "Do you know something about NOPE?"

"Not much. It is a new protest group, isn't it? Protesting something or other. Quite wild, I imagine," she savored her drink. It was really delicious.

JR was amused by the raw expression in her eyes.

He also felt relieved. Their assumption was correct. Her answer had made it clear that she was neither a Believer, nor a Follower. She would be able to tackle the job he had for her, without any bias or conflict.

She decided to accept his bait. "Okay, let's test your theory. Tell me, why would they kidnap her? They need loners, rebels, or ultra-rich. She is none of those. So, no use to them."

"Wouldn't it be a Koh'noor in their shaky crowns, if they could tote her around as their flag bearer?"

"But she would not agree to it. Bakul would not allow it."

She stared at him. "Is that why they murdered him?" She tossed her hair into place and sat straighter. "No, Chief. That does not hold water. They cannot be that stupid. Pia does not move without Bakul. To convince her, first they would need to convince him. If that's the case, they would have kidnapped him, not killed him."

"Your logic is sound, Sonal." He got up to refresh their drinks. "But suppose they considered their chances of brain-washing both of them impossible? Suppose they considered him an unnecessary nuisance? Suppose they believed if they got rid of him, they would be able to brainwash her?"

Sonal stared at him, "Good questions. One more. If logic required that one of them be left alive, who would fetch higher ransom?"

JR nodded, "You got it."

Sonal thought about it, then shook her head vehemently. Her hair again fell over her eyes. Pushing it away impatiently, she moved to the window. "I have heard all kinds of things about NOPE. One that everyone—those for it *and* those against it—say is that NOPE is not money-crazy. It only wants grass-roots participation, and political clout, to achieve its goals."

"Don't these two items go together? Can they achieve these goals without finances to fund their activities?"

She simply stared at him.

He glanced at her thoughtful face, "That's your assignment, R-Seven. Come, let's have dinner. It's getting cold."

She made no move towards the dinner table. "What's my assignment? NOPE? How does that compute?"

JR ignored the question. "I don't believe it. The whole evening you have been bugging me to take you to Virunga. Now that I've brought Virunga to you, you are letting the food go cold."

"Look who's complaining!" Smiling, she moved towards the table and picked up a plate. Giving it to him, she took another one for herself.

Serving him some salad, she said, "Haven't you kept me in suspense long enough? Why don't you tell me what surprise you have cooked up for me? What you want me to do?"

He took his plate to his desk and stood leaning against it.

"You are officially resigning. You will contact NOPE and tell them you left us because you hate the Establishment. You want to be their disciple and work for their cause. As an insider, whatever you learn, you will let me know."

She gawked at him with offended, unbelieving eyes. "You want me to be an informer? a . . . a *spy?*"

"Tsk! Tsk! my dear. The correct designation is 'Investigative Reporter.'"

She replaced her plate on the table, moved back to her chair, and clutched its back firmly with both her hands. "Chief, would you tell me something right now? Not stories. Not half-truths. But the whole truth?"

"Have I ever lied to you, R-Seven?"

She clutched the chair harder. "How can you entrust such a sensitive job to me when you do not trust *me?*"

"Not trust you?" He was really surprised. "Why wouldn't I trust you! Of course I trust you." He shook a finger at her, as if to say, *you have been working here, haven't you!*

"No, you do not trust me." She shook her head and brushed away her truant hair. "You keep track of me seven days a week, twenty-four hours a day. My condo, my Visi, my hovercraft are bugged. Even a chained rabid dog has more freedom than I have."

JR stared at her fuming face, at her bright aquamarine eyes flaming with suppressed outrage.

How did she learn about it?

Every possible precaution had been taken. There was no way for her to find out. How did she find out? When?

"You are wondering how I found out?" Wry humor jeweled her attractive eyes. "I may not be very intelligent, Chief, but I am not so dumb either."

Our mistake, he wanted to say. We knew you are exceptionally intelligent. But apparently we underestimated you.

"Why, Boss?" she was asking. "Why am I your prisoner? I know the other Space News employees are not kept under such hellish surveillance. Why I have been singled out? Is it by any chance because once you were my teacher, and you think I'm still that immature, ignorant, impetuous girl who did not know the difference between . . ."

Not able to complete whatever it was she was about to say, she strode to the dinner table. Turning her back to hide her face, she started piling heaps of food upon her plate.

JR felt he was having a nightmare. What she had just said, could not be real. He tried to clear his thoughts. If she knew about it, then everything they had recorded could be wrong. She could have calibrated her behavior to confuse and beguile them.

He pushed a button on his arm-rest.

"Space Priority." A strong voice, oozing with dark authority snarled through the receiver on his desk.

"Cancel all surveillance on R-Seven."

"Noted, Sir." The Voice had apparently recognized who was speaking. It inquired respectfully, "The network apparatus, Sir?"

"Remove and destroy. It will not be needed again."

"Acknowledged, Sir. Consider it done. Space Priority out."

"Space Priority!" Sonal breathed hard. "I am that important?"

"Is that why you were refusing to work, R-Seven? So that I will fire you? And you'll run and hide somewhere, where . . ."

"Don't sidetrack, Chief." She moved to her chair and started attacking her dinner as if she had not eaten for days. Taking care of shrimp and vegetables indiscriminately, she said decisively, "No more questions. And no assignment either. If you cannot tell me the truth, count me out. Right now."

JR looked at her regal face. At her clear eyes that hinted of untold monkeyshines. Her slim, attractive body. If he took her in his arms and kissed her, would she respond?

No. He could not do that. It was forbidden. Even more importantly, it might spoil their business relationship.

He could not reveal the truth because he was oath-bound. He had accepted the responsibility knowing the sacrifices it would require. To find a way to accomplish that difficult task, without telling her anything, was an integral part of his job.

Sonal Neera looked at his brooding face and wondered—was he making up a story, or telling her the truth when he said that once upon a time he was her teacher?

Was he really the person for whom she had written and torn so many love poems? Was he really the star-rider, the shimmering knight of her dreams? The person because of whom she had not able to love anyone since he had suddenly disappeared from her life?

What would he do if she slipped both her arms around him and kissed him hard? Would he pull her in and respond?

Would she like that kiss? Would she like those lips? Those strong arms that looked like as if they could crush a mountain.

Her whole body tensed. Leaving the plate on the side table, she moved back to her chair, sat down quietly, and looked away.

JR panicked. He thought she was rejecting him, would get up and leave. Then all night—all future nights—he would lie awake, wondering what he could have done.

That would not be so bad as would be the result that they would assign someone else to take care of her.

He came to a decision. No doubt, he was oath-bound. But every job must give room for exercising one's discretion. If they would not approve, they would have to find someone else. He would know he did not fail because he did not try his best.

"Sonal," he murmured softly, "I can tell you what you want to know. But you know me. I don't believe in hand-outs. You have convinced me you are right. I'm willing to make a deal."

She looked at him suspiciously. What she needed to know had no room for any negotiation. JR anticipated her answer. Not giving her a chance to reply, he quickly asked, "If I answer your question, would you also answer one of mine?"

She stared at his poker face. What kind of a question was it that needed such bargaining? Could it be about those foolish days when she was so secretly—so hopelessly—fawning over him?

Whatever it is, she argued with herself, if I do not accept his challenge, my curiosity will never be satisfied. I will never know why I have felt imprisoned since my childhood.

She came to a decision—she was done with brooding. No matter how difficult it would be, she must deal with him at his level. "Okay, that's a deal."

It was difficult, but she found strength to compose her face and looked at him, "Chief, your mind can operate without coffee. Mine cannot. Without it . . ."

He looked crestfallen. "I'm not just guilty! I'm double-guilty! First, I spoiled your evening. On top of that, I forgot about your Mexican coffee. Shall we go to Virunga?"

She laughed and decided to take his cue, "Why not? Since you have been snooping and know more than me what I like."

He moved towards her. She shot up from her chair and skipped ahead of him towards the door.

Glancing back to make sure he was following, she thought, Is it true? In real life, does it really happen? If one wishes upon a star, can one's dream come true?

Should she forget the past? Should she look up a new star tonight and make a new wish. . . .

8

... *Standing Against the Wind*

. . .

"If you wish upon a star," Kumiko wrote in her diary, "it does not matter who you are." She sighed. Ninety-seven. Just eleven times more and she would be done.

Written one hundred and eight times, would the words create the magical spiral she had willed for herself? If done right, would her incantation's earthly force take charge of her life's quest and launch it towards its elusive orbit?

Engrossed in her thoughts and the work she had forced upon

herself, she sat unobtrusively at her corner desk, her head leaning on her left elbow. Her cheek rested lightly on her half-open palm. The overhead light illuminated her lively face.

Anyone who chanced to look at her would have felt impressed by her single-minded concentration on her job. That is, until the observer found that her devotion was not applied to anything related to her job at Space Central.

It was not that she did not know what that nosy busybody—if it happened to be a supervisor—would say. *That* she knew very well. It was just that tonight she was not worried. Tonight there was not anyone around to interrupt her, or to keep her busy.

For several months, she had been trying to complete this ritual. The words needed to be written one hundred and eight times without any interruption. Whenever she had started, for one reason or another, she had had to leave it unfinished.

She was only a reserve trainee cadet in the Space Flying Corps. Often it seemed to her they were pushing assignments on her that had nothing to do with her job. She did not mind it. She loved working at Space Central. That, however, often meant she could not find time to fool around like everyone else.

Tonight she had started on her secret project with very high hopes. The other volunteers manning the crucial stations had their own New Year secrets. They had no time, no reason, to bother her.

Finally, she had done it. Finally she had achieved her goal.

Tonight something should happen. If her Earth elements were true and fearless and dynamic, tonight something would happen.

She looked to her left. Leaning back in his chair, his feet sprawled under his table, Pushpak Prado Powhatan was staring at the space-screen shadowing his face.

Poor Pushpak!

Kumiko knew, just knew, what he was thinking. His rebellious thoughts would be on that space shuttle scheduled to leave in a few days. His mind would be under an endless assault of questions that had no answers.

Right now, if he were at home, he would be daring anyone and everyone by knocking out his punching bag. Here he had no punching bag. Here he had only this tantalizing space-screen, a constant reminder of that soon dashing-away dream. This electro-dynamic barrier, if he tried to bang it, would not deflate even an insignificant micro-inch.

Pushpak. She tried to send her thoughts to him. Why don't you let me be your punching bag? Why don't you relent just a little bit and give it a try? Just once . . .

She got up and moved towards him. Standing close, she lightly touched his shoulder with one finger. He looked up. Her limpid, dark eyes, as always, seemed to be hiding some new mischief.

"Hi," moving to a side chair, she leaned on its low back. Pushing his thoughts back, Pushpak gave her his best smile. "Hi, yourself," he said as warmly as anyone could.

"What's bugging you, Robin Hood?"

"Bugging me?" He wagged an accusing finger at her. "Your eyes always see things that are not there, Ms. Robespierre."

She scowled. "Listen to me, Prado," she said imperiously. "If I'm your spooky Lord Robespierre's current heir apparent, you are not so far behind. Believe me, if you really want to do something about your problem, you need to join my group."

Pushpak Prado groaned. Why was everyone *always* telling him to listen to them? And which one of her innumerable clubs was she talking about now?

He had long ago stopped keeping track of her headline catching, colorful and mysterious, clubs and associations. But he dared not tell her that because that might endanger the endearing light she always had for him in those lovely, limpid eyes. So he smiled. A broad, cheerful smile that could dim the midday sun, and leaned farther back in his chair.

"You are such a lousy optimist, Kumi," he said roguishly. "You think your Brown-shirts will accept me? No. I guarantee you, one glance at me and they would disqualify me right away."

"Elements! Fire and Water and all that's Holy!" Kumiko exclaimed, exasperated. She dropped down in her chair, pulled it forward and leaned towards him. "You big dope! You know, saying that, you're insulting our NOPE."

"I am?" he hoped his eyes were expressing suitable surprise and that prompt space-touching surprise would let her be merciful, and make her forget the terrible insult he had so ignorantly heaped upon her beloved organization.

"Of course you are," her dark eyes blazed thunder and fire. "Listen to me, Prado. NOPE is *different.* It's not like the others. NOPE cares. It really does. It's the most precious club you can find. And its philosophy is very simple and down to earth. You'll like it."

"What makes you so sure?"

"I know you, don't I? Like you, in NOPE we're trying to buckle the current winds. *Never One Penny Ever.* That's our motto.

Our Watchword. Our name," she smiled and the fire in her eyes obeyed. "Isn't that clever, Prado? Most everyone can adjust it to their own currency—*Never One Pound Ever, Never One Paisa Ever . . .*"

"Very clever," he nodded in agreement. "But never one penny or paisa for what?"

"I joined it only because I thought you would approve." Pouting her lips, she got up as if to return to her station.

Pushpak grabbed her hand. Time for a showdown, he thought. Time for pushing her to the goal line, then snatching the lead.

But trying to snatch away her hand, before he could speak, she had resumed. "You want to go to the Moon and they won't let you go. Has it ever occurred to you . . ."

He grabbed her other hand also and she struggled to get free.

". . . how many others there are like you? Not just folks in engineering. There are traders, and contractors, and photographers, and builders, and you name it."

"Hold on! Listen . . ."

His words fell on unlistening ears. Without stopping, she continued in the same breath, "They won't let you space-trade. They won't let you find space-jobs. They won't let you do anything! To fund their precious space program, they have this mandatory tax—one to ten percent of your income-credits. You can not refuse it. You can not escape it. Even if . . ."

Needing to breathe, she stopped glaring at him accusingly as if he was personally responsible for the offending tax plan.

My chance, Pushpak thought. But, before he could sneak in a word she demanded, "Tell me—give me one reason why we should donate our hard-earned credits to fatten the space syndicates? No taxation without participation. That's our goal. If we can collect the needed signatures," she glanced at him appealingly, "we can demand a meeting with the United Earth Council."

"You know what, Kumi. I'm going to stow away on the next space shuttle."

"No, you are not!" she snapped. "You got no criminal mind. You don't want to rot on some obscure reform island for the rest of your precious life. And," she wagged a finger at him, "don't try to change the topic."

"Who's changing the topic!" His mood changed and he grew

very serious. "I was only trying to tell you that for me and everyone like me, that's the only way open. The space syndicates don't just control the Earth councils. They also run the United Earth Council. What's wrong with your friends? Do they live on some other planet, that they don't know that?"

"Politics!" she scoffed. "Who cares for it! We are only interested in following the time-tested rules. Democratic methods. As long as possible."

"*As long as possible?* What happens when it seems impossible?"

"We have a meeting tomorrow. It's very important."

"All meetings are important."

"No. This one's different."

Pushpak did not say anything. Just waited for her explanation, which he knew would come, even if he tried to stop it.

"A couple of time-shattering items are on the agenda," she said enigmatically. "One of them concerns your precious Spacepol."

"My Spacepol?"

"They have killed a popular hero, kidnapped his partner, and are now fabricating evidence to frame NOPE for both."

Pushpak Prado blinked. There was no need to ask who this precious hero was. The news was still getting splashed on all the newscasts.

Suddenly the image of a very young, very impressionable, very distraught girl, trying to forget the sight of spilled blood, shadowed—crowded—his mind.

"What evidence do they have?" he asked somberly.

"Spacepol doesn't need any evidence."

"Of course they do. They are not above our time-tested laws."

"Will you join us? Help us? You are badly needed."

"I may. If I can persuade my Grandma."

"What has your Grandma got to do with it?" Kumiko asked belligerently. She was losing patience. If his grandmother refused, would that mean she would have to start all over again?

"Nothing," he replied, elaborately bowing to her in her chair, as if she were royalty. "Just my habit. I never do anything without telling her."

Without giving her a chance to pounce again, he touched a panel on his chair, "P. P. Powhatan. Personal call. Record ID, time, and duration. Do not record conversation."

"Noted, ID, time," the mechanical voice of the Visi-Central stated. "No recording. Will time it. You may commence, Mr.

Powhatan."

He punched his grandmother's numbers. "Hello, Grandma. Hope I didn't wake you."

Her wide-awake eyes lit up with joy. "Prado, my son! You changed your mind? You coming right now?"

"Grandma, I want you to meet someone. This is Kumiko. Say hello, Kumi."

"My regards, Grandma," Kumiko bowed respectfully. "You know, Grandma, your grandson is impossible. I did not want to intrude upon your privacy so late at night."

"No need to apologize, my child. I love knowing my grandson's friends. I know all his friends. At least, that's what I thought. How come Prado never told me about you?"

"Grandma, life history later when you are fixing her breakfast. I just called to tell you I'm bringing her with me. And Grandma, we'll be late. So, please, don't delay your dinner."

"What's so important that you want me to eat alone?"

"It's my fault, Grandma," Kumiko crossed her fingers behind her back. "I'm pestering Prado. He wanted to leave as soon as his watch was over to be with you before dinner. But Grandma, we have this special meeting. If he misses it . . ." she left it unsaid.

"Fine," Grandma happily nodded her acceptance. "No problem. I want him to attend all meetings. He can't let down his friends. I won't allow it." She pointed a long finger at Kumiko. "But you promise? You'll bring him over as soon as your meeting is done."

"I promise, Grandma. I won't fail. If I do, I'll let space gobble me alive."

"Shss, child! You should not speak such words." To soften her rebuke, she smiled and said affectionately, "Don't get too late children. I won't eat until you come." Waving good-bye, she switched off the Visi at her end.

Kumiko heaved a big sigh of relief. "Your Grandma's a very fine person," she told Pushpak with firm conviction. Then a thought came to her and a mischievous smile lit-up her eyes. "You know what, Robin Hood?"

"What, Ms. Robespierre?"

"She would like us to be ringmates. That'd make her very happy. I could see it in her eyes. Why are we delaying it, Prado? Why don't you make me your ringmate right now?"

"Because, I'm not yet twenty-one. And you're only seventeen."

"Eighteen."

"Not for another seven weeks."

"Okay, we will wait your precious seven weeks," she sighed.

"Meanwhile, I thank you for coming to the NOPE meeting." Impulsively, she took hold of both his hands in her own.

At the touch, Pushpak again remembered his brief encounter with that frightened stranger—his last customer at the Energy Station. Her image sharp and clear, offering him those new century earmuffs, again flickered in his mind.

He closed his eyes and pulled Kumiko towards himself. She instantly threw both her arms around his neck. He bent his face over hers and kissed her.

The image of the tearful stranger, staring at his chest, his shoulders, his eyes, grew stronger. He kissed her harder.

Kumiko panicked. This is not a *get-acquainted* kiss, she thought. This is a *farewell* kiss. He is leaving me. He is going to stow away on that blasted spaceship. But he is afraid of doing so. He needs me.

She tightened her hold and tried to imitate a kiss she had seen so many times in the movie, *The Cobra Keepers*.

I need to go with him, she told herself fiercely.

He is exceptionally intelligent. But not in such matters. His mind is incapable of imagining—pre-conceiving—matters that require deception of any kind. If he tries to stow-away alone, he will be caught. I'll find a way to evade Spacepol, as have so many others. May Elements protect and nurture NOPE. They have lots of people. They won't miss me. But my star-infatuated friend is totally helpless. Without me, the winds opposing him won't let him run very far. . .

"Robin Hood," she ruffled his hair, "Listen. We'll stow-away together. I'll come with you."

"What about Spacepol?"

"May Thunder drown Spacepol!" She kissed him and snuggled closer. "Let them try to find us. Just let them try?"

Her touch tingled Pushpak's nerves. Again the memory of the stranger whose looking-glass eyes had sought his fellowship, shadowed his mind.

He decided to forget the matter of space exploration for a while, and embark upon another venture, equally unexplored, equally mysterious. His fingers moved towards the buttons on her blouse.

Busy conceiving, kindling their own fireworks, they did not see the dazzling fireworks exploding upon the space-screen.

***

As if enjoying the star-challenging fireworks so much he could not move his eyes away, Daniel O' Shaughnessy Shostakovich stood rooted near his large window.

He was, however, only giving his unexpected visitor time to unwind and relax. JR's opening words were that he had come over to consult with Daniel about the Orpheum murder. But Daniel knew the reason could only be Sonal. In that case . . .

Jayarath Rao Agashe, Chief Editor of the New Space News and Chairman of Intra Planet's Board of Directors, was trying to find words to offer his resignation from his taking care of Sonal Neera. He was not succeeding at all.

His mind was wandering. After the Seven-Day War, when the United Nations was abolished and replaced by the United Earth Council, old Danny O' would have been given any title, any position, that he wanted. But he declined every offer, all the suggestions, and retired to this small island in the Gulf of Siam.

Why? Why suddenly overnight, would a super-dynamic person like him make himself an unreachable recluse?

Was it disenchantment of some kind? Or a secret cover that required absolute anonymity? If the latter, for whom? Earth syndicates? Space shakers-and-movers? Why had Spacepol gone along with it? Except refusing to remove his name as their Consultant-On-Vacation, why had they left him alone?

Did it have anything to do with his interest in Sonal Neera?

Why was he so much interested in her? Was he her surrogate father and like many others was not willing to acknowledge it?

If he was her father, why was he reluctant to at least tell her? No doubt, he belonged to the Presurrogate Age. But . . .

Daniel's admirers were fond of saying that the once-upon-a-time chief trapeze artist of Spacepol was not just a symbol of Earth unity. He was much more. He was the breathing, moving soul of the new United Earth. If Earth could produce more sons like him, her shaky existence could become less precarious.

As a proof of their deep-rooted conviction, they cited his qualifications, and physical appearance. He had the flaming red hair that he had inherited form his Irish grand-uncle coupled with the light copper skin that he got from his American-Indian great-grandmother. His nose, given by his Jewish father, was long and distinguished with a pronounced bridge. And his sparkling, slanting eyes reminded of his pretty Japanese mother. His tempered voice held a distinct Oxford accent, giving away the sports fields where he had developed the quick agility of his karate-tight muscles.

No one knew exactly how many Earth languages he had mastered during his lengthy career in different professions or how many medals of valor he had earned during the pre-united Earth wars. Known galaxy-wide for his never-failing intuition, and negotiating skills, they said he had the power and skills to turn around and bend any wind that dared to blow against his beloved Earth.

Tonight. Although he was alone at home this new-century-heralding-night, with no one to see his clothes, he was immaculately dressed, as if, instead of a long night's dreamless sleep, he was ready for a full night's work!

As if sensing JR's thoughts, the ex-admiral stirred.

Without turning, he spoke as if he was continuing an unbroken conversation, "It could be an internal squabble. We have been watching them for some time."

We? JR wondered. Watching who?

Taking a sip of delicious jasmine tea, JR cupped his hands around the steaming cup and silently waited.

Daniel turned. "We need a new face. A person not known to anyone in the crime-world."

To do what? JR wanted to ask, but he simply offered, "Well, we can try to recruit Pavan."

"Pavan? One of your reporters? Isn't he the one who is determined to forget all his education and training, and wants to devote his life to sports?"

JR nodded. "That's the one."

"Why him?"

"He has an intuitive mind. Loves uphill challenges. And his spy career began without our planning it. He was at the Orpheum."

"I have never regretted accepting your advice," said Daniel picking up a small Visi from a nearby shelf, placing it between them on the teacart.

JR punched the numbers. Pavan's tousled head and sleepy face appeared instantly on the small screen.

"Hello, Chief?" Despite his disturbed sleep, he sounded quite alert. "Have you . . ." Then he saw the face of a stranger and stopped.

"I'm sorry, Pavan, I woke you."

"It's OK, Chief. What's up? Good news? Or bad?" Will you

introduce me, he wanted to ask, but did not.

"Pavan, when I called the Peace Guards, they told me to contact Admiral Shostakovich. They believe the person who got killed was a Jalangan."

"A . . . who?" Pavan's sleep suddenly fled. Feeling wide awake he straightened up and finger-smoothed his hair. His feet dropped down looking for his slippers with his toes.

During this exchange, the ex-Admiral was quietly studying the handsome oval face. He decided he could trust this young man. "Jalangan," he offered. "Very difficult to learn anything about them. Membership is by invitation only. A new member needs to be sponsored by at least seven members in good standing."

JR placed his cup on the tea cart and glanced towards the Admiral. "*Jalangan?* The name sounds so strange! I have always wondered about its origins. Does it mean something?"

Daniel smiled—the first time since, sporting a closed face, JR had arrived uninvited in his old, precarious, dented shuttle. "Well?" he drawled, "it stands for a kind of slogan."

"Don't they all!" Pavan stifled a yawn. "Overnight they keep sprouting to reform something or other."

"This one's a mouthful. Ready? Listen to this—*Join And Laugh At Noah's Great Ark.*"

Rudra! Pavan thought. These days one comes across weird names. This one's the craziest. Is this Admiral-person serious, or joking? He stared at Daniel, at his carefully-combed, flaming red hair. At his copper skin. At his navy-green oriental eyes. Wow! So much like mine! Now I know how mine must look to the others.

From his childhood memories, a picture flashed—the Admiral playing and winning the Natvar Chess Tournament. He recalled how fascinated he was by his challenging, mind-gripping game.

"What do they do?" he asked. "Make noises for the protection of wildlife?"

"Philanthropy is not their cup of tea." Daniel moved and sat down near JR "They build boats. Big ones. The new ones that everyone now calls *islands*. They almost have a monopoly."

"You live and learn!" Pavan exclaimed. "I thought World Islands, Inc. was monopolizing that market."

"World Islands is a subsidiary. JALANGA is the holding company," Daniel explained. "It has cornered several inter-sector monopolies. World Islands is just one of them."

"Wow!" Pavan was impressed. "How did they manage that? My

textbook says no one is allowed to own more than one."

Daniel smiled. "Textbooks are just launching pads, Pavan. If you do not know that . . ."

"Sorry, Admiral. That was a very careless statement." JR spoke quickly to cover his embarrassment, "One of the monopolies is that ad company that is doing such a fantastic job of marketing them. Everyone, even those who cannot afford them, are hankering to get one. Life in those weather-controlled sanctuaries can be very comfortable."

"Exactly," Daniel nodded amiably. "The Regulatory Councils have left them alone because breaking the monopolies may invite trouble with the job pools." He paused, then continued. "Spacepol got interested in them only recently due to some communication irregularities."

The ex-Admiral paused and glanced at the attentive faces. Neither one said anything. So he continued, "They have the best attorneys money can buy. So on the surface, everything seems perfect. But, the more we look," he drummed his fingers on the table, "the more it seems the people holding the various titles are not the decision-makers any more. The question is, if there is a shadow ruler behind the throne, is it a person or a shadow cabal? If it's the latter, where is the cabal headquartered?"

The silence that ensued Spacepol's secret chief's speculation was finally broken by JR "That invites many questions, doesn't it?" He glanced first at Pavan, then at Daniel.

"Go on," the ex-Admiral prompted.

"If it was in-fighting, was this murder due to personal vendetta, or secret shifts in the balance of power? If the latter, would it stop here, or have others been targeted? If the victim belonged to a faction, would the faction try to seek revenge? If Spacepol was checking, why had their mole failed to alert us?"

Pavan was feeling bewildered. If the victim was a Jalangan, why was the news media advised to announce Bakul's cremation? Could he ask? Or would that be considered inappropriate?

Finding their eyes resting on his face, he decided to ask. "We do not want to alarm the shadow rulers. Is that why the real identity of the victim has not been disclosed?"

"What would you say," the Admiral's long fingers played some obscure melody on the table, "if I asked you this question?"

Pavan did not hesitate. "You have two more reasons. One, we do not know if that Jalangan was their target. Someone may have wanted to kill Bakul. He got sick so unexpectedly, the killer did not know he had been replaced by his understudy. If that was the case, if the killer finds out Bakul is still alive, he will try again."

They were both listening intently. Seeing the look of approval on their faces, Pavan's face brightened up. "The second reason is even more important. If the killer knew the person on the stage was not Bakul, he still grabbed that chance to kill the Jalangan. If we reveal it, he may kill Bakul just to confuse us."

"Very good, Pavan. Excellent." The chess master was delighted. "Now, I also want you to tell me what this dilemma means. What kind of priorities does it set for us?"

"Well . . ." Suddenly Pavan felt he had said more than what he should have. If he wanted to prove to JR he was no good at anything except sports, he should have kept his mouth shut. "If we can find Bakul, many of our questions can be answered. I could have never believed he is such a coward. Why is he hiding?"

"He is not the only one." JR got up and moved to the window. "Two others who can throw light on the enigma, have also disappeared—Pia Payal and Maya Kiran. Are they with him? Or did they fear for their lives and fly away independently?"

"No, Chief. Pia is not hiding," Pavan hoped his face was not telling them he was lying. "The Space-V just announced it a while ago. She will attend the Twin Films Award dinner. If you want to question her, you can reach her there. Andrey would not have announced it if she was not with them. . . . Just like Pia. She never misses a confirmed appointment. You can bet on her."

"I wouldn't." The Admiral sounded troubled. "We have mastered the art of manufacturing masks to such a perfection. . . ."

"No!" Pavan added extra emphasis to his "bursting with shock" voice. "They wouldn't dare crown someone else in Pia's place if they want to remain in film business. If someone tries to imitate Pia, she would not have any place left to hide her face. No. No one—*no one*—can step into Pia's shoes."

JR and Daniel exchanged glances. Ah! To be young and chivalrous! It was not so long ago . . . At least, it did not seem that long ago, when they themselves would have sprung like this to protect their heroine's image and prestige.

"Let's hope you are right, Pavan." Daniel turned and extended his hand towards his visitor. "JR, old chap, thanks for coming."

JR decided to pigeon-hole the question of his resignation for the time being, and accepted the friendly hand. "I came because, if I had not, you would have disturbed my sleep." He smiled. "By the way, Pavan is volunteering."

"Is he?" Daniel asked. He liked the young reporter. He knew what to say and, even more important, what not to say. That was the kind of person he needed. "Is that so, young fellow?"

Volunteering for what? Pavan wondered. Where JR was concerned, you never asked. "Certainly, sir," he replied cheerfully.

"In that case, I'd like you to attend a meeting for me. Think you can do that?"

"What kind of meeting?" Pavan asked eagerly. "Where?"

"We have reason to believe the Jalanga Board of Directors is meeting tomorrow. We know Jal-Eleven. We can isolate him. We can make sure he does not attend the meeting. Someone is needed to replace him. Can you do the job?"

Pavan stared at him. This Admiral-person wanted to throw him in the wolves' den? A sports reporter, who did not know the ABC's of spying! He glanced at JR's expressionless face, then looked back at Daniel. "Admiral, assuming you can get a mask," he asked, "is my height and weight the same as Jal-Eleven's?"

Daniel glanced at JR His navy-green eyes silently said, "you have given me the right person, my friend."

"All your questions will be answered. Report at eleven at Space Central, ninety-fifth floor," the ex-Admiral ordered. Remembering Pavan had never served in army or navy, he softened his voice and added encouragingly, "I will personally make sure you are thoroughly briefed."

Glancing at Pavan's apprehensive face, he smiled. A friendly, fatherly smile. "Meanwhile, sleep well tonight. You are going to need all your energy the next few days."

This was permission to sign off. "Thank you, sir. I'll be there." Pavan smiled and switched off the Visi at his end.

But he did not feel like going back to bed.

Sleep had fled. All the theories he had formulated about the murder were gone like a passing whiff of dying smoke. What he had just heard could only mean one thing—that it was not a simple murder case. What had happened was not a routine, everyday crime. It was not a lover's quarrel that in a fit of insanity makes a person forget his humanity and impels him to raise his hand blindly.

This crime was so complex—had so many ramifications—that he could not even start to guess where its roots could be hiding.

Whatever it was, it was definitely not a play with which one could play rough and tumble, and quickly sew up the winning score. It was more like a wily spider's web that had more loaded, sticky bases than any umpire would like to face in any game.

If Bakul was not the intended victim; if JALANGA was the kind of outfit that old Daniel suspected; if the killer boomerang had found its target; if Jalangans were controlling the fibers of this murder-mystery, and they had jumped ball. In error, or not—it would do no good to home-in rashly on their treacherous trap-door.

The only practical lead off, from Spacepol's point of view, would be to try to work from within. . . . No doubt, that's why Daniel wanted him to impersonate a Board Member. But with all due regards to Daniel and his brilliant advisers, should he allow them to push him in a murky web, about which they did not have adequate knowledge?

Who did he know who could back him up? Who could help him achieve a good running start? No one.

In that case, shouldn't his first priority be to find where Jalanga's Shadow Council was headquartered? If there was a shadow council, wouldn't it be located on some obscure, junky space-station, where no one would suspect its existence?

Maybe not. If JR's right—and generally he is—for a criminal, the best place to hide is the most obvious one. He thinks no one would go there looking for him. If this theory has any water, then the shadow cabal has to be at Jalanga.

In that case, wasn't Spacepol right in sending him to Jalanga? It seemed like it was. If its orders were too confining, as perhaps they would be, that was, no doubt, the reason it had not succeeded until now. Should he prepare himself to out step its orders to do what must be done to solve the mystery?

Rudra knows! In this century, that is rapidly spreading its wings to fly away . . . no, even in the preceding ones, wars never started with big bangs. They erupted due to the simmering socio-political fabric getting kindled by a tiny, malcontent spark.

Was this murder a warning? Was the present uneasy peace, established by the Seven-Day War, about to be thrown to the fish? Was Mother Earth gearing itself for some new kind of world order, based upon new kinds of socio-political ruling units?

He remembered reading somewhere, "The most important events are often determined by trivial causes." Who said that? Yes, Cicero. So long ago—Sixty B.C.— in his *Orations Philippicae.*

It took centuries, he thought, for the fragile city-states to evolve into the unwieldy body they called United Nations. Like any organism growing old, losing its breath, it died. Now the imbalances created by a deathly power struggle in this globe-circling corporation could trigger a new global war. The life of the present world order, called the United Earth Council, could be the shortest among all the previous political units.

Feeling very unhappy, he moved towards his night table and tried to clear it to locate his favorite picture cube. "The history of Peace, my dear Nicole," he said addressing the face smiling in the cube, "is always written by the Fingers of War. Let's hope—just hope—that this cruel murder is not going to trigger the first Global War of the new century."

He picked up the picture cube in both his hands. A small butterfly skittered away leaving behind a small feather. As he picked it up, a long forgotten ditty began to warble in his mind . . . *But for the robin and the wren, a spider would overcome man. But for the robin and the wren, a spider . . .*

"Well, Funnyface," he softly murmured, "if they wake me up in the middle of the night and talk intrigue that won't let me sleep, should you be allowed to sleep?

"I know you won't come here. Should I come to your place? So that both of us can huddle together to find a way to penetrate the incredible web of this mystery? Haven't you said so many times," he touched her nose lightly with a long finger, "you wanted to don the robes of a spy."

He replaced the cube and looked at her three-dimensional image. No, he decided. She had not yet forgiven him for missing the vacation at his Nau-Shera Island. This second transgression would clinch it for ever. She would never speak to him again if he ruined her chances of keeping herself fully awake for the coming midnight celebrations. She needed her sleep tonight.

What about Pia?

On the Space-V, when he had heard that the Twin Films would be presenting her the award at the midnight dinner, he had wondered how Andrey could have made such a reckless decision.

Pia had left a message on his tele-diary to tell Sonal she was going away for at least a month. No doubt Andrey was using an impersonator and would need to be exposed.

One person's poison is another's nectar. Andrey's stupid mistake had given him the heavensent opportunity to sidetrack his unsuspecting boss and the all-knowing admiral.

But if he contacted Pia, she wouldn't be content to just talk through the time-ripples. She would come over. That would jeopardize not just her safety, but all their fragile plans.

Who else?

Should he call Sonal? Star-touching Sonal. A resourceful person, who was never afraid to try anything.

She may also be sleeping. Should he call her now? Or should he wait until morning?

He sighed: there was no time to lose. Before *volunteering* at pokerface Danny O's Spacepol office, he must prepare a surrogate fellow-spy about whom the Space Security had not yet learned.

If he could do that, Pia's plan would not be endangered. Earth would not have to fight alien invaders.

Now that Pia was away, if he could accomplish that, all by himself—wouldn't the inscrutable chess dragon be impressed?

Ah! Then the possibilities . . . then the possibilities. He grinned from ear to ear.

No. He should forget about Nicole. She was not the spy type, and more important, she was not one of them. She might not be able to keep the secret covered.

Sonal was not Nicole. She would not mind getting wakened in the middle of the night.

He moved to the comlink and clicked Sonal's numbers.

***

Her comlink bleeped. Sonal Neera stared at it with surprise.

How did it get re-activated? Before going to bed, she had disconnected it. Since then she had not touched it.

Only one way, she decided. At the first rays of the shyly peeking dawn, the efficient Ringaroo must have activated it.

Then, let him answer it. She had given him strict orders—she was not to be disturbed. By anyone. For any reason.

Dressed in a loose muumuu, she was watering her plants. Ignoring the persistent beeps, she proceeded to the next window. As she bent over them, her miniature yellow and red roses, nestling in gleaming brass pots seemed to nod and whisper, "What are your plans for tonight?"

"Tonight," she told them, "I'm not going to close my curtains. I'll leave my windows open. In my half-sleep, I'll curl up in the cozy lap of fireworks and star-rocketing revelry keeping awake all the street lamps. When the whispering glimmer of the new day's first breath will try to softly cloak my closed eyes . . ."

"Yes?"

"I won't tell you. At least, not right now."

Her comlink was still bleeping.

"Ringaroo? Where are you?"

Her robo-Major didn't answer. He had gone away somewhere, without asking her permission.

When I get the chance, she thought, I must fix his circuits.

He has started taking too many liberties.

In her nightrobe, with her hair all mussed, she did not feel ready for anyone's eyes, especially when she could not even guess who was at the other end. She accepted the call activating only the incoming image.

"R-Seven, come over right away." It was JR, his voice vibrating with stifled urgency surprised her.

Then she realized it was not just his voice. His reddish thread-tinged eyes and crumpled clothes seemed to to be saying he had not slept all night. It looked as if he had not even glanced at the forlorn looking cup of black coffee sitting near his hand.

Sonal was frightened—what had happened?

Was there another murder? Did someone else get killed? Crazy people! She softly muttered. Can't they wait to get rid of each other, until the new century is, at least, a few days old?

Her glance moved to the minute hands ticking away on the cuckoo clock. It was almost noon. Twenty minutes to twelve.

So! In the Japanese Sector, the New Year had already arrived. There, the new century was already a half-hour old.

She closed her eyes to better envision the laughing faces.

All the singing and dancing. On the rooftops. In the people-rippling, multi-colored streets, children would be blowing balloons. Huge, big balloons of every possible color, popping up the pathways . . . And the dark eastern skies, glowing gold, and green, and blue, with shimmering, cascading light displays. . . .

"Sonal? Are you there?" The deep baritone filled her space. As if just by his voice, he would catch hold of her. In his waiting eyes, worry now seemed to be gaining the upper hand over his century-old-tiredness.

"Yes, Chief. I'm here," she replied softly, reluctantly.

"But we had agreed. Today is Sunday. My day off. My first day of Freedom. I intend to enjoy it."

"Later. Not right now," he ordered. "I expect you in my office within half-an-hour." The screen went dark.

The stern command tinkled her to the core of her being.

Staring at the blank screen, she thought. Yes! There is no doubt about it. He IS my ex-teacher. The one for whom I had written and torn so many poems. The one whose memory assaults me whenever I come across someone who could be my ringmate.

Standing against the wind, I whispered your name . . . .

Her body trembled. "Okay, Chief, I'm coming," she told the blank screen, and hurried towards her sonic shower.

9

. . . Time for
Stratagems

*"Will you walk into my parlor?" said a spider to a fly,
"'Tis the prettiest little parlor that ever you did spy."*
—Mary Howitt: *The Forest Minstrels*, 1821

. . .

*Why doth the spider spin her—artificial web thick in one—place
and thin in another? And, now useth one, and then another knot,
except she had an imaginary kind of deliberation, forethought and
conclusion.*

—Michelde Montaigne: *Essays, II*, 1580

. . .

"Our Honored Guest. Please, wake up," the robot's respectful
voice repeated a third time. "Your shower is ready."

Maya Kiran heard, but decided not to open her eyes. They
should not find out she had regained consciousness until she sorted
out the questions in her mind.

She tested her muscles. Her hands and feet were free. She was not tied up any more.

Her pillow was soft. Waterbed comfortable. Room temperature just right.

The subdued humming sounds of massive machinery, doing its routine jobs in a space rotating habitat, was not there. That meant she was not on a space station.

She was not in any land-condo either, because she could not hear any of the routine earth sounds—hovercrafts, land autos, Peace Guard sirens, distant drums and shouts of people on the crowded streets marching for one cause or another.

That left only one possibility. She was on an island. A very modern, very luxurious, very comfortable man-made island.

Was it possible that was she was still on Hunter Island? That everything she had experienced was merely her old nightmare? Nothing more than that old dream that had expanded itself and acquired additional dimensions?

But the bed that was just like Shaku's, the one that they had purchased together, was not a waterbed. Her pillow was not a goose-feather pillow. The sheets were never so smooth, like real silk.

How about the conversation she had heard, as if in a dream, when she had felt her body dumped on a bed and her feet getting untied? "Why this stranger? Why didn't they kidnap Pia?"

"Be glad they didn't. Pia is a karate champion. Sports four black belts. She can make mincemeat of ten like us."

So! Pia was not here! That meant Bakul was not either! Had they moved them somewhere else? Or had that two-tongued Blueface mesmerized her, lied to her?

How about the necklace she could feel against her neck? Upon her chest? She never had it before!

She moved her hand to touch it. The robot waiting near her feet misunderstood her gesture. He thought her chest was hurting. He stepped forward. "Honored Guest, are you not feeling well? Shall I call our doctor?"

"No, don't," she snapped. Opening her eyes, she looked around the room as if to memorize it and its contents. Then pulling herself up, she propped herself against the goose down pillows. "Where am I? What's this place?"

"My programming forbids me to answer your questions, your Ladyship."

"Who is your Master?"

"My programming . . ."

"Your programming!" She scowled. "Then how can you help me?"

"I cannot let you get hurt, Visitor Mistress."

"Okay, fine. You stand guard outside my door until I call you. I don't want anyone—not even your Master—to come in."

"Your wish is my command, Honored Guest," the robot smartly stepped out and closed the heavy, ornamental doors behind him.

Fine mess I have gotten myself into, Maya Kiran thought. Bakul and Pia are not here to help me. How am I going to get out of here?

Entering the bathroom, she faced the mirror: No. This was no dream. She was awake. The blue pendent was still hers.

If it was not given to her in her nightmare, if she touched it, would the magic still work? With one touch, would that blue giver reappear? With one finger she touched it, and instantly the reflection of the blue stranger appeared on the mirror.

"I want to see you in person. Right now," she demanded.

There was a soft whisper of air behind her.

She quickly turned. He was there. But no threatening blue veil this time. Only that friendly smile, and those impossible eyes that could be only genetically engineered.

"Who are you?" she demanded. "Where am I?"

"Too many questions!" Those golden eyes, flecked with that lovely green, smiled warmly. "You are safe. That's all that matters."

"You got me kidnapped! You call that safe?"

"We got you out unhurt. That was our only objective."

"I was in no danger. My friend's home has always been my home. That room has always been mine. Neemu has always taken care of me. If you had not messed up the security shield, those robo-kooters would have burned to cinders as soon as they . . ."

"Maya," he interrupted showing tolerance. "Your suspicions are valid. You don't know me. But believe me, I *am* your friend."

He leaned against the huge, ornamental mirror, and contemplated her ready-to-brook-no-nonsense face and eyes. "If I decide to trust you, can you keep a secret?"

"Try me."

"I will. I'm not supposed to tell you, but I want you to feel comfortable. You see, Earth's map is about to change. Hunter Island is about to drown. You'd have drowned with it. I was at my wit's end. How to save you? The kidnappers did me a big favor."

Maya Kiran laughed. "Earth's map is about to change? Doomsday is here? And you are the Pundit to forecast it? Why not forecast it on Space-V? Why save only poor me?"

"Because . . ." with one blue finger he lightly touched her cheek, "You are a very special person. Do you know, Maya, why you often call yourself *kiwi*?"

She shrugged. She did not understand what that had to do with anything. "It's just a word," she said, "that I read or heard somewhere. It does not mean anything."

"No. It does mean something. It is not just a word. It is a very rare, very precious bird. It wants to fly, but it cannot."

"So? Sometimes we all use nonsense-words." That's part of being human, she wanted to say. Being a computer product, you won't understand it. Something on his face stopped her.

"Do you remember?" he was saying, "in the Baby Care Center, in your first craft class, nothing that you made satisfied you. Shaking your fist at whatever you made, you used to tell them defiantly, "I'll make you fly. You'll see. *One day I'll make you fly.*"

"Funny! Funny! You're a surrogate child of Freud or something?"

But he was not smiling anymore. "You're obsessed with the idea of flying, my dear," he checked himself, then continued, "because you can fly. Soon you will. That's all."

She glared at him. "Kalki! What kind of a joke is this?"

"Not a joke," he assured her. His engineered eyes, flecked with that mysterious green, looked desperate. Then it seemed as if he had made up his mind. "Different life-forms," he offered mildly, "have different capabilities. You have yours."

"Sure! Why not! You have fallen in love with me. So you want to believe I'm one of your kind. And you can teach me to fly. Where are your feathers, sir? And where are mine?" She spread out both her hands and fluttered them like imaginary wings.

"Temper! Temper!" He placed his long, lean blue forefinger under her chin and lifted it up. "It's time for you to meet your kidnappers. They won't harm you. Just obey their orders."

"I will do no such thing."

"Oh, yes! You will." He smiled that charming, mesmerizing smile. "Now close your eyes."

"Why should I, if you are going to teach me to fly?"

Without answering, he placed his hand upon her eyes. It felt cool and friendly. She quickly moved her hands to remove it. Before they could reach it, it was gone.

He was gone.

"Okay, Sir Blue Person," she threatened the blank mirror. "This time you got away. Not next time. I learn quickly."

She moved to the closet that was more like a small room and rummaged through the shabby dresses piled one upon another. *Kalki save me!* She breathed hard. *Who lives here? A junk collector?*

Suddenly she had an inspiration and she started whistling. Carefully, methodically, she picked several items—a cleaning lady's uniform, a nurse's cap and apron, a beggar's tattered shoes, a Peace Guard's heavy, black stick. And to top it all, she chose glass and bead jewelry of every kind for every part of her body— arms, wrists, waist, feet, neck, and hair.

"Gorgeous!" she told the stacked pile. "You are simply stunning. You deserve a thoroughly clean body."

Testing the water in the antique looking, oriental bathtub, she turned towards the huge mirror and touched her pendant. As the blue reflection appeared, she shook a threatening finger at it. "Whoever you are, you cannot boss me. No, sir! No Way! I'm Bakul's Rakhi-Sister. The one he calls, *Vagabond Island.* You just watch me. You just watch."

She moved towards the bathtub, then turned back and told the now-vacant mirror, "No more 'Protection-Talk, please'. MY Rakhi-Brother isn't kidding when he calls me a 'Space-Enchanting-Stand-In'. I don't need to obey you. I'm perfectly capable of handling my kidnapper, whoever he is. So don't interfere, just don't."

A few relaxing minutes in the bathtub cooled her temper.

Pouring lots of fresh-smelling, bubble bath oils in the hot water, she began to hum her favorite shower-song:

Mask-Maker, Mask-Maker, make me a mask.
An alien face, that's all I ask.
A Mermaid riding an angry whale,
Or a Kiwi rocking a raging gale.
Mask-Maker, Mask-Maker. . .

In their office, Andrey and McMillan had not spoken a single word for almost an hour, which was very unusual.

Andrey sat in a corner, in an easy chair, his eyes glued to the book in his hand. McMillan was pacing back and forth, from the window to the door, his mind roiling with the explanations he would have to offer Pia when she would walk in, sparking tongues of fire that could burn their whole planet.

"Jumping Jehoshaphat! Where is she?"

Andrey Voznesensky did not move. He was not really reading the book in his hand, but he pretended as if he were and had not heard. Over the years he had learned, when the rush of adrenaline was propelling his friend, it was best to leave him alone and let him work it out at his own pace.

"If we had an EYE in her room we would know what she's doing," McMillan glared at his partner. "But you quashed the idea."

"Now wait a minute!" Stung by this uncalled-for accusation, Andrey threw away his book in a corner. "You were the one who had such elephantine qualms about violating a young lady's privacy."

"Gotcha!" McMillan laughed. "Finally, I got your eyes off that blasted book." He moved to his chair and sat on its arm. "Want to send Robo-M to fetch her?"

"We have Robo-C-Five there, with orders to bring her over right away. If he hasn't, there must be a reason. Maybe she is still unconscious. Maybe those mindless Robo-Guards gave her too heavy a dose of whatever it was that you gave them."

"Well?" McMillan drawled and glanced at his antique grandfather clock. "We will give it another ten minutes. If she's still not here, I'll go and get her myself."

He did not have to. A few minutes later they heard the heavy tread of the Robo-Server. McMillan quickly moved to his chair and plunked himself down, trying to compose himself. Before he could, the robo entered. Behind him shuffled in the person they had so successfully kidnapped against all possible odds of every kind.

As she entered, Andrey and McMillan both jumped up from their seats. Not due to respect for their hostage, but due to sheer surprise. The dark-skinned woman, with shuffling feet and stooping shoulders who stood before them, squinting at them through dark-ringed eyes, had no resemblance to Pia Payal. Or to be more precise, to her understudy whom they had watched performing Pia's role with such exceptional skill.

Who was she?

Even the whole galaxy's make-up would not transform this

grotesque hag to resemble that exquisite understudy. No matter how desperate, no theater manager would dare to bring this hunchback on the stage to impersonate anyone.

Trying to make one of her eyes look smaller, Maya Kiran was scrutinizing them. One was tall and lanky, with shaggy hair; old-school-Englishman written all over him. The other in his late fifties, a true-blood Russian type, looked like a clean-cut menace. He could be a problem. She stifled a sigh.

Andrey's blood had turned to ice. Before his throat could close shut by the shock, he managed to croak, "Who are you?"

They had not recognized her. Maya Kiran's pulse beats wanted to jig and dance.

She had never applied her own make-up. Working without her maid's help, without any expertise, with unfamiliar supplies, she had been worrying if she had succeeded in camouflaging herself. Apparently her efforts had paid off. How much?

"Better not make me wait, lady," Andrey barked.

Maya Kiran's mind spun with visions of problems awaiting her.

She may have succeeded in hiding her body, what about her voice? If she answered, wouldn't they recognize it?

Fiercely telling herself not to touch the blue pendant hidden under the layers of her costume, she decided not to open her mouth. If she did not answer, what could they do? Or to be more precise, what would they do?

Andrey and McMillan's eyes met, asking each other the same question. Who was she? The understudy's maid? How could the Robo-Guards make such a terrible mistake? They had seen the stand-in's three-dimensional holo. . . .

Watching Andrey getting nowhere, McMillan decided to try.

Trying his best to sound friendly, he asked courteously, "What's your name?"

Maya Kiran was glad that her blue pendant wasn't within easy reach of her hand. *You are merely a superfluous anchor,* she told it silently. As Bakul says, I'm a 'Vagabond Island'. Used to doing my own thing. I don't need any anchor. I don't need *you.*

"Why don't we all sit down," McMillan suggested. It sounded more like an order.

Maya Kiran saw no harm in that. She shuffled to the nearest chair. Giving the Robo-Server permission to withdraw, Andrey and McMillan lowered themselves in theirs.

"Now, let's begin from the beginning." McMillan sounded as if they were all sitting in his breakfast parlor, enjoying good old British tea and scones. "First I tell you about us. We are film producers. My name's Milan. My partner's, Andrey. *The Cobra Keepers* was ours. You must have heard. It helped Pia Payal win the Galactic Movie Queen Award. By the way, did you vote for her?"

A dense fog lifted from Maya Kiran's mind. *Kalki Above And Beyond!* she thought. They must have called the hospital. They must have been told Pia was there. They must have discovered my trail. They intended to kidnap Pia. Not me. That explains it. That explains the whole thing. Her pulse slowed down. But she did not reply. Did not move a single muscle.

McMillan leaned his long frame forward. Putting his palms together, he steepled his fingers. "We do apologize for bringing you here, but we had no choice. We needed you. If we had asked, you might have refused."

They looked at her, waiting for her response.

Maya Kiran considered the situation. She could not just sit there. She had to say something. Do something. . . .

She could play the part of a mute. But she did not know how a mute person behaved. And she did not know sign language. If she refused to speak, they might torture her.

What were her options? What was the best option? She stared at Pia's portraits hanging on every wall.

***

Staring at Pia Payal's portrait, Jal-O was trying to figure out his options. When he accepts the Earth Lokani position, would he be better off by having Pia at his side? Or without her?

The answer would depend upon how the Earth people would respond to her bonding with him. Would they like it if their favorite movie queen quit her work? Or would they rebel?

Snatching off his true-skin mask, flinging it towards his night table, he strode across the room to his full-length mirror. The track lights hanging over the mirror hit his body. Bathing in its milk-white light, both hands on his hips, feet apart, he stood staring at his face.

Gingerly, with one finger, he traced the familiar outlines. Shapely nose, beautiful, neatly spaced teeth, full lips with primrose stripes . . . and the regal-looking third eye in the middle of his wide, imposing, forehead.

On my home planet, I was considered exceptionally handsome, he thought. There I used to parade around in simple clothes, because I was so proud of my regal, aristocratic appearance.

Why is it that on this water planet that is so varied, that nurtures such diverse life-forms—some with such grotesque and hideous attributes and shapes—whenever I look at my face now, I dislike it so much? Every day more and more?

Why doesn't it look handsome anymore? Why is it that every time I look at it, it seems more and more like an ugly, alien face?

What is the reason? Why have I begun to dislike my birth concepts of beauty and started considering these earthlings perceptions as my own? Have I really been here so long that reality has started twisting?

He shivered.

No, he fiercely told himself. If my face seems so strange to me, it's only because I so rarely get a chance to see it. Here I never see this kind of beauty on another being's face. If I had at least one person of my species here, my face would not seem so alien to me. And I would not begin to dislike it so much.

If I tried to explain this to Lord Kito, would he understand? Or would it make him wonder about my psychological equilibrium? When the others learn about it, would it give them another excuse on a platinum platter to clamor even more for my immediate recall?

Should I call him right now and pose a hypothetical question? If I do so now, before Operation Earth Shield has been triggered, would he wonder about my real reason?

When I accept the position of Lokani here, they will be so furious they will plan to kill me, not help me. Considering that, isn't this the best time to make them send someone?

Quickly moving towards his night table, he located the spot on the wall that only he could see. As he touched it, a small panel moved. He pushed his finger into the tiny hole and pushed another button. A large panel slid out holding a small, metal cube.

Placing the cube on the floor, he placed both his palms on its both sides in the two locking plates. The upper lid fell back, and a long cylinder popped up.

Just then a loud, sharp knock sounded on his door.

Annoyed, he glanced towards it. The security shield was on.

The lock-plates glowed red. That meant they must be glowing red on the other side of the door also. Who had the courage to disturb him when this *DO NOT DISTURB* sign was so clearly on?

Was it malfunctioning and not glowing on the other side?

The knock was repeated. A little louder. "Sire?" Through the heavy, security-shielded doors, his Robo-Major's voice sounded very distant. "The Eagle Boats are arriving. What are my orders?"

Jal-O glanced at his wristwatch. The boats were not expected for another forty minutes! Why so early?

This was not a good omen. Not a good omen at all.

He snapped shut the cube. Palm-locking it, he replaced it on the panel and pushed it back in its secret vault. The small hole closed. The colorful tapestry on the wall hid his secret.

"Master," his Robo-Major was saying, "I know it's early. Should I direct them to the pleasure rooms?"

"Patience! Patience!" he muttered. Adjusting his mask on his face, he touched a bead in the gold chain around his neck to deactivate the security shield and ordered, "Enter."

The huge, ornate door slid on its grooves. The Robo-Major stepped in and the door automatically slid back.

"Had they signaled they would be coming early?" Jal-O knew glaring at Earth-robos was useless. But he glared anyway.

"No, sire. The robo-watchers just spotted them and they called me right away. I know if you had called them ahead of schedule, you would have given me my orders. That's why I took the liberty of intruding upon your privacy."

"You did the right thing," Jal-O assured him. "Take them to the Council Room and stay there even after I take my chair. Leave only if I order you to leave."

"Orders noted, sire. I'll obey," the Robo-Major saluted and withdrew. The door closed behind his back.

Jal-O leaned back against his chair. Closing his eyes, he tried to relax and organize his thoughts. But the question kept intruding— why are they coming early? Eager to initiate the new century's festivities, or seething with revolt?

With a sigh he heaved himself out of his chair and headed to the shower.

His robo-cleaner had laid out his clothes on the dressing couch. As always, he had chosen with admirable discretion a business suit that was not too formal, and could also be worn for the planned revelry.

Taking only a brief shower, he dressed quickly, adjusted his face mask, and picked up the two files he needed for this critical meeting.

He had reached his bedroom door when he remembered that this meeting might last longer than usual. If it did, his robo-cleaner would need entry to take care of the evening chores. Jal-O quickly back-tracked to palm-lock his file cabinet so that he would not have to security-shield the bedroom.

The Council Room was not very far. Ordinarily he would have walked. But right now, he wanted to go through the files once again and refresh his memory.

He pressed a panel near his door and his indoor carriage dropped down from the ceiling. Sitting comfortably, he punched in his destination and the slowest possible speed. The chair lifted itself a few inches above the floor and started gliding forward on its magnetic beads embedded in the ceiling. He opened a file and tried to concentrate. This was more important. Pia's problem and the consultation with Lord Kito would have to wait.

The chair stopped near the Council Room. Stepping down, Jal-O punched the code to send it back.

The smoked glass doors were open. With measured, unhurried, steps he walked to his seat behind Jal-One's chair. On his way he noticed the three vacant chairs. In the others, the council members waited quietly. Bodies taut. Both hands on the table. Not looking at each other. Not talking with each other.

Tonight, he thought, one of those three chairs would remain empty. Was this the reason they had violated the rules and arrived early? If that was the case, how would it affect the agenda that he had prepared so carefully? By some miracle, would they just ignore the empty chair and get on with the meeting? Or would they create trouble? Just trouble, or serious disruption?

Jal-O felt a little nervous. He looked around. His Robo-Major was standing unobtrusively in a shaded corner. That gave him some relief. Quietly sliding in his seat he started arranging his material. Just then, the harbor door slid open and both the remaining members walked in.

Are they together? Jal-O wondered. Is it just a coincidence that they anchored their boats the same time? Or have they broken the council rules and revealed their identities to each other?

On his home planet, Jal-O had always taken great pride in his skill of decoding his fellow being's thoughts and actions by their body language. But the human beings he found a very difficult species. Whenever he had tried to orient his action and decisions on the basis of their body language readings, more often than not he had found himself wrong. He had learned to restrain himself.

I should keep quiet, he thought, and let Jal-One open the meeting. If the question of murder is raised, I'll quietly listen as long as possible. If the discussion starts getting out of hand, then I'll intervene.

Pleased, he congratulated himself. How many others could have framed a logical strategy so quickly! Not many. Ready now for anything, he relaxed, resting his hand lightly on the file that contained his agenda for establishing a new kind of political framework for the unsuspecting planet, Earth.

As Jal-One tapped his monitor to start the meeting, Jal-O thought, there is no reason for me to worry. Operation Earth Shield could not be in better hands. Even Lord Kito is not capable of executing what Kato would. Kato, his Robo-Super, whom Pashka had designed according to Jal-O's specifications.

They gave me this assignment, he reminded himself, only for one reason—none of their favorite super-achievers are capable of designing the kind of positronic brains that I can. And Kato is my best. He is the culminating product encompassing all my learning and experience—my crowning glory. He is the only force, the only pawn I need, not just to outsmart Lord Kito and his clique, but to crush them and achieve my obscure career's only objective.

In his mind he envisioned Kato bending over the LDM to launch it, triggering a new future for this unique water planet and its new Perpetual Lokani.

***

The small shuttlecraft settled down over the swirling sand.

Its hatch doors opened, releasing ladders. Two figures, totally shrouded in long gray robes, emerged and quickly clambered down.

They had scanned the area before touching down. Still, they wheeled on their heels and glanced around. They were alone and there was no place for anyone to hide. As far as their eyes could see, it was just sand and more sand. No structure of any kind. No lights. Just the two of them. And their small shuttle.

The taller one threw back his face-cover, revealing a young face and younger-looking eyes. "Kato, we should have a test run before we unleash this thing. Once unleashed," his eyes took in the land around him, "there's no turning back."

"Master-Consultant, if you do not have the courage to use this machine," the Robo-Mechanic asked, "why did you volunteer for this job?"

"Who says I don't have the courage?" the human snapped. "You are a machine. You do not know. Any machine, no matter how good, is not allowed to start servicing without routine tests. From what I've heard, it's space-clear—this beauty's just been manufactured. It never had a test run."

Kato was a robot. And robots have no way of feeling anger. But even for Kato this conversation had been going on too long. *If I could feel,* his logic-circuits were saying, *I'd feel glad that I'm a robot. If I were human, I could easily murder this obnoxious, warm-blood-flowing-being, who keeps hammering away at the same senseless argument for no logical reason.*

His positronic brain had been considering the problem since the human had started arguing like a broken record. An answer clicked and he changed tracks. "What do you think it is?" he asked. "It *is* a test run. The first one. This area, as you know, was chosen with great care. There is no life here of any kind, human, animal, or vegetable. This land is absolutely useless."

The young man's eyes said he was not convinced.

Checking furiously, Kato's logic circuits quickly found the reality a blood-flowing-being *would* accept. He moved to face the mortal being. Using a cajoling voice, he repeated deliberately, "Absolutely useless! So useless that despite the horrible paucity of land your planet has been experiencing, no one has tried to develop it for anything." He paused for effect.

"*ANYTHING,*" he repeated forcefully.

The young man moved to the shuttle ladder and leaned against it. Yes! he thought, history tells us our world was not always like this. Once upon a time we had much more land. But using technology indiscriminately, we destroyed two-thirds of it. In those plentiful days, everyone was so busy grabbing the maximum leverage from everyone else, that no one bothered about the ecological effects of their heedless activities.

Some of them no doubt talked about it, but mostly for their personal benefit, for their ego satisfaction, for their prestige and image enhancement. No one took anyone seriously until it was too late and the climbing waters started gobbling the land masses containing agricultural land and manufacturing plants.

Then, when the problems could not be pushed away from their door-steps anymore, the people tried to solve the problems by building artificial land. The encroaching waters kept drowning the false land. So someone had the brilliant brain wave of manufacturing boats so big that they would be self-sufficient like small islands.

But no matter how good they make them, a man-made island cannot perform like a natural island. Cannot function like and replace Earth-land. Even more importantly, if we go on like this, in the not-so-far-away future, we won't have any natural land left. But no one is bothered about it. Every micrometer of Earth is now under the direct control of United Earth Council. And its Conservation Department believes the only job is to make sure that whatever land we have remains un-utilized.

"Kato," he softly murmured, "Earth is such a unique planet because we have two precious items, rich land and life-sustaining water. But like anything else, to keep these two alive, nature needs equilibrium. You know what one of our ancient philosophers said about these items such a long time ago?"

Kato's logic circuits energized. If his memory did not contain the information, he required it for future reference. "What?" he asked. "Who?"

"Name was Shakespeare. In his book, *The Tempest,* he declared, *I would give a thousand furlongs of sea for an acre of barren ground.* Whenever I'm working on one of my land reclamation projects, I always remember it."

To exert better control over his butter-fingered chatterbox, Kato moved closer. "We are getting behind schedule. If you still have unanswered questions, we must scan the briefing tape again."

"No, Kato. That's not necessary. I remember the briefing," said the chatterbox, looking very much like the "lost soul" in the movie, *The Cobra Keepers.* "Torpedoing this land-scooper will not destroy this land. It'll create a big lake here that'll be used in many ways, including fish nurseries that will feed thousands."

The young man heaved a deep sigh. "I have not forgotten anything, Kato. The problem is that basically I'm a land-person. The harum-scarum drowning of all this land," he spread both his arms as if to embrace it, "is making me very unhappy."

"Sire," Kato's logic circuits knew how to utter a reproving sound. "Even at this last minute, you are labeling it harum-scarum! And you call yourself a NOPE member!"

"Of course I'm a NOPE member. You are a robot, but NOPE's

philosophy and objectives were explained to you. You know very well. NOPE does not believe in destruction—of any kind. When they hear about it, they will perhaps cancel my membership."

"No they won't," Kato asserted. "On the contrary, to express their gratitude they will proudly parade you all over the galaxy. By your bravery, you will have single-handedly brought down the present political hierarchy crawling on their knees."

"I'm not so sure about that." The young man sat down and dug both his hands in the cool sand. "Threats and blackmail don't work on our planet. They may trigger world wars, but they don't bring rulers down to their knees."

"Ordinary threats, yes. Ordinary blackmail, yes." Imitating humans Kato stamped his foot. "But this will be no ordinary threat. When they receive your ultimatum," Jal-O's super-robo continued, "that if they refuse NOPE's demands, all the irrigation land under their control will be drowned, they *will* come crawling to your feet right away. You can be sure of that."

The young man did not answer. He kept filling his fists with cool sand and letting it pour down through his fingers.

Kato squatted near him to be more persuasive. "I know you have degrees in Geology and Terra-Forming. But you must have read some history. Do you remember when the first atomic bomb was blasted over Hiroshima? Its purpose was not to kill human beings. It was a threat. A blackmail. To stop the war and establish peace. And, it had never been used before. *It was a test run.*"

The young man looked up. The remaining sand in his half-closed fists trickled down. "I guess you are right. They are right." He rubbed his hands together to clear them of sticking sand. "Okay, let's bring down the magical wand and set it up. It's almost eleven. Not much time left now."

Kato climbed up the ladder, went inside the shuttle, and reappeared rolling a big, cumbersome, steel box-like object. Hooking it to steel ropes, the robot gently lowered it. Then throwing down a couple of small boxes, he again disappeared inside their shuttle.

The young man moved slowly. Reluctantly. Opening a box, he took out the torches it contained. Setting them up in a wide circle, he started lighting them.

Kato reprogrammed the shuttle for take-off. Switching off the automatics, he clambered down to take charge of his precious LDM—the Land Development Machine, converted to Land

Destruction Machine.

Lighting the last torch, the young man softly whispered, "My fellow NOPE members, I agreed to drown this land only for securing NOPE's objectives. Not for any personal benefit. I hope you will understand that."

"You have not eaten anything all day, Master-Consultant," Kato said. "Why not have your dinner now? The return journey won't be very comfortable on hungry stomach."

"Fine, Kato. Let's plug you also so that you don't feel any energy loss on the return trip."

"I'm OK, sire. Once fully charged, my energy lasts several days."

"Come on Kato! You know our customs. When in company, we do not eat alone."

"You're right, sire. I will obey." Kato took out a cord and a battery from a box, opened a panel under his arm and plugging himself, sat down and closed his eyes.

The young man opened another box. Taking out a table cloth he spread it on the sand and started taking out his dinner.

The energy pouring into Kato's frame was pulsating in his synchro-cyclotronic brain. The young man got up. With quick, soft steps, he made a half-circle, keeping a safe distance from Kato. Reaching the LDM, he quickly made some adjustments in the controls. Without disturbing the unsuspecting robot's energy-induced euphoria, he swiftly returned to his waiting dinner.

The torch light seemed to flicker with pleasure. A broad grin illuminated the truant NOPE leader's worry-flown-away face as he plunged his fork into the cold bean salad.

10

... Don't Think Twice

I breathed a song into the air,
It fell to earth, I know not where ...
And the song, from beginning to end,
I found again in the heart of a friend.
—H.W. Longfellow: *The Arrow and the Song,* 1841

. . .

We are in the world like men playing at tables; the chance is not
in our power, but to play it is; and when it is fallen, we must manage
it as we can.
—Jeremy Taylor: *The Rule and Exercises of Holy Living,* 1650

. . .

Sonal Neera was halfway through her lunch when she realized that on the other side of the table, JR was not really eating. If he was not hungry why had he ordered practically everything on the Virunga's lunch menu? Just for her?

Taking a small sip of cranberry wine, she glanced at him speculatively, "Chief? What are we celebrating?"

Her voice brought him back from wherever he was, but not completely, "Celebrating?" he inquired absent-mindedly.

"When I walked in, you had said first we'll have a 'working lunch'. If this is a working lunch, I'll . . . I'll eat my hat."

The smile that her words brought to his fireworks eyes quickened her pulse. "You never wear one," he said as if that took care of that problem. "Well, if you have to know, this lunch is supposed to give us enough ammunition. Me, to work here alone; you, to stay up late tonight."

She put down her fork. "Late? Not me. My plans are to enjoy the Ringaroo Special he has been planning for me for weeks, then applaud the fireworks on Space-V. Then . . ."

"Well," he drawled, "you can watch Space-V when you return from the meeting, although I doubt it will adjourn that early."

"What meeting? I'm not Pavan. I never attend meetings."

"Remember? You promised to check out NOPE activities? Tonight they are having an important meeting. This would be the best time to contact them. Everyone who is someone will be there. You will learn a lot that we need to know."

Sonal Neera's heart sank. She kept her fork moving in the Prawn Curry so that JR would not get suspicious, but suddenly she was not hungry any more.

On her way here, thinking about yesterday's conversation, she had fashioned succeeding flood gates to protect her fragile stakes. She could withdraw her resignation on the condition that she'd be given a desk job. That would allow her to remain close to JR and find out if she still loved him. If the answer was *yes*, she would do whatever was needed to kindle his dormant emotions and awaken his feelings.

If the answer was *no*—possible, because that kind of proximity might create the familiarity that would smoke away that faraway memory-glorified magic—it would allow her to forget him and get on with her separate life.

This possibility, no matter how remote, had frightened her. Therefore, quickly closing this gate, she had opened another one. If he interpreted her request for a desk job as her refusal to work as a *spy,* she could change tracks and agree. Then reaching there, she could use a simple trick—get lost and never come back.

What if with all the resources open to him, he would manage to trace her, bring her back, and wouldn't let her get away?

That was not just a possibility. That could really happen. Considering that, wouldn't it be best to use another time-honored strategy? Work as a double agent? Take advantage of Space News. Advising it, using the knowledge gained from it, help NOPE?

She lifted her fork, but changed her mind. Putting it back on the plate, she smiled her best smile. "You really think I'm that charming? I'll just go there and say, 'Here I Am,' and they will open all their secrets for me?"

He laughed, leaned forward, and with a light touch moved the hair falling over her eyes. "No one who knows you has any doubts about your magnetism. But for the kind of job you will be doing for me, I have to consider your other qualification—your creative and exceptionally resourceful mind."

She fumed inside. How could she forget how charming he could be? Why didn't she think of answers beforehand to such classical clichés? Such beguiling maneuvers?

"I know you," he asserted compellingly. "I know you can do the job." He raised his glass, "Come on, let's drink to your success."

Dictator, she thought. *Shogun, Drill Sergeant . . .*

Then without any warning, a question popped out of her, surprising her by her own audacity, "Chief, if you won't mind, can I ask you a personal question?"

He felt a premonition of what she was about to say. And he felt a little afraid.

His mind urged him to stop her. To advise her to let it remain unsaid, as it had for so many years. A memory flared up in his mind of those long-ago, gone-forever days, when . . .

He squirmed in his seat.

Sonal Neera of the truant hair and aquamarine eyes, he wanted to say, *you are not the only one who has been standing against the wind. There was a time when I was younger, chockfull of mountain-touching aspirations, and believed this world was made just for me.*

In my ignorance, I let them thrust upon me certain duties. Responsibilities—irreversible and unchuckable. Therefore, my wind-tunnels have been much tougher, Dear. You cannot guess how much more complicated. How much more atrocious . . .

Instead, keeping his inspiring mask intact, he simply asked, "Sonal, you are not my subordinate any more. You have resigned. Why do you still keep calling me Chief?"

Caught off-guard, she could only ask, "What should I call you?"

"How about Jay or JR, like everyone else?"

"No." She glanced at him dubiously. "I couldn't do that. Those words won't come to me. I'm not used to them."

"What else would you prefer? The word *Chief* doesn't seem appropriate any more."

"How about," she glanced at him and there was a sudden mischief in her luminous eyes—the kind that he had never seen there before. "How about the name I have been calling you since I was that high?" She moved her hand a couple of feet above the floor to indicate how young she was.

"No, no, that high." He lightly held her fingertips and raised her hand a few feet. "At least that high."

She quickly withdrew her hand, and said accusingly, "Again your evasive tactics? You don't want to answer my question?"

"Fire away."

"You may not like them."

"Try me." His tone was light, but without those despotic templates, his expressive hazel eyes looked very cautious and thoughtful.

Feeling awkward, Sonal Neera glanced away. But, even evading those waiting eyes, she found it impossible to phrase the question that now stood between them.

Now that she had mentioned a question, she could not take it back.

She had to know.

Pushing her chair back, she moved and stood behind him.

Holding the back of his chair, making sure that her fingers were not touching him and trying very hard not to sound nervous, she asked in a small voice, "Do you have a ringmate?"

She could hear her own breath, but not his reply. She felt afraid—she had angered him.

But JR was not angry. He was thinking—we need to sort out this thing between us. If we don't clear it, we won't be able to work together. If we do, her life may become easier. She may regain herself. Feeling free of the unreal walls she built around herself, she may move out into a circle of friends her own age, so that in time, she would be able to find someone to love. Someone whom she will not consider unreachable like an eagle.

He left his chair, turned, and stood facing her. Taking her face lightly in his palms, he softly murmured, "Sonal, attraction is rarely one-sided. And love? Love is like a shadow wheel. It touches not just ringmates, but many other relationships. Yes, even in this age of tenuous Surrogate links."

He took her hand. Pulling gently, he steered her towards the long, comfortable guest couch. Seating her in a corner, he sat near, but at a comfortable distance. Then resting his arm on the couch, so that it would be behind her head but not touching her, he said in a very friendly, companionable tone, "For certain things, I'm oath-bound. But not to a member of the opposite sex, I assure you."

Seeing her smile, he felt encouraged, and continued, "I can't mention those promises. *To anyone.* Under *any* circumstances. But yesterday, realizing how much it's hurting you, I had promised myself that under my personal responsibility, I'd bend the rules a little and confide in you, hoping you would not mention them to anyone. You will keep them a secret."

He waited, as if he expected a response. But she just sat looking at her hands resting quietly in her lap.

He lightly touched her fingers. Getting no response, he let them go, "I was surprised to hear you think Pia Payal is your sister. If she is one of you . . ."

Her expression changed. "What do you mean, *one of us?*"

"Sonal," he took one of her hands in his own. "You are not alone. There are six others. We had secret orders. No harm must come to you, under any circumstances. That's why you were under such close surveillance, not because we suspected something."

She looked bewildered, "Why? Who are we? What have we done? Who are the others?"

"Who are you?" he echoed. "That I do not know. What have you done? Nothing, as far as I know."

"Then why? Why suspect us, imprison us so horribly?"

"You were not supposed to know about it. How did you find out?"

"Chief! Why can't you ever answer a simple question?"

"You don't ask simple questions, R-Seven," he smiled. But seeing the impatience in her troubled eyes, he quickly added, "To be frank with you, I can't figure it out. Since you all started walking and talking, you could not have sneezed without our knowing about it. Why suspect a six-month-old baby? Beats me!"

"However," he said reassuringly, comfortingly, "you have nothing to worry about, believe me. All of you are perfectly normal, with above average IQs. None of you has any deviant tendencies. Your psychographs indicate that you are incapable of harboring or developing a criminal mind."

"Then, why the Big Brother Eye?"

He leaned back and put both his hands behind his head, "As I told you, I've given it a lot of thought. And I've wondered, could it be that your genes were programmed in one of those experimental labs, and they want to keep tabs on the results. Just a wild guess—perhaps a hundred percent wrong. Come to think of it, why don't we make it your second project. You help me find out."

She was not listening, "But I'm the only one who was born on the Surrogate Island? Pavan and Pia were not."

"Pavan? What he got to do with it?"

She cursed herself for speaking without thinking.

How childish I am! she thought. Pavan had insisted on a secrecy-oath. He told me about us—about me and Pia Payal—only after I took that oath. Stupid me! Why do I keep breaking it!

Wait! Can't I justify it on the grounds that he gave me the job of finding the fourth person, and JR may be hiding that information inside his space-garrison mind?

"Who is not answering the question now?" JR was asking.

"Chief?" she requested endearingly. "Please don't tease me. I want to know who are the others. What are they doing? Where can I find them? When can I talk with them?"

"Spoken like a true journalist, R-Seven," he glanced at her quizzically. "If I had the answers, don't you think instead of banging my brains about it, I would have solved this puzzle?"

Finding her lost in thought, he added softly, "But, I think you have the answers."

"Me?"

"Someone told you Pia is your sister. We can ask him. Who is he? Or is it *she*?"

Yesterday, she would not have told him. But today was another day, "Like you, I also took an oath, Chief," she said softly. "Perhaps, I can also bend it a little. But it won't be of any use, because that person does not know."

"How do you know that?"

"Because he told me to help him find someone else."

JR could not remain seated any more. He got up, walked to his desk, and turned back. He did not even realize he was pacing back and forth because his mind was churning. If old Danny O' were caught in this situation, what would he do?

Sonal's troubled eyes followed his advancing and receding feet. He says he does not know the others, but he knows about the psychographs. How? Does he know the Guardians of the others? Is there a committee? When and where do they meet?

It would not hurt to ask him, "Chief, why don't we ask the other Guardians?"

"Guardians?" He stopped in mid-track, "Oh, you mean others like me. I wish I could, R-Seven. But I don't know who they are."

Suddenly an idea struck Sonal Neera, and a cold shiver ran down her body, "Chief?" she asked, "are you . . . are you one of the Seven?"

"Me?" He looked so appalled, obviously the idea had never even occurred to him.

"Think about it, Chief. Can it be some kind of a chain? Each person sheltering another. Wouldn't that be the easiest way to ensure their joint protection, and also to keep them together?"

JR stared at her. Her theory, no matter how improbable it sounded, seemed to make a lot of sense.

She glanced at him, and then glanced away. "Do you know what I think is the worst thing? The most horrifying part of it?"

He just glanced at her, his clear hazel eyes looking like two big question marks.

"Not just me and Pia, all of us could be brothers and sisters."

"What's so horrifying about it?"

"They may have also learned about the others. Any time, if one of us is attracted to someone, wouldn't we wonder if he or she is our brother or sister? Knowing this, until all of us find each other, we will never be able to bond a mate."

She looked so miserable, so stricken, he felt melted down to his inner core. Quickly moving, he sat down next to her and put his arm around her. "Sonal, that's not the reason I never bonded. And I feel quite sure that I'm not one of the seven."

"Why? How can you be so sure if you don't know the others? Not even their Guardians?" If you don't know them, she thought silently, how do you know about their psychographs and the rest?

"I just know it. I feel it in my bones."

"How logical and scientific!" she smiled. "I did not know you were capable of using such folk methods for solving double-Dutch mysteries." She snuggled against his arm, "If not, then why did you scorn the ringmates who must have crossed your path?"

In answer, he ran a finger, lightly like a feather, on her cheek.

Seeing her closing her eyes, he took her face between both his hands and kissed her, lightly at first. As she responded and threw both her arms around his neck, he pulled her closer and kissed her harder.

In between the shared kisses, he softly whispered, "You are not the only one who is keeping a name for me. I also have a name for you."

"Honest?" Pushing back her truant hair, she traced a finger on his lips. "Tell me. What is it?"

"First, you tell me."

"That's not fair."

"Why?

"First things, first. I mentioned it earlier. You said it just now. It's your turn. Mine will come after half-an-hour."

"That's fine with me." He kissed her eyes, her lips, and, moved down her neck. She giggled, and tried to move. He pulled her closer and his fingers found the buttons on her dress.

She held his hand, "Don't I have to go to this NOPE meeting?"

"Oh!" he groaned. "The blasted NOPE meeting!"

Either he had forgotten or was feigning it. Either way it did not matter, because finally she had found him. He was hers. He had waited for her, and if necessary, would wait longer.

Strength from his powerful arms flowed into her. She felt secure. Confident. Happy.

"If I have to travel, I need to pack a few things."

"Good," he mumbled, without showing any signs of releasing her, "I'll help you pack."

"Then let's go." She started to move, but he pulled her back. "Do you really want to go? Because, if you don't . . ."

"Oh, yes." She tried to dangle down her feet. "Can't give up the chance of learning to be a spy. Can I?"

"Not spy, my dear—investigating reporter," he smiled, and released her.

Moving to the door, encircled within the boundaries of his demanding arms, she remembered her friends—Shakeela, and Roxy, and Maya Kiran.

She wondered where they were, what were they doing, Was the soon dawning New Century also coming to them with such a delightful promise of unbuckling a waiting future? A future, that despite being so well camouflaged, was beckoning with such delightful and sparkling promises.

Wasn't the fact that it was so well camouflaged, a part of its magical attraction?

***

Camouflaging herself, Maya Kiran had succeeded in protecting her stakes—had secured her future. But under her captors' threatening eyes, she did not feel so sure any more. Suddenly she had an inspiration, "Ye th . . . th . . . thot I . . . I . . . I Pia?"

Suffering snakes! Andrey shivered—*She stammers!* Her body we could somehow hide by our cameramen's tactics. How would we hide her speech?

"No. Pia could not make it," McMillan was groping for the right words. If he made any mistake, she might again clam up. "So we thought as her understudy, you could take her place." He paused, then continued, "Our make-up artists are good. They can make you look like Pia. You would like that."

Another curtain lifted. So, they know who I am! They know I'm not Pia! Now what? The crooked shoulders disguise was a mistake. They can force surgery upon me. If they disrobe me, they will find out I'm perfectly OK. Then what?

"Ev . . . Ev . . Evryon kno . . . kno . . . knoz . . . P . . . P . . . Pia refuz a look-alike . . . in th . . . thet . . . thet moovy," she stammered.

"Quite true," McMillan nodded. "But in that popular play, *Spider's Stratagems,* she had one. Your mistress."

Another curtain lifted—They think they have kidnapped my maid. Wonderful. Just great! My blind strategy worked. Now, if I can somehow take advantage of this Kalki-blessed miracle . . .

"Weeell," she yawned and tried to get up. Purposely slipping, she tried again, and stood holding on to the back of the chair, "You cu . . cu . . cud call th . . . the tha . . . thater . . . . fa . . . fa . . find th looka . . . look-alike. I . . . I got to go. Impo . . . Important mating.

"What meeting?"

"N . . . n . . n . . NOPE Mating. My frr . . . frrnds waiting. They g . . . g . . . got my tickets . . . For m . . . m . . . many cann . . . carnival shows," she improvised. If they'd buy her lie, she'd have to go somewhere. If that Blueface really knows something that no one else knows. If her not-so-secure hiding place, the Hunter Island, is about to malfunction—break down or drown, wouldn't a NOPE carnival be the best place to get lost?

Her admission about NOPE membership jolted Andrey so much, he suddenly found his voice, "You are a NOPE member?" He spat the words.

"Ye askin l . . . l . . . li . . . like . . . ye ss . . . . ss . . . . seen a . . . a ghost!" She smiled a very crooked smile, "I'm a . . . a . . . . a human, a . . . aain't I? And, th . . . th . . . this n . . . n . . Nopefest be th . . . the best show . . nn . . nn . . . Not so?"

Mother Earth, forgive me, she thought. Let my Rakhi-brother never find out I just praised NOPE.

"We need someone to attend our dinner tonight," Andrey knew their plans had misfired. But now there was not enough time left to send the Robo-Guards back to Hunter Island to pick up the elusive understudy. He felt like a sinking man grabbing at quickly disappearing straws, "You are a nice person. You can help us."

"Naw! Ye d . . . d . . . do me a b . . . . b . . . big honor, Sir. B . . . b . . . . but I'm j . . . j . . . jus' a . . . . a . . ." frantically grabbing, she found her own straws. "Furchoon-teller. A . . . a . . . a sykik. N . . . n . . . No actris."

Holy Toledo! Andrey's eyes seemed to say to his partner, *That's all we need! A fortune teller! How lucky can one get?*

Enjoying their stricken faces, Maya Kiran decided to enhance the frail web of her falsehoods. If a time comes when they find out how outrageously she had lied, hopefully it won't matter. Hopefully by then, she would be lost in the NOPE crowds, and they wouldn't be able to catch her. "Ye d . . . d . . . decent people. I'll hu . . . hulp ye. Give you a psychic spell. B . . . b . . . but, ye dunt wa . . . . wa . . . waste your dinner. . . . ."

It seemed like a glimmer of hope. "If you think we are decent people . . ." Andrey started to say, but she cut him short. "Bbb bad for . . . fortune. Cancal dididinerr . . . No Space-V. tt . . tonight. Earth shakes. Wa . . wawater all over. S . . . s . . . save yor money."

She is not a psychic. She's crazy! Andrey and McMillan exchanged a glance and silently agreed.

Quickly moving to his desk, Andrey pushed a button to call the Robo-Guards. She is a lunatic, he thought. Perhaps harmless. But still a lunatic. Better to send her wherever she wants to go. The sooner we get rid of her, the better it will be.

The guards flanked her to escort her out. At the door she turned, and waved a limp hand at them, "Mm . . . Mm . . . May the urth be with ye . . . al . . . alwez."

If they don't return my greeting, she thought, that would mean they are convinced, and they won't recall me before the hovercraft leaves.

They did not return her greeting.

The Robo-Guards matched their steps to her slow, crooked walk. Finally, when they reached the hovercraft, they helped her in and took their seats in the cockpit. Without looking back, one asked, "Honored Guest, where would you like to go?"

These metal-heads, Maya Kiran thought. They would not know the difference between stuttering and natural voice. "To the NOPE carnival," she replied in her natural voice. "You know where it is?"

"Yes, your Ladyship. It will take about eighty minutes. Please, relax. You can watch Space-V or read a book. There's also wine and snacks in that cupboard near you."

Maya Kiran leaned back and closed her eyes. If I call that blue liar-conniver, that dumb, egotistic-dictator, and tell him the whole story, will he admit how wrong his advice was?

She picked up a book and tried to forget him for the time being, but his mesmerizing golden eyes, flecked with that haunting-green, kept hovering on the pages of the book. His seductive voice kept haunting her thoughts.

If he's not just an accomplished actor, she mused, if he is a real person, wouldn't it be fun to get to know him . . . If he is an actor, so what! Didn't tonight prove that I'm not just a stand-in? I'm a star in my own right! If he is an actor, wouldn't he admire it?

Should I surpass Blueface? If I put on Pia's face, will he recognize me? He wants me to be his puppet. Can I turn the tables? Make him my puppet? Impress him so much that he will obey me, do what I want, without his even realizing it?

The idea was so intriguing, she moved to the washroom to put on Pia's face.

As her own face emerged from the layers and layers of that lurid make-up, admiring it, she decided. Hiding somewhere near the edges of the carnival, she would call him.

11

. . . Pawns Cross
The Squares

It is a double pleasure to deceive the deceiver.
—Jean De La Fontaine: Fables, II, 1668

. . .

When the Himalayan peasant meets the he-bear in his pride,
He shouts to scare the monster, who will often turn aside.
But the she-bear thus accosted rends the peasant tooth and nail,
For the female of the species is more deadly than the male.
—Rudyard Kipling: The Female of the Species, 1865-1936.

. . .

*S*tanding near the edges of the NOPE Carnival, Sonal Neera was cursing herself for having wasted all her life living like a bumming puppet. Someone tells you to study, you study. They tell you to eat, you eat. They tell you to move, you move . . .

Then suddenly, without any warning, they throw you to the wolves! If they had taught me how to find my own way, I wouldn't be standing here now, wondering what to do, where to begin.

She moved towards the gigantic billboards, revolving and blinking brightly, enticing everyone to follow their choices—Music Circle, Magic Land, Sports Stadium, Space Rotunda. . . .

The crowded, nerve-racking, mucked-up land-cities had nothing in common with this clear-air magic land. But it was not just the sullen despondency of the whining city that was missing here. Something else seemed to be missing from this supercharged, buoyant medley. Sonal wondered what it was. What was missing?

Moving from one billboard to another, suddenly she realized what it was—the striped green uniforms, human or robot, always dotting such crowded city carnivals, were not around. Their sparkling green hats, that could always be spotted no matter where one was, were not a part of this vast panorama.

Why? she wondered. Is NOPE really such a powerful organization that the Park Island Authorities had to bend their rules for them, as they would not for any one else? Why would they do that? Because of its assertion that where *"NOPE walks in, CRIME walks out?"* Violence is as human as apple pie. Why would they believe such an illogical claim?

She remembered what JR said was NOPE's motto. *Do not get into a fight if you can avoid it. If you can't avoid it, see it through. Don't hit if it is honorably possible to avoid hitting, but when unavoidable, never hit soft. Don't hit at all if you can help it. Don't hit a man, if you can possibly avoid it. But if you do hit him, put him to sleep.*

No wonder, she thought, SpacePol was wondering about their links to Bakul's murder. As to the Peace Guards, instead of getting rid of them, shouldn't they have been dispersed here generously? Shouldn't the people with such a motto be the first and foremost candidates to deserve them?

Reason and logic, she reminded herself, often have no working relationship with one's missing or overbearing clout.

But NOPE's decision to mothball the Peace Guards was creating a very serious problem for her. Since they were not around to give her directions, whom could she ask where the NOPE Council was holding its meeting?

Feeling very helpless, she again glared at the life-size holos towering above the billboards. Eloquently describing the marvels that awaited her, their eye-catching messages portrayed fun, food, and games to dazzle and delight her body, heart, and mind.

It seemed as if whatever one would wish for recreation was there. She just had to make a choice and move in that direction. Before her distraught eyes, every few seconds the picture-perfect holos pirouetted giving directions for reaching those endless attractions. Ghost Castles, Tomorrowlands, Vampire Kingdoms, classical and folk dancing shows, theaters, wrestling, fire-hoop jumping competitions, Bearland, Disneyland, Peacock Puram and Tigerland

. . . She just had to decide, look up, and find it.

But none of them, not even one, mentioned the existence of a NOPE Council Conference Bubble!

She wondered if JR was given wrong information about the location and time of their meeting? Here, no one seemed to have debates and meetings on their mind. Instead, they all seemed to be celebrating with all they had—*LIFE* and all that it means to live.

Disturbing her despair, a young couple came strolling in her direction, their eyes glued to the billboards, arms entwined around each other. Not aware of Sonal, the girl threw her free arm in the air, as if to encompass it all. "What a night!" she exclaimed.

Her escort pulled her in close. "Just made for us," he replied taking her in his arms. Hugging her tight, he kissed her, and they laughed. The lights of the billboards fell upon their faces, making them look like ephemeral Earth-spirits on a Shakespearean stage. Sensing Sonal's eyes they shyly smiled, waved a tripping good-bye, and, taking a few quick steps, jumped upon a moving walkway.

Watching them disappear, Sonal's depression dug deeper. Among all these people recklessly rushing over the fleeting expressways towards their waiting fun, how would she find someone willing to spare a few minutes to guide her? Would they even know if there was a meeting going on? Or care?

JR's image smiled in her mind. "Just find Kumiko," he had said, "and everything will be all right."

"Kumiko who?"

"Just Kumiko."

"What do you mean *just Kumiko?* Everyone has the right to have a second name of their choice."

"Yes," he had nodded in agreement. "But she prefers not to choose. She prefers to remain *only* Kumiko."

That had sounded ridiculous. Quite unheard of. "Why?"

"Who knows!" JR was smiling, but his hazel eyes held a curtain of mystery. "Perhaps for no reason. Or perhaps because . . . because she is a seventeen-year-old, space-hypnotized Cinderella."

Sonal did not understand, and would have asked more, but something in JR's demeanor had deterred her.

Sensing it, JR had continued. "Like many of us, she is standing on conflicting crossroads. One road she is seriously contemplating is NOPE's march for space-faring freedom."

"Fine. No problem. I'll find her," Sonal had asserted with confidence. After all, how many seventeen-year-olds would be there in a planning committee's meeting.

No problem indeed, she now thought wryly. Among these thousands of people interested only in enjoying themselves, why should anyone care about a scatterbrained Cinderella's existence or her whereabouts?"

"A penny for your thoughts?"

A friendly voice reached her, disrupting her reverie. Sonal Neera glanced in that direction.

Lost in thought, she had moved on, and had reached a Food Bubble displaying lots of exotic items. The fellow behind the counter was smiling at her expectantly.

She returned his smile. "Just a penny?"

"In NOPE," leaning his elbows on the gleaming counter, he rested his chin in his hands, "a penny means a lot."

"I'm new here," she admitted. "I'm thinking of joining your club. How do I go about it?"

"Very easy." He grinned, "Start by sharing salt and water with us." He waved a hand at his display. "What would you like?"

She could not recognize the items he was selling, and it did not seem the right time to start experimenting with strange foods. Suppose she got sick? But that was not the right answer. "I appreciate your offer." She shook her head ruefully. "I won't be able to afford it. Short on credits. End of the month, you know."

"Oh! Don't worry about that. Tonight, you can't pay for anything here. Everything's for fun."

She did not believe him. "You mean, you are going to feed all these thousands of people free?"

He laughed. "Who do you think we are! Space Tycoons?" His expression was so funny, Sonal laughed with him. He waved towards the torch-lit tables where only a few sat here and there. "As to thousands, we wish everyone was more interested in food. But they are having so much fun, no one wants to waste time eating."

"So you are going to lose lot of business today."

"Told you. No business today." He again tried to explain. "You see, what we do here is this—we donate whatever we can for our cause. When we finish what we brought, we fold up and join the fun. So how about helping me close early?"

"If you put it that way . . . What do you suggest?"

"Now you're talking." Picking up a large plate, he started piling it up with a medley of delicacies.

Sonal looked at the huge servings with consternation tugging at her heart. What was that yellow thing topped with lots of almond-cheese? The medley of exotic looking vegetables was perhaps OK, but what was that with lots of brown sauce and mushrooms?"

"Enough! Enough!" She tried to stop him. "I just ate a while ago."

"That's how you keep paper-thin?" He handed her the over-loaded plate and again leaned on his elbows.

Whatever the items were, they were delicious. When she started eating, she found she was quite hungry. Trying to finish it all, she said casually, "It seems everyone in space is here tonight. If some one wanted to find somebody, one would never succeed."

"You think so? That's not so!" He proudly beamed. "We are most organized. Very efficient. You go to *LOST AND FOUND*. They can find anybody. *ANYBODY*," he repeated for emphasis.

"Terrific." Placing her empty plate on the counter, she beamed at him. "Where is it? Which way do I go?"

"I'll show you." His elbows immediately came off the counter. His expression said her request was a real space-sent blessing. He was itching to leave his Food Bubble. A robo-cleaner had emerged from the shadows to pick up the empty plate. Ordering it to take care of the counter, he guided her to the nearest moving walkway.

They passed bubbles offering everything under the sun. She thought, later I would like to visit Garuda Circle. No, perhaps first Luna Nest.

"Bearland is to the West." He was pointing, "Inca to the East and Eagle Mountain is South.

"And there in the center of everything," he pointed proudly, "is our Lost and Found. We have it here," he explained as if to a child, "because when children get separated from their Robo-Mothers, they point their compass towards the center and step on the walkways that bring them here."

He smiled. "Tonight we have been very lucky. Until now." His eyes sparkled with pride. "We haven't heard *Lost and Found* calling any parent, even once."

Enchanted by it all, Sonal's eyes followed his finger. The small Lost and Found Bubble loomed large in the clear space around it. She stared at it because she was not prepared for the contrast that suddenly materialized before her eyes. The small structure was not merely simple, homely, and unadorned. Sitting there all by itself, it seemed very forlorn and lonely.

Noticing her guide's feet stopping, she turned and offered him her hand. "Very nice of you to take so much trouble and come with me all the way. Please accept my million-zillion thanks."

"No trouble. None at all. Glad you're here." He lightly touched her fingertips. As the next expressway began to take him back, he turned and waved. "May we always share salt and water."

"May the Earth be with you always," she returned the greeting as he moved away with a final wave of his friendly hand.

Slowly moving towards the forlorn looking Bubble, Sonal Neera thought, sitting here alone, all by itself, amidst all the noise, music, and distant laughter, this Lost and Found Bubble is, no doubt, the only place no one wants to visit.

Instead of diminishing, its loneliness was enhancing by the sight of one solitary person behind the empty counter, his head bowed over a piece of paper on which he was drawing something very intently.

Noticing her, he turned the paper upside down. "Welcome."

His smile said he really meant it.

He looked very young, but his voice was deep and strong. It seemed to her she had never before seen such clear brown eyes.

He was asking in his caring, heart-warming tone, "You lost someone?"

Feeling self-conscious that he might think she was staring at him, she shook her head. "No, I want to meet someone. The fellow who just left," she waved in that direction, "said you would find her for me."

"Just say the name." His rugged, chiseled face looked very confident.

She tried to hide the anxiety that suddenly constricted her throat. "Kumiko. She doesn't have a second name." Did that sound strange, she wondered, and again wished this Cinderella had a second name.

But apparently the Lost and Found fellow didn't find it strange. "Fine," he responded as if it was the most commonplace thing, as if he dealt with people who disdained a second name all the time.

Punching a few buttons on his console, he picked up his megahorn and spoke into it in a ringing voice. "Lost 'n Found calling," his tunnel deep voice boomed. "Kumiko, please report.

"Lost 'n Found calling. Kumiko, please report . . ."

Replacing the megahorn under the counter, he pointed a finger towards the night sky. Sonal glanced up. Above the crowds a skywriter was moving gracefully, weaving in large, smoky letters, "Lost 'n Found needs you, Kumiko. Please report. Lost 'n Found needs you right away. Kumiko, please. . . ."

Glancing towards the expressway, he solemnly stated, "She'll be here soon." But the anticipatory brightness in his expressive eyes belied his somber demeanor.

There is something more here than his job of helping me, Sonal thought.

To fill in the awkward silence that fell between them, she said apologetically, "I'm sorry, I interrupted your work."

"Oh! It's really nothing. Just a rough sketch of a spaceship that's been haunting me." He turned over the drawing and spread it before her eyes.

"Wow!" she exclaimed. "It looks terrific to me. Why not approach the right people? I'm sure they'll love it."

"No they won't."

He sounded so sad, Sonal was touched. "Why not?" she asked encouragingly.

"Because," he began, then he recognized the stress in her demanding voice and he smiled. "We won't achieve inter-galactic travel in our lifetime. Our Space Syndicate Controllers. . . ."

"You are a very kind person," she said.

"Why? What did I say?"

"Dignified those ruthless demons for whom our planet is now only a barren bull; who give their bloodthirsty blitzkrieg such respectable names as mergers, reorganizations, and selective promotion of Earth Interests; who . . ."

Before she could run out of words, they heard quick clip-clop of rushing feet.

"Elements! Why all the ruckus?" a young voice behind them demanded. "Do you want the whole galaxy to know you want to see me?" it affectionately chided.

Turning, Sonal saw a young girl approaching them. Some might not consider her pretty, she thought, but in her own way she certainly is very attractive. JR had said she is seventeen, but she looked younger. More like fifteen.

"Just doing my duty, Ma'am," The Lost and Found fellow gave her a mock salute and turned towards Sonal. "You have at your service," he flourished an arm as if presenting royalty, "our most eminent Junior Membership Director, Ms. Kumiko."

Kumiko glared at him sternly. But the pride and affection bursting in her sparkling eyes belied her fierce stance.

She turned towards Sonal. "Has he introduced himself? Our maverick member who doesn't listen to anyone?

"Except my Grandma." He winked at Sonal.

Kumiko ignored the remark as if he hadn't spoken and continued, "the most reluctant Lost-People-Pilot NOPE could have found, Pushapk Prado Powhatan."

"Wow!" Sonal exclaimed. "What an imposing name!"

"It has gone to his head. So many important positions available and this forsaken one is the one he chooses!"

"No one else wanted it," he reminded her. "You *did* sound quite relieved when I volunteered for it."

Kumiko apparently knew how to turn a defeat into a victory. "Ha! If I hadn't agreed, you'd have sneaked out at the first chance you got and closeted yourself in your precious *Robin Hood*." Before he could reply, she turned to Sonal. "And you are . . .?"

"Sonal Neera. Previously of the New Space News—a disenchanted quitter. I have been wondering what to do with my desultory life and how to move forward in the New Year. I have been wondering about joining NOPE. Someone in my office had mentioned your name. So I thought if I could talk with you. . . ." She left the thought unfinished, dangling in the expectant air.

But Kumiko didn't need her to continue. "Elements!" she protested, "don't sound so apologetic! You did the right thing. Without knowing us, how can you decide whether or not to join us! Come, I'll intro you to my boss. In fact . . ."

"Is this . . ." they heard someone behind them asking hesitantly, "Is this the right place for a person who feels lost?"

Kumiko and Sonal turned as one and saw a young female looking at them apprehensively. Her clothes were outrageous, and make-up even worse. She did not seem to belong in this world.

"You've lost your friends?" Kumiko asked.

But her question got lost in Pushpak's surprised outcry, "Space Almighty! Look who is here!" His joyful bellow startled them all. "Have they found the killer?" he asked the outrageous nursemaid. "Do you think he could be hiding here?"

Kumiko whirled, anxiety reigning supreme in her dark, anxious eyes. "You know her? Who is she? SpacePol?"

"Naw!" Trying very hard to slow down the heartbeats slamming against his chest walls, Pushpak grinned in his most heartwarming, most delightful, manner.

"She's just a theater person." To reassure Kumiko, he lightly touched her shoulder. "She's no SpacePol, Kumi. She's just a stagehand. You know, the people who fix curtains and things."

Kumiko was not satisfied. "What killer?" she asked.

"That snake-begotten ruffian who killed that famous play's hero. You know the one running longest at the Orpheum?"

"Oh, that!" Kumiko breathed hard. "You were there? You saw the murder?"

"No, but she was. That's why I asked her." To stop any further discussion, he blandly added, "She is my friend."

Kumiko's eyes sought Sonal's, as if to say *Elements! What outrageous friends he finds! Totally out of this world!*

"Okay, you take care of her." She dismissed both of them for the present from her mind. "Come, Sonal Neera. We're getting awful late. If the Shadow's report gets started before we get there, Zorro will chop off my head."

As they turned, Pushpak called, "Kumi?"

"What?" She half-turned.

"Would you please leave your meeting a little early? As you know, Grandma won't eat until we get there."

A peace offering? Kumiko smiled. "I promised, didn't I? Have I ever broken a promise? Meanwhile, have fun. Both of you."

She took Sonal's hand. "Come. We have to change a couple of express lanes quickly. Zorro won't wait for us."

Sonal was used to walking at a quick pace. But she found it hard to keep pace with Kumiko. Skipping slightly ahead, she was asking, "Since you were a newsperson, perhaps you can tell me."

"What?"

"Why so much ruckus about one lousy murder? I mean, people get the knife or what-not all over, all the time. Half the time no one even hears about it. Why is everybody so shook up over this murder-suicide?"

"Perhaps because the victim was such a special person," Sonal temporized. "What do you think?"

"What do I think?" Kumiko slowed down, "When I remember it, I remember that old saying, *Never be a pioneer. It's the early Christian that gets the fattest lion.*"

Sonal stopped in her tracks. "Meaning?"

"I wish I knew," Kumiko shook her head ruefully. "I just remember it. The words just pop up in my head. That's all. Come. Don't stop. We are almost there."

"You mentioned a report? Is it about that murder?"

"We are there. See that large, square Bubble? That's us. Come." Kumiko's feet moved faster. The doors were closed. Giving Sonal an enigmatic glance, Kumiko softly knocked. The door instantly slid open.

To Sonal, the gathering seemed very informal. Dressed in festive clothes, they sat in uneven clusters, listening to the speaker at the podium. As Sonal entered, heads turned.

"Friends," Kumiko said without wasting any time, "let me intro someone. This is Sonal Neera. An ex-New Space Newser. Wanting a new spot, she came over to meet us. Let's welcome her."

Hearing the loud applause, Sonal felt very self-conscious. The speaker at the podium sensed it and raised his hand to quiet the gathering. "Sonal Neera, our honored guest, please have a seat. We have to take care of three more items. Then the meeting will be open for discussion and introduction of new members."

He smiled pleasantly, to encourage her by letting her know she was not the only one who was new and perhaps feeling uncertain. "Kumiko," he added. "We are still talking about the rumor that SpacePol suspects us for Bakul's murder."

"I was saying," a round, fat man, with bushy eyebrows whined from a corner, "it's not important. Let's not waste more time on it. First, tell us about Falcon, who betrayed us. Why do you want to keep him under wraps?"

"Wise people don't indulge in unsupported accusations, McAdoo. You know that." The Speaker's eyes reflected frustration, but his voice was cool and friendly. "We have all known Falcon for a long time. We all know how dedicated and trustworthy he is. Without knowing all the facts, we cannot put him on trial. We must wait until we hear from the search party."

"If we don't hear from the search party?" a woman with small, beady eyes, and hawk-like nose asked in a shrill, reedy voice.

"Then we will just have to meet again, won't we?"

Almost all the heads nodded in assent.

The woman with beady eyes got up. Her companion also. He was a tubby little fellow who looked as if he had been poured into his clothes and had forgotten to say 'when.' Together, they waddled towards the door. The gathering seemed to heave a collective sigh of relief. Sonal smiled. What a pair! she thought. *What Pavan would have said, if he saw them?*

And the Speaker? Pavan would have admired his smooth handling of the ticklish situation. No wonder he was their leader. She could not guess his age. He was thin and short, with a thin angular face. A couple of deep scars on his forehead disappeared under his thinning white hair. One on his left cheek ran all the way down his neck, and disappeared under his shirt collar.

Where did he acquire all these scars, she wondered. In the Seven-Day War or in midnight drunken brawls?

Half-listening to the discussion that was going around and around in circles, she wondered if she should tell them they were worrying needlessly. The rumor they had heard was false. SpacePol did not suspect them. They suspected the JALANGA.

But she remembered she was a spy. JR had emphasized one item more than once—her job was to listen and learn. She should talk only when necessary. The less she was noticed, the better it would be.

Her mind wandered and she remembered the young woman who had joined them when they were leaving the Lost and Found. Unless she had a double, which Sonal doubted, that woman had to be Maya Kiran. Why was she dressed like an eighteenth century floozy, cape, apron, and all? Why had she told the Lost and Found fellow she was a stagehand? If she was here to perform in a play, she would have told him she is an actress. If she was replacing Pia, she'd have dressed like her. Why was she trying to hide her identity?

Could it be because she is involved in the Orpheum murder and is trying to evade SpacePol? In that case, why would she attract attention to herself by flaunting Pia's mask? Pia must have called her. After the meeting, when Kumiko takes me back to them, should I ask her? She was pretending she did not know me? I didn't want to embarrass her so I kept quiet. If I had called out her name, . . .

Sonal's untimely reverie was broken by the loud bleeping of a podium-mounted spacelink.

The council member who was speaking stopped mid-sentence. Zorro moved and accepted the call. Listening, his expression turned very grave. Without saying anything, he punched a button on the podium and a wide screen rolled down on the side wall. The stereo speaker sputtered with space noises, but the picture on the screen was quite clear—a lonely looking desert, with no redeeming features except a few dim-lit torches leaning in an uneven circle. A hovercraft sat in a corner. Near it stood two Robo-Guards in their yellow hats and two tall figures in striped green uniforms. The search party. Sonal breathed hard.

The one who came barely to the other's shoulder, spoke without any preamble. "They were here." he pointed towards the spots with his hand torch. "Their shuttle landed here. Here, they camped a heavy object. Falcon's engraved knife. Perhaps he had his dinner."

"But," the taller one added somberly, "there's nothing here to indicate where they have gone. No debris. No . . ." Suddenly he stopped and stared at the spot from where they had picked up the knife. Leaning upon one knee, he started to dig in the sand.

His searching fingers found a folded piece of paper. He quickly unfolded it. "It's Falcon's handwriting," he said throwing his torch light upon it.

The room suddenly grew very quiet.

In that hushed silence, the voice emerging from the spacelink sounded unnaturally loud. "Friends," reading the note in his bright torchlight, the taller one intoned. "This machine I'm carrying can mean the end of our world as we know it. I'm trying my best to do something about it. If I come back alive, I will tell you all about it. If I don't, nothing will matter anymore anyway. If you believe in God, pray for your Earth tonight. Pray for your world. Falcon, signing off."

There was no wind on the desert. The paper in the Green Guard's fingers was as stiff as his fingers, as his whole body, as the body of every listener in the Council Room.

On the screen the smaller one spoke in a very sad, very gloomy voice. "This is obviously their last rest stop. Why didn't Falcon leave a clue? He knew we are just steps behind him. Did he change his mind, turn traitor, and decide to evade us?"

The taller one shook his head. "No, I don't think so. This message is clearly saying this is their last stop. He was not planning to go anywhere from here. Something must have gone wrong. The next move was unexpected and unscheduled. That's why he was not able to leave another clue, as he had at the previous stops."

He paused, then continued. "Well, nothing more we can do tonight. You all can go home. But don't switch off your com-links. We need to keep in touch." The Green Guards saluted, and the screen went dark.

Someone spoke from the middle of the room. "If *they* have really invented a Doomsday weapon, could they have killed Bakul because he found out about it? Falcon had said, JALANGA . . ." He stopped in mid-sentence because suddenly all the lights went out.

In the ensuing confusion, they heard a thud and a crash. Those who had brought hand-torches tried to find their bags. Someone shrieked. He had stepped on a body. In the blinking lights of the distant carnival filtering in through the transparent walls, they saw the last speaker lying face down on the floor.

Pandemonium shrieked in the Hall. Several rushed towards the fallen member. "Hold back. Hold back!" someone shouted. Others tried to form a ring around him. "Please, hold back. He has fainted. He needs air."

Just then the lights came back as suddenly as they had gone out. Everyone started moving to peek at the fallen body.

There was a circle around him, formed by anxious members trying to isolate him, to make it easier for him to breathe. One pillowed his head. Another one held his feet. Turning him around, they noticed the poison darts sticking in his neck. It must have been a very lethal poison. He was already dead.

The Guards! Sonal thought frantically, *where are the guards? Space Almighty! Why doesn't someone call them right away?*

Then she remembered. There were no Guards. They had been excused because NOPE believed in non-violence. Holy Space! When JR hears about it, what would he say she should have done? Should she try to get out and call him?

Someone must have beeped the Guards on his porta-link, because just then a bevy of green striped, green helmeted men rushed in. Two of them strode towards the body. The others blocked the exit.

Before they could say anything, the lights went out again. Through the half-open door and the Bubble's transparent walls, they could see this time all the carnival lights were also gone.

What had happened? Had the Park Island Energy-Generator overloaded and fused?

Outside the half-open door, the carnival loudspeaker started emitting meaningless sputterings. Then a clear voice came through. "Please remain calm. Please, do not move. Please remain where you are until we get the lights back. Please . . ."

The voice stopped. In the torchlit silence, they stood and huddled quietly, staring at each other. Questions circling and revolving in their minds. But no one felt ready to say anything.

The loudspeaker sputtered again and a strong voice boomed through. "Kumiko, can you hear me? Kumiko, I can't reach my Grandma. I'm leaving. Will call you."

Kumiko's feet moved towards the door. But she restrained herself. Being a logical person she knew her effort to reach him would be useless. First, there were the Guards blocking the exit. They wouldn't let her leave. No way! If, by some miracle she succeeded in persuading them, it would still be useless. Without energy, the pathways wouldn't be running. No matter how fast she ran, she would not reach Pushpak's hovercraft before he took off.

Despite all the courage she could always muster during any crisis, she felt scared. She could easily handle what she could understand. How does one deal with disasters that seem so incongruous? So incomprehensible?

Why was Pushpak's grandmother so worried? Who are the mysterious *they* the fellow who just got killed had mentioned? He was hit as soon as he uttered the word JALANGA. Does it mean JALANGA spies have infiltrated NOPE? Was it they who killed him?

Does it also mean that from now on they would have to close their doors to public and have closed meetings?

What was Falcon hinting in his sand-buried note? How could anyone have invented such a space-shattering weapon that Falcon spoke of in such awe without SpacePol's knowing anything about it?

Isn't that impossible?

Falcon is a very scrupulous scientist. He would not have used those words if they were not true. In that case, does this energy blow-out have anything to do with that blasted machine? Is the world really going to end tonight? If it is, why couldn't she end it in Prado's arms? Why had all her efforts to keep him close to her tonight failed?

Someone nearby was sobbing. She wanted to reach out to her, but someone was already turning to comfort her. Kumiko wondered if the mourner was related to the victim? What was he trying to say? How had Bakul known so much about JALANGA? Had he tried to infiltrate it? Who are they anyway? She never heard of a terrorist group bearing that name.

But the name sounded familiar. She vaguely remembered hearing it somewhere. She tried to remember when, where, or in what context she had heard it. Were they terrorists? If yes, why hadn't SpacePol confined them to an isolated Terrorist Island?

If the world was about to be annihilated, why would JALANGA remain untouched? Wouldn't it die also? Didn't the Jalangans care for their lives? Were they some new kind of blood-thirsty kamikaze whose self-hypnotized minds could find pleasure and self-esteem only in senseless, nameless death?

Elements. Fire and water and all that's holy, please hear me. This is Kumiko's promise. She closed her eyes and breathed hard. *These JALANGA—no matter who they are, I'll find them before tomorrow's sun touches the evening's horizon, and I'll avenge my friend's slaughter.*

She opened her eyes. Outside the Bubble's transparent walls, a couple of torches flared. Suddenly an image of leaping flames flashed in Kumiko's mind and she remembered when and where she had first heard the name, JALANGA. It was a long time ago.

She was only eleven then, going on twelve. One day on her way to the gymnasium, she came across a huge fire that was engulfing a sixty story building. Smoke-helmeted, masked, yellow-robed firemen were swarming all over. Some onlookers were trying to help them. More were coming. She also got off the expressway.

Hovercraft ladders were picking up people from balconies. Others, tumbling from windows onto tarpaulins, were getting whisked away to waiting air-ambulances. There was one balcony that the ladders were not able to reach due to the overhanging branches of the nearby trees. A young girl was leaning over the balcony. Despite the coaxing from below, she would not jump. Behind her back, the fire was leaping, moving forward. Soon, it would reach the balcony.

Kumiko did not hesitate. Picking up a long rope, looping it on one shoulder, she clambered up the nearest tree. She tied one end of the rope to a strong branch, and the other end to her waist. She would try to reach the balcony. If she failed, the rope would hold her until they could rescue her.

Mother Earth, water, fire, and all holy elements, our lives are yours. In our hour of need, please make me succeed. Silently saying this prayer, she aimed for the fire-threatened balcony and leaped. She made it with inches to spare. Quickly scrambling up, she untied the rope from around her waist, and touched the stranger's shoulder. "Come on. Let's go."

The frightened girl was gazing at her with incredulity and wonder in her huge, big blue eyes. In reply, she only clutched the railing harder.

The flames licking the windows behind the balcony were leaping out. Soon their necks and backs would get scorched. Kumiko forcibly loosened the stranger's fingers, bent the girl's body forward on the steel railing, and toppled her. As soon as rescue workers lifted the stunned girl off the tarpaulin, Kumiko herself jumped.

Landing on the balcony, Kumiko had sprained her toes and the stranger had burns and blisters. As they waited for the ambulance, she glanced at Kumiko shyly. "You saved my life. I do not have words to thank you."

Kumiko smiled. "Think nothing of it. If I were up there and you down here, you'd have done the same thing."

"No, I couldn't have." The girl shook her head. "I live in a one story cottage. On an island. Until today, I didn't even know I was so afraid of heights. This is," not wanting Kumiko to think she was a coward, the stranger quickly added, "my first landside trip."

"Wow!" Kumiko was impressed. "You live on an island? All the time?"

"Yes," the stranger nodded. "I'm attending a special school. Learning robo-manufacturing. Because I topped my class, they gave me a land vacation. What a mistake I made accepting it! I'll never take land a vacation ever again."

"Don't say that! It's not *that* bad! This fire was an exception. We rarely have a fire. Tell you what." Kumiko pulled out a piece of paper from her pocket and scrawled her vid-diary number. "When they release you, call me. I'll take you around my city. We'll hit all the tourist spots. When you are sightseeing," she added, "it makes a lot of difference who your guide is."

"That's true." The girl had smiled for the first time. "But if something comes up—if I have to go back before I call you—you call me. On Jalanga, where I live, only members are allowed. Or guests. You can be my guest."

"Okay, but nothing will happen. Our hospitals take very good care. Before you leave, do call me. My name is Kumiko."

"Kumiko what?"

"Just Kumiko."

The girl had smiled a second time. "I'm Pashka. I also declined a second name." She felt a special kinship. "Kumi, when you come to visit, let's reinforce this like-thinking. This kinship that's so rare. Let us be Rakhi-Sisters."

Before Kumiko could reply, the Burn Unit Guard had come over with a wheelchair. Pashka was whisked away. Her words hovered in the air. Kumiko waited for a few days. Pashka never called.

A few months later, in her mail Kumiko received a silver bangle with Pashka's name and vid-diary number engraved on it. Kumiko loved it. It was the first gift she had received from a five-minute friend. Pashka's memory had faded, but she had always worn it. Now touching it, she thought—Pashka. I hope you still remember me, because I'm coming over. I hope you would still like to be my Rakhi-Sister and tell me all about your Jalanga.

Quietly she moved towards the washroom. A Peace Guard eyed her, but seeing which way she was headed he did not stop her. Entering the washroom Kumiko softly closed the door and peered through the eyehole. No one had followed her. No one was near the door. No one was glancing in her direction.

Breathing a sigh of relief, she quickly stepped into the broom closet. The door automatically closed behind her.

She groped in the semi-darkness, found the lock, and pressed her palm against it. The secret escape hatch slid open and she walked out into the dark shadows. The hatch quickly closed, leaving no tell-tale sign of its being there.

She hurried to find a public comlink to call Pashka. She did not know how far Jalanga was, but she was confident. She would find it before the rays of the morning sun. If Pashka was still the same old Pashka, she would tell her what's cooking in Jalanga.

12

... *Time-Blasted Traps*

*DEBOUT! LES DAMNES DE LA TERRE! DEBOUT! LES
FORCATS DE LA FAIM! LA RAISON TONNE EN SON
CRATERE, C'EST L'ERUPTION DE LA FIN. DU PASSE
FAISONS TABLE RASE FOULE ESCLAVE, DEBOUT, DEBOUT,
LE MONDE VA CHANGER DE BASE, NOUS NE SOMMES
RIEN, SOYONS TOUT! C'EST LA LUTTE FINALE GROUPONS-
NOUS, ET, DEMAIN, L'INTERNATIONALE SERA LE GENRE
HUMAIN. (On your feet, you damned souls of the earth! On your
feet, inmates of hunger's prison! Reason is rumbling in its crater,
and its final eruption is on its way. Let us wipe clean the slate of
the past—on your feet, you enslaved multitude, on your feet—the
world is to undergo a fundamental change: we are nothing, let us
be everything! This is the final conflict: let us form up and,
tomorrow, the International will encompass the human race.)*
                    —Eugene Pottier (1816-1887): *L'Internationa—LE*
        (in H.E. Piggot, *Songs that Made History*, ch.6, 1937)

. . .

God moves in a mysterious way
His wonders to perform,
He plants his footsteps in the sea,
And, rides upon the storm.
—William Cowper: *Royal George,* (1731–1800)

. . .

*I*n the JALANGA Council Room, Jal-Eleven was feeling bored by the endless data the wall-screen was unrolling. Were the others, silent and motionless like time-frozen petroglyphs, interested in all that, or were they also bored and chafing at the wasted time?

There was no way to find out. Everyone's face was fully covered by their JALANGA-crested veils. Even their eyes were not visible because the eyeholes were covered by a thick, black net, sporting vision holes.

In fact, whoever had designed their robes had made quite sure that no one would be able to identify even the toenails of the persons hidden inside. The loose, head-to-toe robes with long sleeves ended in gloves so that even their fingers were not visible. Carrying the camouflage to the Nth degree, even speculation about their actual heights was made meaningless by the platform shoes that many of them wore.

That was not all. Since one can be recognized by one's voice, they did not speak. They typed their comments on the consoles fixed on their armrests. The words projected on the wall screen.

Except for the minor differences in heights, the only identifying marks were their membership numbers embroidered in yellow gold on their left shoulders. Contrasted by the black color of the robe, they glistened with unnatural brightness.

Sitting straight up in their high-back chairs, both hands on the table, they were occupying three sides of a long, wide table. On the fourth side, the wall was fully covered by the spacelink screen. With its figurine-etched brass frame, it was the only ostentatious item in the Spartan room.

The room was extraordinarily large, with a very high ceiling curved into the walls. The walls curved into the floor. There were no windows. Light came from touchglow panels encased in the walls.

Other than their chairs, the only furniture in the room was a mahogany table. On its polished surface sat a small, white marble sphere. If anyone had a bug hidden somewhere, the sphere would glow pink and would continue to dim and brighten until the bug was removed and deactivated.

During the lifetime of this Council, it had happened only once when the Council was barely a week old. The snooping member had to swallow a cobra venom pill and the details were entered into the minutes of the meeting.

Finally, the last figures rolled in, and the computer voice fell silent. The vacant screen waited, but no one had any comment. Jal-One moved his eyes. He glanced at Jal-O, then at the others. What is he seeing, Jal-Eleven wondered. Is there some kind of device embedded in his eye patches that the others do not have?

The silence was jarred by Jal-One's moving his chair closer to the table. He sat even straighter so that his back seemed almost rigid. Without any more delay, he punched on his armrest console. "All of us have, no doubt, heard the news. Does anyone here know anything else about Jal-Two's murder?"

The silence in the room was deafening. The screen waited. Jal-O glanced at their rigid backs and wondered if he should say something. But the time did not seem right. He held his silence.

Jal-Eleven couldn't take it any more. He rapidly punched his console and the screen read, "I think it's time we discarded our veils. We should know each other. We should know who we are."

Jal-One's fingers jerked into motion. "Eleven, you are out of order. Review of constitutional changes is not on today's agenda."

"Neither is Two's murder," Jal-Four lashed out. "I agree with Eleven. Until he died, we did not know Two was Bakul. SpacePol suspects NOPE, but everyone knows NOPE doesn't need such methods. If the truth is not revealed, they may never catch the killer."

"I agree," Jal-Seven quickly added his weight to their comments. "We must talk with the news media. We must hire a detective. Why would anyone kill a beloved hero? Because he was one of us? In that case, are we also on the hit list?"

Jal-O felt very uneasy. The cowardly human minds were trudging towards forbidden grounds. If their fears were not quashed before they got out of hand, it could be disastrous.

"Pardon me," he intervened, the only one who was allowed to use his voice because everyone knew who he was. "With all due respect, may I remind you that this is not the right time to waste your energy on such a tangled, untimely item."

They all glanced at him with surprise. He was their employee, not supposed to speak unless ordered to do so.

Jal-O, however, ignored their shock. Before they could reprimand him, he continued smoothly. "Operation Earth Shield's time has come. All your energies are now needed for launching the new world order that you have so painstakingly planned. Granted, each one of you is equal to a thousand. Still, at this time you cannot afford divided attention.

"With your permission," he respectfully bowed, "I'll now ask Keno-M-One to display for your pleasure the transmission from Kato-S-One. M-One, do you have the tape?"

His Robo-Major quietly moved and pushed a panel near the screen. A small tray slid forward bearing a black tape and a portable spacelink unit. Inserting the tape in the unit, he placed it near Jal-O and turned it on.

The wall-screen transformed itself. Looking like a 3-D theater screen, it depicted a dark, torch-lit desert, and a robot helping a human moving a heavy machine towards a waiting shuttle.

Trying to keep his tone devoid of all emotions, Jal-O softly intoned, "Per your Plan, we selected a radical NOPE leader to push the button. You will recall we had two problems. First, if we had given him an inhabited area, he would have torn the contract and accepted the death penalty, but would not have pulled the trigger. Second, we needed a NOPE-guarded route so that when SpacePol investigated, they would believe that only NOPE was responsible."

On the screen, the machine was getting loaded on the shuttle. Behind it, the human and the robot climbed in. The ladder was pulled in, and the door slid shut. The engines hummed. Slowly climbing up, the shuttle streaked out of the camera's range.

Jal-O switched off the video. "To solve these problems, we secretly programmed a map on the machine's memory tapes so that it would reject the desert that you just saw as the last stop."

He stopped as if he expected a comment. None came.

"For security purposes, the preceding activity was not recorded. As planned, when the NOPE leader tried to switch on the machine at the spot they just left, it did not respond. It merely projected the map where it wanted to go.

"At that point, Kato apologized to the NOPE leader for making a navigational error, and bringing him to the wrong desert. They are now heading towards the spot that all of you have chosen so carefully. The NOPE leader now has no option. If he refuses to trigger the LDM, Kato will tie him up and do it for him."

The Council Members sat silently staring at the blank screen. They had participated in the planning of this event and had waited for it. But now that the time was here, they were feeling apprehensive. It would work, but then what? How would it affect their future lives? Personally and collectively?

Jal-O glanced at his wristwatch and turned on the video again. The camera hidden on the second desert picked up the descending shuttle. The shuttle circled once and touched down. Its door opened and the ladder dropped. The robot and the human brought down the Land Displacement Machine and set it up.

The human fiddled with the machine and said something to the robot that the camera-audio didn't quiet catch. The robot squatted near the machine, opened one of the plates, and started checking something. Climbing two steps at a time, the human quickly entered the shuttle and disappeared inside.

Jal-O squirmed in his seat. Humans! he thought. Always forgetting something! Always last minute delays!

It was too late when he realized that the human was not delaying anything.

On the screen, the Land Displacement Machine turned blue, and started rotating, glowing red. At the same time, the shuttle engines started humming.

Taken by surprise, the robot scrambled up and ran towards it. But the shuttle did not wait for him. Quickly lifting up, it started to climb away.

The robot waved his arms, then rushed towards the camera hidden in the nearby bush.

"Master," he shouted, "Master Falcon said due to location change, the lock-time needed correction. He needed the time-punch and went up to get it. That was a lie. He is not an honest human. He is a crook. You fell in his trap. I need to be rescued. Please, send someone quickly!"

The request was useless. As Kato was speaking his last words, the LDM was emitting ground-penetrating flames. Within seconds, the land it was sitting upon started to sink, taking the machine, the robot, and the camera with it.

The screen went blank.

It worked! They breathed hard—*now what?*

"Now the real work begins!" Jal-O said softly, self-effacing, in a frighteningly neutral voice.

But his mind was burning, churning like an atom-splitting oven. *Falcon! The Hellish-Fiendish-Crawling-Worm! Why did he kill my Kato? For this inexcusable, brutal crime he must be punished. I will kill him. No matter how fast he runs, no matter where he goes, I'll catch up with his running feet and kill him.*

***

Keeping up with Pushpak's running feet was hard work. On top of that Maya Kiran's rebellious mind was furiously scolding her. You dumb Kiwi! Why didn't you get lost in the crowds as you had planned? Why didn't you politely decline this maverick's absent-minded invitation? What are you going to do in a strange house, under the questioning eyes of an old matriarch?

When she was told that *Spider's Stratagems* would be folded forever on New Year's Eve, her immediate feelings of sorrow and uncertainty for her future had quickly changed to a kind of grim anticipation. I won't work for six months, she had told herself. I'll move around, visit the places I've been dreaming about and spend some time with Shaku and her family. Perhaps, just perhaps, Bakul and Pia would like to join me in my planet-wide wandering.

And if Pia won't have me as her understudy in her new venture, as she didn't in *The Cobra Keepers,* I'll join some space-opera crew where life would be fun and not such hard work.

Considering what she had been going through since the curtain fell on *Stratagems*, it seemed as if until then her life had been a dream holiday. Until then, roles in Pia's plays had been handed to her on diamond platters. Life was comfortable and predictable. Every day swept away with pleasure and fun.

To make it absolutely perfect, Bakul was always there to tease her, to make her laugh, to make her life a golden, cherry blossom swing gently swaying in the warmth of his friendship and affection.

Yes! It had been perfect. That's why her nasty Blue Wheel Nightmare had started receding. Had become less frequent. Had become an ordeal that she could easily forget with the first rays of every dawn. But now resurfacing, it had taken on a life of its own—not only had it become real, it had also gained additional, absolutely ridiculous dimensions. To make it worse, Bakul had disappeared. Without his Shavian support, moving alone she found each step posing a new danger. To top it all, there didn't seem any chance that days like the old ones would come back soon.

Her thoughts broke—Pushpak was slowing down. She glanced ahead. A four-seater sat alone in a corner of the crowded parking lot. Was it their destination?

If it was, she liked it. It shimmered softly in the shadows and lights lent by the far-away flickering torches. A kaleidoscopic fireworks display was beaming down upon it from the skies. Its ID plate proudly proclaimed—*ROBIN HOOD*.

Pushpak was looking at her uncertainly, as if not sure whether or not to feel embarrassed. "Kumiko named it," he said as if an explanation was needed. "Her idea of a fine joke."

"Why? I think it's a splendid name." The appreciation in her voice sounded quite genuine.

Pushpak did not answer. He strode ahead to punch out the parking meter. Seeing the blue light circling the hovercraft disappear, Maya Kiran moved towards the co-pilot's seat and climbed in. She watched with fascination as Pushpak's long fingers flew on the console, programming the controls.

As the hovercraft climbed, it seemed to her as if they would collide with a sprouting rocket or a spilling, gyrating, syncopated Catherine wheel. But it steered clear as if it had eyes. Soon the cacophony of the fireworks dimmed. Only the starlight remained.

Next to her Pushpak's whole body appeared tense. He was staring at the panel pulsating console as if trying to triple the speed of his powerful craft by sheer force of his will power.

Maya gently touched his arm. "She is all right. I'm sure."

He glanced at her, smiled, and tried to relax. "I'm glad you're with me."

"Nice of you to invite me. If you hadn't, I don't know what I'd have done. You see, I'm . . . running away."

"Why? What have you done?"

"Nothing. I've done nothing. That's the whole problem. Since childhood, since I can remember, I have always followed someone. Been someone's shadow. It is ridiculous, because I've always wanted to be me. Something more than someone's shadow."

"A shadow? A stage-person like you?" He wanted to put his arm around her but restrained himself. "If you ask me, I'd say anyone who knows you would say you are pretty independent."

"But you don't know me! I'm not who you think I am." Almost defiantly she pulled off her face mask.

"Holy Lorelei!" he exclaimed. "I thought these things were only fiction. Don't tell me they are real!"

The look of awe-buffeted wonder on his face was out of this world. No one could have looked more astonished. Maya Kiran did not say anything. She smiled and twirled the mask.

He touched it with one finger and found his voice. "You are clowning like Kumi. Having New Year fun. You are really not an actress!" It was not a question; simply a statement.

"Oh, yes. I'm an actress all right. But, I'm not Pia Payal."

"Who is Pia Payal?"

She was stunned. "You don't know Pia Payal?"

She stared at him with total disbelief. Then watching him grinning, she realized he had scored one. Well, okay, she thought, I'll get even. Soon.

"Want to guess who I am?"

"Don't have to guess," he stated smugly. "I know. You're Pia's little sister. Have always followed her steps. But now you are having second thoughts."

"Nope," she shook her head. "Guess again."

"I give up."

"Not so quickly. You get three guesses. Try again."

"Okay, gimme a clue. What's your name?"

"Which one? My birth name? Given name? Or my chosen one?"

He looked at her sparkling eyes, her starlit face. He wanted to say, I don't know your name. I have no idea who you are. But since first I saw you, I have felt like my whole life I've been waiting for you. When you are near me, it feels like during all of the gone-by centuries, we have always been bond-mates. As if . . . as if we have always walked together on the changing shores of life. We have never been separated. You are the one for whom my life has been always breathing. And, would keep on breathing just for you. Do you think that's possible? Does it make sense?

No. It did not make sense. So he said instead, "How about the one chosen by me?"

Maya Kiran shrank within herself. Oh, no! she thought, is it happening again? Just when I thought I had planned a no-nonsense escape, am I about to be cornered again!

"My chosen name," she quickly offered, as if that would extinguish the silent quest on his earnest face. "Is Maya Kiran. Until the *Spider's Stratagem* folded, I was living as Pia Payal's shadow. And now . . ."

"And now?" he echoed, silently chiding himself. She hardly

knows you and you wanted to give her a name! How stupid! Wouldn't that just make her despise you?

To avoid looking at him she was looking out. A dark object looming ahead startled her. "Pushpak, look! What's that?"

He had been totally absorbed in her. Surprised by the sudden fright in her voice, he glanced in the direction her finger was pointing. There, not very far below, something globular, something dark and lifeless, seemed to be slowly rising above the surface of the ocean. Feeling fascinated, quickly switching the controls to manual, he reduced speed and started circling down.

Whatever it was, it seemed shaped like an egg. As it emerged, slowly but steadily, it's circumference seemed to grow bigger and bigger.

"What is it?" Maya Kiran whispered. Now that the first shock was over, she was more curious than frightened. "A new kind of island?"

"Not unless . . ." Pushpak was maneuvering the hovercraft to bring it closer to the strange object. But he was not able to fully concentrate. You have already made a rotten mistake, his mind was furiously scolding him. Don't make another. Just don't.

Leaving the thought dangling, he stated, "We need to get closer. Islands are required by Universal Law to display their name and ID. If one disobeys, penalty is immediate destruction, by any citizen, no matter who the owner is."

"It's width seems disproportionate to its height! See, it's getting wider!" Maya Kiran was staring at it as if, if she tried hard enough, her eyes would penetrate its mystery. "Look! It is bellying ocean life. It will kill them all."

"Well, it's rising very slowly. The living beings would have time to get away. But the plant life . . ."

Circling down, even in the dim starlight, they could see the uprooted plant life floating around the dark, mysterious object. Strangely, nothing was sticking to its smooth surface. It appeared shiny and clean as it emerged as if someone were wiping it lovingly with the New Wipex.

Was it their imagination, or a trick played by the starlight? Or was it really some kind of transparent yellowish halo enveloping the base of the dark object?

"Pushpak," Maya said without moving her eyes. "If this thing is a newly emerging mountain created by colliding down-side Earth plates trying to eat-up each other, I'll eat a whole spaceship."

"No you won't. Not my spaceship."

A roguish smile twinkled in her eyes. "You know what I mean."

Mountains grow in centimeters. In centuries. Not like that! Not before you can blink your eyes!"

"I'm not a Geomorphology major. You tell me. Could a huge volcanic eruption somewhere down there may have pushed it up?" He was pushing buttons to reduce speed to get closer, "One thing's for sure. As far as I know, no natural phenomenon was ever born with such a smooth blue surface."

"Blue or not, maybe that's what it is? Just a big piece of rock?" Maya Kiran sounded as mesmerized as she was feeling. "Is that how the Himalayas rose centuries ago? But Pushpak, it doesn't look like a mountain. It looks more like a pyramid! Or a pagoda!"

"So it does!" Pushpak nodded. "It doesn't look like a geological formation at all. I wonder who had the money to build such a gigantic object? I wish," he sighed wistfully, "I had one of those convertible crafts that can float on water."

"I'm glad you don't. If you did, you'd get so glued to this thing, you'd never move from here. Come on, let's notify someone."

"Notify who?"

"How do I know? The Coast Guard. The Ocean Patrol. SpacePol. Somebody?"

"I know *THAT!* What I meant was, whom can we find? No one's around. Everybody's on a galactic, drunken vacation."

"Then?"

"Not our responsibility. They'll find out soon enough. We don't want to get involved with them. Let's go and get Grandma. She knows about such things."

"What things?"

"That's it! Best idea I've had so far. I'm going to call her."

He quickly punched her numbers. "Grandma. Hello, Grandma."

"Ah! Prado? Don't tell me you are not coming!"

"Grandma, I want you to see something. I am going to pan the cameras. See that blue thing twinkling under the starlight. To me it looks like something man-made."

Her mid-summer eyes seemed to grow larger as she stared at the screen. "You know, Kaku," her strong voice sounded husky, full of odd emotions, "I think the ancient legend has come true."

"What legend?"

"You come home right away. I must brief you."

"Shouldn't we first call the Ocean Patrol? Coast Guard?

Somebody?"

"No, my son." She had regained her composure. Her voice was strong again. Strong and authoritative. "They will find soon enough. I don't want you to get involved. Not yet. Get out of there before anyone arrives. And remember," she wagged a finger at him, "bring your new friend. Don't leave her somewhere on your way. It's important."

"Sure thing, Grandma." Pushpak had never seen his grandmother lose her cool. It disturbed him. He quickly punched the new coordinates and, circling away, increased the speed to the maximum allowed by Universal Law.

As they veered away, the side screen showed lights of two distant aircraft speeding towards them.

"Look, Pushpak!" Maya Kiran exclaimed. "Your Grandma was right."

"She is always right." Pushpak was staring hard at the controls as if somewhere there answers were hidden to all the questions that were whirling in his mind.

Maya Kiran understood. She sat quietly, not touching or looking at him, trying her best to give him as much space as he needed to grapple with his turbulent thoughts.

In those unguarded moments, the image of the blue stranger crowded her mind. When the two Robo-Guards had released her at the periphery of the Nope Carnival, she had sought out a solitary pillar. Hiding behind it, she had touched the blue pendant hidden inside her dress.

The deep baritone voice that had, in such a short time, become so familiar, had almost instantly responded. "It's not fun and games, Maya," he had chided her. "You do not need me. Remember, you must not call me when I'm not needed. And no one—*NO ONE*—must learn about me. It's our secret. You must conceal it."

"But—"

"No buts. Just remember." Then for no reason, the voice had lost its anger. In that ancient, smooth and friendly manner, he had added, ". . . and, Kiwi, remember this also—there's no when or where. Like a whisper of air, I am never very far from you."

Those words, that voice, coming through that pendant, seemed to have penetrated every pore of her skin. She had shivered. Was it her imagination or was he really in the gust of wind that had just then ruffled her hair?

Now, in Pushpak's hovercraft, moving speedily towards an unknown destination, she wondered if that vanishing blue person was connected to this strange object that was emerging from the deep depths of this solitary area. This object had such a shiny, sparkling blue surface that it seemed to match the color of his skin.

What if everything he had told her were blunt, shameless lies? What if it was he, or his kind, who were responsible for the murder in the Orpheum? What if Pia and Bakul were prisoners inside that mysterious blue object? She shivered.

"Cold?" Pushpak asked, glancing at the life-system control needle. "She lives some distance from here. But we'll be there soon."

"Pushpak," she said in a small voice. "There always have been stories about witchcraft. Could they be based upon real truths?"

He misunderstood her question. "My grandmother is a direct descendent of a very ancient healer of an ancient tribe. They were called Maya. Similar to your name, isn't it?" He looked at her and smiled reassuringly.

"In those ancient days," he added, "they were called *medicine men*. Their heirs secretly managed to keep the ancient knowledge alive. If some ignorant people labeled it witchcraft, how does that matter? Doctor, engineer, professor, aren't they just labels to distinguish one profession from another?"

"Profession?" Maya Kiran looked up at him. "Well, I guess that's one way of putting it."

"You know, I've thought about it. History's truths are based upon the writing historians' perspectives. Legends have theirs. But based upon what? If in those ancient days, when we hadn't even invented the wheel, extra-terrestrials were visiting us, if a human glimpsed a spaceship booming away . . ."

"You know, you're right. It never occurred to me. That would certainly be considered magic. The stuff of which legends are made."

"Exactly," Pushpak beamed at her. "See there? Those city lights? My grandma lives in that ancient city. Nothing on this planet can move her from there."

"I bet something can."

"What's that?"

"Concern for your safety."

He grinned. "What do you bet?"

"The moon." She moved her hands encompassing the distant

image, as if she owned it. "Or, if you wish, those ancient city lights."

"Those city lights." His grin broadened, and he started switching over the controls to manual, preparing to land.

In the starlight, Maya Kiran saw a medley of mysterious emotions on his enigmatic face. She lightly touched his hand. "Pushpak, would you listen to me? It's late. If Grandma went to bed, we won't wake her up. It can wait till morning. OK?"

Her fleeting touch sent chanting currents coursing through his veins. *Would I listen to you? Of course I would!* He nodded, smiled, and placed his arm companionably around her waist.

She did not respond. But made no effort to move it away either.

Looking ahead, Pushpak started to whistle a tune he often hummed when flying alone:

Yonder there, not so far. That flickering, flaming star.
All night burning bright, is not a candle, nor a meteor.
It's only me. Merely me. Calling your fugitive name.
Wherever you are
Can you see it, Love?
That far-away fenced-in-light.
That is just my knocking heart.

***

JR was knocking and knocking. But in his maddening nightmare, the door to the Star Stairs was not opening. Actors and actresses, in blood-dripping masks and costumes, were rushing up and down the stairs. But each time he took a step, the door slammed shut in his face. "I'll burn it!" He was shouting, banging at it. "Where's my laser torch? I'll burn it" . . .

Suddenly there was no door. No stairs. He was in Pia Payal's red-hot dressing room, shaking her shoulders, goading her. "Tell me. Tell me. You must tell me or I'll throw you down the stairs." She was struggling and he was bashing her head against her mirror. "Tell me. No one recognizes Maya Kiran in your role. How did Sonal recognize you? What did you tell her that you have not told me? Tell me . . ."

The bleeding statue whirled and faced her. It was not Pia. It was Sonal. He was not in Pia's draconian room. He was in Sonal's seven-senses arousing bedroom, and she was smiling at him seductively, "Chief, your mother never told you? You should not enter a lady's bedroom without knocking?"

"I knocked."

"No, you did not."

"I knocked."

But the robo-girl, flames leaping from her red eyes as she beat his chest, was not Sonal. It was Maya Kiran. She was crying and hysterically screaming, "Answer your spacelink, you Heartbreaker! Answer it, you old fire-eater. Answer it . . ."

The shrill, non-stopping spacelink bleeps finally penetrated JR's nightmare. He turned and groggily pushed the button on his armrest. The spacelink's speaker exploded. It spluttered unintelligibly, stopped, sputtered again. JR felt like shaking it. Instead, he decided to switch it off and go back to sleep.

Before he could, a clear voice came through. "Time for Time Hawk Three. They have exploded the LDM. Two? Do you read? I will now . . ." the rest of the communication was lost in atmospheric interference.

Jolted fully awake, JR stared at his sputtering machine. Who had exploded what? Switching it off, he rubbed his eyes.

The voice had sounded like Pavan's. And the correct codes were used. What was he talking about?

He glanced at his wristwatch. It was already past midnight. Waiting to hear from Pavan and Sonal, he had fallen asleep in his office chair. In his absence from the waking world, the New Year had sneaked in and he had missed the chance of welcoming it. He had missed the chance of watching the colorful celebrations.

As always, life had again cheated him. Even on this historical day, that would soon belong to the realm of cherished legends, life had not spared him.

Through the half-open windows, he could hear the far-off voices on the street. With sleep-heavy feet, he walked to the window, opened a shutter, and looked down. A blue balloon, floating up, missed his fingers by inches.

"Aren't you on a warp-drive?" he chided himself. "So you missed the sight and sounds of clanging bells and flying balloons? Big deal! Midnight comes every night. And Space-V will be replaying everything again and again for weeks. How does it matter if you had watched it then, or, would do so later?"

Why not watch it now?

He reached for the remote on his side table, called his robo-server to bring his dinner, and switched on the Space-V.

But the screen stared at him blankly.

That's strange, he thought changing to the Inquiry Channel. Big, bold letters told him in several languages to tune in to Channel Q. *My God!* he thought, *They've triggered another war!*

Quelling the strange, prickly heat in his backbone, he quickly punched in Channel Q—the Emergency Channel to be activated only in case of a major war.

The screen depicted a strange scene—tall buildings rapidly sinking under rising waters. Animals floating—dead or dying—rotting vegetation. Hydrofoils, canoes, kayaks, rowboats, tugs, sloops, trying to rescue the drowning men, women, and children. The bluestar-studded, Space Cross ambulances homing in towards the disaster area. . . .

Shooting stars! What kind of a joke is this! Which scum of the Earth had the bright idea to air such a hellish movie this night? This night of all the thousands of nights?

Then he saw the mute button light. He clicked it off and the anchor person's somber voice broke in, ". . . the reason for not spacecasting the midnight celebrations. Until we hear more from the Ocean Patrol, we have nothing else to report."

"We repeat. It has not yet been established why the Energy Station in Sector 3209 blew up around midnight. It had so many backups and fail-safe systems, such a massive breakdown was absolutely unthinkable. It should not have happened. We have been told the United Earth Council is doing everything that can be done. Meanwhile, Sectors 3208 and 3210 are taking steps to take over the load. Please, remain calm and stay wherever you are. There's no need to panic. The global peace is intact. We repeat . . ."

The robot had wheeled in his dinner. JR pushed it aside and switched on the mute button. His mind had become a melting pot of burning questions. Is that what Pavan was trying to tell me? Why his transmission got lost? Did someone stop him? Did he get disconnected by this infernal holocaust? Is he safe? Where is he?

Had Pavan ignored his instructions? Without telling him, without his permission, had he left Jalanga? . . . followed someone to the stricken area? Is he in some kind of danger? Sector 3209, the Space-V said. And Sonal is . . .

By Space! Sonal? What about Sonal?

She was always itching to go the extra mile without any thought in her one-track mind about her personal safety. She was on Park Island, lying half in Sector 3208, and half in 3209. Her image, floating lifeless on the swirling waters, swam before his eyes, and he shot up from his chair.

The only way to find her would be to go there.

He rushed to his bathroom to freshen up and change. It did not take him long.

Tying up his shoes, he glanced at the Space-V. The disaster scene was still the same. Large ships and various types of aircraft had now joined the rescue effort.

He got up and picked up his coat from the table where he had dropped it when rushing to the bathroom. Just then, his doorbell chimed. The night-security screen showed the grim face of Admiral Daniel O'Shaughnessy Shostakovich.

Holy Space! If, instead of calling, the Thought-Admiral found it necessary to come rushing, the news must be really bad. Would he be able to keep his cool in the presence of that thunder-hook Eagle Eye?

Trying to calm the butterflies roiling in his stomach, JR clicked on the security route to his office, waved away his robo-server, and strode towards the door to admit his unexpected guest.

"Do come in, Admiral," he said, opening the door. "I had fallen asleep. Just woke up and switched on Space-V."

The admiral searched for something on JR's face. Not succeeding, he moved towards a chair and perched on its arm. "I've come to pick you up."

"Where are we going?" JR asked, adding in the same breath, "Have the shadows reported?" He had to know right away.

"Pavan's shadow called when Pavan landed on Jalanga. He is still there. When he leaves, we will be notified right away. Jalanga, I understand, is quite safe."

The ex-Admiral, Spacepol's secret brain, waited as if he expected a comment. JR simply stared at him.

Realizing it was a bad sign, the ex-admiral softly continued, "According to Sonal's shadow, she out-performed herself. Not only did she find Kumiko without losing any time, she also managed to get invited to that meeting. Seems there was some trouble in the Council Bubble. That's where we are going. Let's go."

What kind of trouble, JR wanted to ask.

But the Admiral's closed face seemed to forbid any questions. Keeping step with his brisk, impatient feet, he only asked, "Admiral, if you don't mind, can we take my Sun Eagle?"

"If I can fly it."

"Of course. It's always yours."

Any other time the Admiral would have smiled. He had heard about JR's superstition about flying in someone else's machine. But right now he did not feel like smiling. He said cautiously, "I don't want to pull out the Earth from under your feet, but I think you should know something."

"Why the preamble?" JR asked, maintaining a dignified profile. "You know me! I'm not an ostrich."

The Admiral walked faster, looking straight ahead. "We don't know what's waiting for us there."

He stopped, threw one glance at JR, then started walking again. "Today I'm not a harbinger of good news. Kumiko is our fourth problem. They cannot locate her. Her sky-shuttle is also missing. We never suspected her of anything. Therefore, her navigational controls weren't hooked. And . . ."

"And?" JR echoed, quelling the butterflies fluttering in his stomach.

They had reached the Sun Eagle. Taking the pilot's seat, Daniel energized it, set up the course, then lifted up and quickly gained altitude.

13

. . . Beyond the
Watcher Shadows

The awful shadow of some unseen Power
Floats though unseen among us—visiting
This various world with as inconstant wing
As summer winds that creep from flower to flower.
—Percy Bysshe Shelley: *Hymn to Intellectual Beauty,* 1816

· · ·

*Here and there in the ancient literatures, we encounter legends
of wise and mysterious games that were conceived and played by
scholars, monks, or the courtiers of cultured princes. These might
take the form of chess games in which the pieces and squares had
secret meanings in addition to their usual functions.*
—Hermann Hesse: *The Glass Bead Game*

· · ·

Watching his time-dented Sun Eagle shooting space under
someone else's fingers, JR was not able to relax in his seat. It felt
strange to ride as co-pilot in his own hovercraft.

Why did Daniel need to ride in his shuttle anyway? If he had not brought his own, how had he arrived here?

He had known Daniel to confide in him unreservedly. Why was he speaking in riddles and not answering questions?

Like anyone else, Daniel had his weaknesses. But acting rude was not one of them. He had heard his question. Why wasn't he replying? Should JR ask again? Or would that insult Daniel?

Before JR could decide, picking up where he had left, the Admiral broke his silence. "Before Kumiko disappeared, a NOPE member had been killed. It was like a double-death blow to them, because it had also mutilated their non-violence rule. Zorro, their chairman, called in the Peace Guards. They were moving in when the lights went out a second time. There must have been lot of confusion. When things settled down, they found another body. Worried, Sonal's shadow looked for her. He could not find her."

JR tried very hard to keep his facial muscles under control. The Admiral had no desire to intrude upon his feelings. Keeping his eyes carefully averted, Daniel continued, "The Guards are very tight-lipped. Despite his best efforts, Sonal's Shadow was not able to discover the second victim's identity. Not even if the person was male or female."

"If he could not locate her, that does not necessarily mean something happened to her," JR observed. He had succeeded in regaining control over himself. Sounding confident like his old self, he added, "Sonal has no enemies. Why would anyone hurt her?"

"What if," Daniel asked gently, "they had discovered she is working for us?"

"Sonal is inexperienced. Not stupid. She would not have allowed them to discover *that*." He was not sure whether he was trying to convince himself or Daniel. To convince himself, he added, "You don't know her as well as I do."

"I hope you are right." Daniel shivered, as if an invisible cold draft had hit him, and stared ahead.

Sonal, JR thought fiercely, *when we reach there I must find you alive. You can't go away and leave me behind. If you've been injured, I* will *find the doctor who'll bring you back, who'll revive that dazzling light in your eyes.*

To divert his troublesome, tangled thoughts, JR tried to find another topic. "What do you know about Kumiko?"

"Strong-willed, impetuous, and very resourceful," the Admiral replied succinctly. "Shadow says the guards are really baffled. The Bubble entrance was guarded by six of them. It is the only door. When they wanted to question her, they could not find her. She had disappeared. No one can figure out when or how."

"A person who is not guilty has no reason to run away!" JR looked thoughtful. "She must have been afraid of something. Could it be she killed either one, or both of them?"

"They don't think so. The killer used a dart gun. One has to be an expert marksman to use a dart gun. Kumiko could not have done it, even if she tried. The weapon training, as you know, begins only after one is eighteen. Also, Kumiko was sitting very close to the podium. The darts came from another direction."

"Then what is the explanation?" JR's mind was busy trying to find the various possibilities. "Does she belong to the killer's group and had to disappear when their work was done? Did she panic that she might be their next target? Or, did she figure out the killer's identity and rush after him?"

The Admiral nodded. "Exactly the questions I've been asking myself. The last one seems most logical. And it's worrying me a lot. The killer recognizes her. If she reaches anywhere near him, her breath will be snuffed out before she knows what hit her."

"There is another possibility," JR suggested, only to keep their minds busy, not because he thought it was a better choice. "Murder can be awfully frightening. She may have run away to seek comfort. To visit a friend."

"Why so secretly?"

"If she asked, the Guards would not have allowed it."

Daniel nodded. "But she's not the kind who needs comforting. Generally, it's the other way round. Also, by all accounts, she did not lose her balance. Shadow noticed it. Unlike many others, she looked undisturbed. No sign of hysteria."

"Why don't we go through her data and check out her friends' names?" JR insisted. He wanted to keep his mind occupied, giving it no chance of thinking about Sonal. "If someone has a shady background, we may have something to work on."

"Why not!" Surprisingly, Daniel agreed without any other argument. "Let's get on with it right away." He called SpacePol and told them what he wanted. Emphasizing the urgency, he added, "Don't wait till I get back. Send it right away."

"Aye, Aye, Admiral."

"And Sergeant?"

"Admiral, Sir?"

"Has Pavan's Shadow reported again?"

"Not yet, Sir. But his beacon is green. They must still be on the Island."

"When he calls, you know what to do."

"Everything's ready per your instructions, Admiral."

As he clicked off the line, an idea struck Daniel. Unrolling his tembook, he got lost in it. He looked so absorbed, JR could not start any conversation. Getting free time and space, his mind again started getting crowded by Sonal's defiant images.

Standing against the wind, I whispered your name . . .

Sonal, he silently asked her defiant image, I told you to find Kumiko and stick to her like glue. Why didn't you follow my advice? You had no experience. You knew you weren't trained for this type of work. You were never given a chance of learning it working jointly with an experienced person. It was a mistake to send you. It should not have been done. If you have been hurt, I will never forgive myself. If they have taken your life . . .

He tried to shake off the horrible thought.

No, he told himself. Daniel is worried. That's why he is imagining the worst. Sonal has no enemies. There's no reason for anyone to kill her.

If Daniel had had the slightest inkling that something might go wrong, he would not have sent her there. People always say: *Where NOPE walks in, crime walks out.* No one could have guessed that a criminal would crash a peaceful meeting and kill two persons surrounded by a group who live and die for their non-violence rule.

JR had never felt so miserable in his whole life. Sonal and Pavan, the two persons for whom he cared so much . . . as if they were inalienable parts of his being . . . were both sent to the peak of bursting volcanoes, and there was nothing he could do about it!

Why is it, he thought, that we always send our young to fight our wars, endangering their precious, inexperienced lives, while we sit comfortably in our sheltered cocoons, waiting and watching?

His reverie was broken by the bleeping of the datalink in the rear compartment. He glanced at Daniel and switched on the terminal. A thin strip of paper, bearing the data they had requested, started pouring out. He picked it up and read it aloud:

Kumiko: age: seventeen years, ten months.

Birth date: unknown

Birthplace: unknown

Parents/Surrogates: unknown

Rakhi-Brother: unknown

Oathmate: none

Ringmate: none

Education: Archeology, Bio-Tech, Space-Geology.

Trainee: Space Cadet Corp.

Historical Data: She was found by a Buddhist monk on the steps of his monastery. Her clothes were very simple. But a diamond necklace was around her neck and a typewritten note was attached to it: TAKE NOTE: Do not dare to give a name to this precious moonbeam. Do not show her this diamond necklace. Give it to her on her eighteenth birthday. No harm must come to her. Guard her like a Buddha's eternal candle. KNOW THEE: This is a sacred trust, for which thou are responsible. Take care of her and no harm will come to thou and thine.

Kumiko's Public Self: Anyone who meets Kumiko finds it very easy to talk with her. Even the first time. She makes friends quickly, easily, and likes to keep them around her.

She is the kind of person who can go to a party where she knows no one and leave with new friends. She projects the image of an extrovert who likes to have fun, but deep inside she is a very emotional person. When she is ready to bond, chances are it will be a lifetime bonding.

Her most important characteristic is that she likes to keep things moving, and succeeds in her efforts by thinking quickly on her feet, galvanizing everyone around her.

Kumiko's Deepest Emotions (What She Hates): Kumiko truly hates to be alone, to have nobody around to talk with and not having a new project to keep her busy. She cannot stand it when life doesn't seem to be moving in some stimulating direction. She is the kind of person who can make the most diehard person see things her way and do her bidding. And she hates it if she does not succeed in her efforts.

Kumiko's Deepest Emotions (What She Loves): While she enjoys making new friends, Kumiko never forgets those from her past. She especially loves get-togethers with old friends. She needs them to keep intact the security factor rooted in her childhood. Another positive factor in her personality is that she remembers the good things, not the bad. A thorough optimist, she has a stream of friends and acquaintances flowing through her life at all times—and the more the merrier. No matter what her new venture at any given time, every experience is more enjoyable to her, when it is shared with someone else.

Friends (In alphabetical order): Aruppa, Binakoo . . .

JR stopped reading and stared at the list. "Stars Above! There must be more than a hundred names here!"

His storytelling voice changed to one full of profound astonishment. "For Earth's Sake! She is only seventeen! How could she have already acquired so many friends?"

Daniel smiled. "Well," he drawled, "you just read her analyst's evaluation. According to him, those are just facts. What the interpretation reveals, that's even more remarkable."

"And that is . . .?"

"To put it briefly, he believes she is subconsciously compensating for the conventional relationships she never had, and has intensely missed."

JR considered it and nodded. "I could add to that. Doesn't it seem even more remarkable that not only did she not allow her scarcities to warp her personality, but also she used them in a constructive manner to gain leadership and popularity?"

He again glanced at the list. Again his hazel eyes opened wide with surprise. "Daniel, guess what!"

"What?"

"I see two names here, shouting like red beacons."

The Admiral glanced at him, his eyebrows moving up like two live question marks.

"Want to guess?" JR asked.

"Nope."

"Okay, let me show you. Here and here—Bakul and Pia."

"Probably means nothing. You know how these lists are compiled. They ask you, who are your friends. Unless needed for some reason, they seldom verify. It will be very ego-satisfying for

any teenager to claim two superstars as one's buddies on the basis
of even a brief handshake in a big crowd."

"You really don't mean it!"

"Maybe I do. Maybe I don't." Regretting he had said that, the
Admiral quickly changed tracks. "You know, JR, your logic
generally works. Kumiko being Kumiko, it is possible she may
have run away to visit a friend."

"There are more than hundred names here. How do we decide
which one?"

"Let's see what my logic says. Look under . . . under P. Is there
one named Pashka?"

JR softly whistled. "Pashka! Trainee in robo-sciences. Jalanga
Island."

"Friend or foe? With today's young ones, you never know." The
Admiral sighed. "She could have gone there. I'll alert Shirakoo."

"Shirakoo?"

"You have never met? You will. Soon."

JR looked hard at his friend. There was something in his
expression, in his eyes, that prompted JR to ask a direct question—
one that he had never dared ask before. "Daniel? If . . . if you don't
mind, can I ask you something? If . . . if it won't upset you."

"Heaven forbid," the Admiral's eyebrows arched again. "Did I
ever get upset at something you said? When?"

JR did not hear that. He was trying to find the right words.
"Kumiko? Is she . . . you know . . . is she one of the Seven? Who
are the others? Why are they being watched like this? Are we
afraid they are hidden keys to disaster or . . ."

"If I knew . . ." Daniel interrupted, but left his thought hanging
in the air. His eyes were glued to the control panel, as if right now
that was the only thing that mattered.

"Look!" He pointed towards the screen. "We are almost there.
Time to circle down. Why don't you put all this in the shredder?"

The tactical evasion did not serve any purpose. It only increased
JR's curiosity. By not telling me, he thought, you are forcing me to
do my own snooping.

Shredding the report, JR tried to envision the young girl he had
never seen. In her holos that he had screened, she had seemed quite
charming. In this Age of Surrogacy, he thought, why would anyone
behave so cruelly as to leave a baby on bare cold stones? If her
natural mother did not want her, even in the seventh month, they
could have transferred her to another womb.

Why had her father chosen a monastery, not a rich home, where she could have had anything she wanted?

To find out, he should visit the monastery where she was abandoned. Monks are very resourceful people. They may have discovered her identity. Or the necklace-giver may have revealed it. His note attached to her bio-data only says what they must do on her eighteenth birthday. What happens after that?

Then, merely because she reaches the age when she is legally considered an adult, would he simply abandon her to flounder through life like so many other surrogate kids?

No. One who cares with such an authoritarian voice; who plans such an unusual gift so much ahead of time; he wouldn't abandon her just when her young dreams would begin unfolding. He may be a key to the mystery of the seven. If he is alive, he must be found.

Would the monks cooperate? Would they help in the search? Suppose they profess their priestly indifference—they did their duty. Now she is eighteen, and they are free—could they be persuaded because the necklace-giver sounds rich, and they always need funds? Yes, he promised himself: I'll visit the monastery. As soon as possible.

***

It was an ancient monastery, built upon sloping hills in cavernous, unending caves. Tall evergreens, untouched by greedy human hands, grew everywhere in abundance, providing the kind of cover that no snooping aircraft could penetrate. The villagers living in the shadows of those hills made it their business to make sure that the ancient, weather-beaten stone steps leading up to the monastery always remained hidden by bushy, thorny shrubs. Travel agencies didn't get a chance to get curious about its existence.

The stones, embedded in hard rock, branched in every possible direction so that unless one knew the secret ID codes, one could keep wandering in the thick woods forever without getting anywhere. Those selected few who knew the codes, after an hour's brisk climbing, found the narrow mountain path that ended in a small clearing, bordered by fragrant, wildflowers. There, in its holy water-ringed center, reclined an ancient statue of Lord Buddha. At its edges, on twelve tall pink marble pillars, burned life-glow candles, illuminating the reclining Buddha and the weather-beaten faces of ferocious stone lions guarding the heavy bronze doors of the secluded monastery.

This cool evening, in a small, interior cave, five monks covered in loose yellow robes sat around a small fire. Its low flames flickered, illuminating and shadowing the mythical images painted upon the smooth, glistening walls and the high curved ceiling.

"I still think," one was saying, "since the letter uses the word 'birthday', we should not plan it for the day we found her. It should be on her real birthday."

"Truth can have many faces," the Eldest One decided to intervene. "But a bond forged by Trust has only one."

"I agree," the middle one nodded. "If they had wanted to reveal her actual birth date, they would have given it to us. The fact that they did not means they want it to remain secret."

"Then it's not a birthday gift," the first one protested. "It's a farewell gift. Is it a message that on that day, our mandate is terminated? Our job is done, and from then on, we can forget all about her?"

"What's the difference?" the Eldest One patiently murmured. "Some responsibilities are given. Some are taken. This meeting is not to dwell on those points. The necklace will be given, as bequeathed, as a birthday gift. The only question is, what do they expect? A private giving or a public ceremony?"

"How about something in between?" the third one asked.

"She has chosen one to ringmate." The youngest one put a couple of sticks in the fire and stirred it. "I don't think his grandmother would object."

"Object! She would love it. But she lives in such a remote area, on the fringes of civilization. Who'd like to go there!"

"How about Sonal Neera's land-condo?"

"They just met. Would that be appropriate?"

"What do you suggest?"

They looked at each other. Finally, the Eldest One said, "We'll just rent a place like everyone else—in the Park Island."

"Park Island?" they echoed, and stared at him. "You know how much it'll cost! Who will pay?"

"Funds will come. As they always have." The Eldest One sounded tranquil and serene. "The only time I had my doubts was when we gave those bangles. But our decision must have been liked, because even for those the credits came promptly."

"That was incredible. True foresight." The youngest one's

challenge-loving eyes reflected deep reverence. "If you had not done so, she would not have remembered Pashka. Would not have found a way to reach Jalanga at this critical time."

"What really baffles me," the middle one said, "is how at any given time, she always manages to grab the appropriate choice. We gave her Pashka's ID long time ago. Why had she never used it before? Why now? Are they guiding her subconscious? Or communicating with her secretly? without our permission?"

"Hush! A worthy mind does not linger upon such unworthy thoughts," the Eldest One sternly reprimanded him.

He glanced at their fire-lit faces one by one. "None of you must ever think like that! Do not talk like that! That child is absolutely guileless. She always tells us everything. She is very intuitive and has the right instincts. That is all."

Accepting his advice, they bowed their heads.

Smiling, as if showering upon them a silent benediction, he affectionately continued, "Let's not waste time. The ancient Dwarka has risen. We must choose our roles. And we still need to decide what we will be doing in the coming Jalanga conflict."

He glanced at the youngest one. "Since you need to leave right away, let's begin with you. Do not change your name this time. You are now responsible for Kumiko. You have an excellent excuse for staying close."

"I know," the youngest one nodded. "To plan for her birthday with her approval and collaboration. The project should keep both of us busy, and at a safe distance from the trouble zones. But, Aacharya Shree, one thing I do not understand. . . ."

"Why not ask, son?

"Why I'm always the one chosen for the easiest job?"

"I remember your complaints about Sonal," the Middle One smiled. "Compared to Kumiko, she is a lamb."

"Ah! But now I'm older and wiser. Capable of handling tougher jobs."

"Go on. Move," the Eldest One said with mock severity. "When you reach the base, call before leaving."

"Will do." The youngest one got up, bowed to each one of them, and moved towards the narrow side entrance.

Silence followed his footsteps. He knew they would not resume their deliberations until he was out of their hearing range. Increasing his pace, he quickly walked to his own cave.

He had expected this assignment. Still, he worried about it.

Working with Sonal, he thought, I had begun to have doubts about
my life's goals. When I was recalled, my studies and meditation
renewed and revived my childhood ambitions and resolutions.

Now, I'm again being thrown back in that jungle.

Would I be taming Kumiko, or would she change me? Would
her world help me to decide whether my current objectives are
realistic, or whether I should cancel them to find a place in the
outside world?

He turned a corner and remembered Pavan—fellow-sufferer,
itching to get away from his job—so fond of saying, *one cannot
stop the Ganges from falling into the ocean.* "Right, Pavan," he
told his absent friend. "At this point in time, I am not going to
worry about what may be inevitable!

"Right now, the only item worth worrying about is that maverick
Kumiko calls *Robin Hood.* Kumiko's guardianship would mean
enduring that dropout's presence all the time. I'll have to get used
to that. And I'll have to present him with a cheerful and friendly
face.

"And maybe, just maybe, I'll pull him out of his sacred illusions.
My training as a monk should help me in this thankless task. Yet,
changing his illusions appears more formidable than keeping
Kumiko out of life-endangering situations."

To successfully tackle Pushpak, he decided, he needed to know
more about him. The tapes his guardian monks had given him
might not be sufficient. He should also study Pushpak's
grandmother's life history.

Entering his cave, the young monk quickly opened his cabinet,
found the tapes, selected one, and, inserting it in the videoplayer,
switched it on. The screen lit up with bold, black letters: *Pushpak,
Prado-Powhatan, Age 20 Born . . .*

He impatiently rolled the screen until it again highlighted,
Personality. He settled down to read patiently.

*Prado would never admit it, but his analytic graphs clearly
indicate that he would like to work for the same employer
for the rest of his life.*

*He is the kind of person who fantasizes about life-bonding,
earning the right to have two surrogate kids, owning the
latest model Robo-Major, and flying the latest model
hovercraft.*

One cannot emphasize it enough, when Prado wants to do so, how kind and thoughtful he can be. He can be often found minding other people's chores and letting them feel important. But if their whims interfere with his causes, or his priorities, he can set them straight without their realizing it.

His exceptional intelligence, discreet ambitions, and ability to stay emotionally balanced make him an excellent partner in any venture.

Traits such as these delineate Prado's deep-rooted, emotional resilience. He can bounce back from the sort of misfortunes that prompt many self-reliant people to contemplate suicide. That's because he does not let himself get bogged down in black moods, preferring to figure out some way to regain a fresh perspective.

Prado's irresistible likability and reliability stem from two different sources in his personality. One reason he is so likeable is that wherever he goes, he makes himself fit in every situation. He fits in because he agrees with people. This is the real key to understanding Prado's private self. Underneath it all, he has learned one simple skill well— first and foremost, try to agree with the people around you.

One aspect of Prado's personality should never be forgotten. He does not like to confront anger, his own or someone else's. He hates conflicts. Falling in such a situation, he prefers not to rock the boat and tries to end disagreements before they can escalate. If this tactic fails, he quietly withdraws from the scene.

Whether you make friends with Prado will depend also upon your choice of friends. Once you get yourself in the same group as he is, the battle is almost over. People like Prado are good-natured beings, who, despite their individualistic outlook, are easy to be around. It's easy to win their friendship, because they like to be supportive. They will like you if you make an effort to like their group.

Remember, Prado won't wander far from his chosen group. So unless you start the ball rolling, it is unlikely that your paths will cross or that you two will become friends . . .

The young monk stared at the screen. Can this analysis be trusted? How good, or bad, are these reports? At the downside monastery, they have a big library. In the short time that he has, they expect him to burrow through all the ancient Earth tapes regarding Prado's ancestry.

Wouldn't it be better not to prejudice his mind with other people's opinions, and instead to formulate his strategy according to his own observation?

Aacharya did not always use undeceptive methods. Sometimes one measure of his trust depended upon how expertly you evaded his direction-finders; and to what degree you did not get bogged down in his tangled looplines. Is that what he expected this time?

In the caving silence, he missed something. His parakeet, Kitty-Kat, was not on her perch. If she had been sent somewhere, he would not leave without her. Moving, he opened the parrot-hole shutter and pressed the calling whistle. In a few minutes, Kitty-Kat came fluttering in. Soaring towards her master's hand, she fondly scolded, "It's getting late. Where have you been?"

"Where have I been!" he retorted, affectionately stroking her tiny head. "Look, who is complaining! I come home after working a whole day and you're not here to welcome me!"

"Teepoo called. We were conferring with Pushpin about your precious Sonal."

"Ha! She's not *my* Sonal anymore. You know that. Aacharya himself told you *that*. We are leaving to find Kumiko. From now on that's the only name you know."

"But Sonal is in serious trouble."

"Lots of people to take care of her."

"No. Nobody's there. Kumiko left her locked with lots of murderers."

"What are you talking about? If a spy kills his enemy, that's not *lots* of murderers."

"Won't tell you a thing unless you promise to come with me to rescue her."

He stroked his parakeet's glistening feathers. Should he disobey Aacharya Shree's orders? Shouldn't he forget Sonal?

But if Sonal was in some kind of trouble, he just couldn't forget her. Kumiko was with Pashka. Safe for the time being. A couple of hours delay would not hurt. Surely, Aacharya would understand that.

Not only that. He would save time if he skipped the visit to the downside monastery. If Aacharya had again set up a test for him, he would get demerits if he did not skip it.

If it was not a test . . .

Considering that the person who was in trouble was Sonal Neera, he decided to take the risk.

"Okay, Kitty-Kat, here's what we'll do. We'll take care of Sonal before making ourselves Kumiko's shadow. I need to discuss with the Park Island Program Director her birthday blast anyway. Aacharya Shree can't get angry at that."

"But then," he added, putting her on her perch, "we don't have any time left. We must leave right away."

"I'm ready when you are." Kitty-Kat happily nodded her tiny head. "This time," she coyly cocked her head, "would you please let me talk with Sonal?"

"Don't be funny!" he softly rebuked her. "You know the rules. You can't talk with *anyone* except me and Aacharya."

"Sonal won't reveal our secret to anyone. She won't."

"It's not the question of keeping or not keeping the secret. And you know that. You can't even talk with several monks who belong to our monastery. She has never been initiated."

"So what?"

"It's for your own safety, Kitty. If your secret is revealed, you won't be of any use to the monastery and your life would be snuffed out. If you're not willing to behave, I'll have to leave you here with Aacharya."

"Garuda Alive! Are cadet-monks allowed to get so angry! One can't even ask a question! Let's go. Shall I tell Aacharya we're leaving?"

"Nope. Not right now. He told me to call from the base." He started throwing items in his knapsack. "Since we are not going downside, Park Island would be our base. We'll call from there."

He tested his torch. The battery was down. "Kitty-Kat, I have too much on my mind. When we reach the village, would you remind me to pick up a refill? Park Island may not have any batteries left."

If the storm is still raging there, stay in the knapsack, he wanted to tell her. But he left it unsaid.

It's better, he thought, to leave some things unsaid. When he was leaving her, if he had told Sonal Neera what he had wanted to say, it would have been very difficult for him today to accept Kitty-Kat's request, and face her again.

***

Sonal was wondering whether she would be be able to face Pavan ever again.

She had betrayed his trust. She had abandoned the search she had promised him. On top of that, when leaving for the NOPE meeting, she had not left a message on his video-link. If he wanted to reach her, how would he find her? True, she had not given JR his name. But JR, being JR, would put two and two together. Then . . .

Shaken by the troubling thought, she tried to force it away and looked for Kumiko.

When the lights had blinked out in the NOPE Bubble, they had gotten separated. Now, carefully picking her way in the flashing lights filtering in through the transparent walls of the Bubble, Sonal tried to move to a less crowded area to locate her.

Picking spots in the crowded hall for her feet, her searching eyes moved and paused, moved and paused from group to group, person to person, until they spotted Kumiko standing in a relatively uncrowded corner. When the faraway carnival light flickered on her face, it seemed as if Kumiko was not a part of the nettled life swirling around her. As if making an invincible barrier of her will-power, she was holding it at bay, so that she could roam free in some faraway place, in some faraway time.

Then the lights came back. Sonal wondered if she should join her, or wait until Kumiko remembered her. Before she could decide, she saw Kumiko moving towards the Powder Room. Not knowing how big it was, she decided to wait until Kumiko freshened up and came out.

But time passed. The Guards erected a temporary screen, creating an office. As they called in the first person for questioning, Sonal quietly moved and entered the Powder Room.

It was empty. Kumiko was not there.

Could she have gotten sick—fainted or something? Getting worried, Sonal quickly peeked in the necessities enclosure. It was empty.

Sonal plunked heavily on the couch. Her eyes once again moved around—there was no other door. No window. Not even a tiny fresh air skylight. There was no way Kumiko could have left this teeny-tiny cubbyhole. Then how did she disappear? And why?

Sonal pulled her feet up and rested her head against the

cushioned headboard. To think better she closed her eyes. But her mind was awfully tired. It could not hold onto any thought.

Without knowing she was doing so, Sonal fell asleep. She did not know more than an hour had passed when she felt someone shaking her feet.

Frightened, she quickly pulled in both her feet and sat up. What she saw with her sleep heavy eyes, frightened her even more—a towering figure, colored blue from head to toe, stood near where her feet were a few seconds ago.

"Wake up, Sonal," the apparition spoke in a friendly tone and smiled, a very winsome smile. His emerald-gold eyes, generating their own sunlight, seemed to be assuring her—relax. There's nothing to be afraid of.

Sonal's heartbeats slowed down. "Who are you?" she demanded. "Don't you read signs? It's not the Men's Room."

"Please, forgive me for intruding upon your privacy," he said, but there was not a drop of apology in his gold-honey voice. "You are in great danger. I must take you out of here."

"Why should I be in danger?" Sonal snapped angrily. "I am among friends. I don't need a guard. When I want to leave, I can go by myself."

"You are right," he nodded. "But you cannot go through that door. Outside, someone's waiting to kill you."

14

. . . *Time for Getting Torn*

It is not in the storm nor in the strife
We feel benumb'd and wish to be no more,
But in the after-silence on the shore,
When all is lost, except a little life.
                              —Lord Byron, (1788-1824)

.   .   .

There is no flock, however watched and tended,
But one dead lamb is there!
There is no fireside, howsoe'er defended,
But has one vacant chair!
—Henry Wadsworth Longfellow, *Resignation,* (1807-1882)

.   .   .

Sonal glanced at the closed door, then at the intruder's blue face and gold-flecked eyes. "So what?" she said. "I'm not afraid. In my work, one must always be prepared for anything and everything, including getting torn to bits."

"Don't be ridiculous!" He snapped. "It's not a joking matter."

"Who's joking? Don't you know there's a time for everything? For eating. For sleeping. For hoping. There's a time for getting torn also. Torn by love. By separation. By too much joy. By too little . . ."

"You are a true daughter. You have a streak of . . ."

"Whose daughter?" She pounced. "Who are my birth-parents?"

"Questions! Questions!" He seemed on the verge of losing his temper. "You are an intelligent person. Tell me, how can I make you understand you need my help to get out of here?"

"Without going through that door, you mean?" she asked. "You can manage that? How?" She looked up. "Through that dumb ceiling? Is that how Kumiko disappeared."

"Kumiko didn't live a sheltered childhood. She can take care of herself in emergencies. She is not my problem. I have no idea what she did. But you, I must request that you come with me."

"Funny! Funny!" She glared at him.

His unyielding expression held no room for any argument. Still she asked, "If I refuse?"

He moved and stood against the other wall looking at her.

He came to a decision. From his voice it was clear how difficult that decision had been. "Sonal, it is not a secret any more. You have learned. You are one of the *seven*."

She pounced, "Who are the other six?"

He continued as if she had not spoken. "The routine means of protecting you are not adequate any more. Therefore, I must ask you to wear this necklace all the time."

From one of his pockets, he took out a gold necklace on which sparkled a blue pendant. Before she realized what he was up to, he had moved, and kneeling near her, clasped it around her neck.

Angrily she yanked at it, trying to unclasp it. But the catch eluded her. "What's this?" she exploded. "Dog's chain? Slave's collar?"

"Certainly not!" He was still kneeling beside her. "It is a kind of transmitter. Anytime you are in any trouble, just hold the pendant like this, between your thumb and finger. We will know you need help and you will get it right away."

"Who is 'we'?"

"Sonal! Do you *ever* stop asking questions?" He smiled and got up on his feet again, towering above her.

"How do I know you are not making up stories to kidnap me with my consent."

"Kidnap you with your consent? That's a new one," he laughed. "Why don't you come near the mirror and try your necklace."

She did not move. "I may try it, if you tell me who tried to kill Bakul. I know you know, because you killed that Pia-giddy understudy before anyone could touch him."

He was startled. "How's that?"

"Bakul's understudy plotted to kill him, so that he could kidnap Pia. You discovered his plot. You needed to protect Pia, but you knew, no matter how much you tried, she would not leave Bakul. So you did two things. To protect her, you kidnapped both of them. And, to checkmate SpacePol, you killed the jealous understudy. So you know who he was. You cannot deny it."

"Wow!" he smiled. "Your mind works fast. You'll make a good spy. Keep it up. But right now, how do you say it, be a sport. Try the necklace."

"Not until you tell me about my birth-parents. And what's so special about the seven of us? Is Pia really my sister? Where have you imprisoned her? And the flying snake? Was it planted in the basket to kill Bakul or his understudy?"

"Great Ocean! I give up!" He threw up his hands in mock frustration. "You are impossible! Murder is serious business. You should not . . ."

"I'm a reporter," she reminded him. "An investigative reporter. I was sent here to observe and investigate NOPE. Are you their robot? Are they involved in these killings?"

Hearing the word *robot,* his eyebrows had arched. He smiled. A mesmerizing, captivating smile. "OK I will give you—what do you call it?—a *scoop.* NOPE is not the guilty party. We know the killers. We are watching them."

"Watching them?" she retorted incredulously. "Just watching them? And allowing them to indulge in their killing spree? Why don't you expose them? Ask SpacePol to arrest them?"

"Because if that's done right now, others may go into hiding. Instead of months, it may take forever to clean up this mess."

"Okay, but you still need to tell me about my birth-parents and where you are hiding Bakul and Pia."

"Why should we hide anyone!" He lost his cool. "We don't interfere in anyone's life."

"You *are* interfering in *mine,*" she pointed out reasonably. "I've

got a job to do. How would you like it if someone forced you to
panic and run and leave your work undone?"

"I concede your logic." He smiled and his gold-green eyes
dazzled. "Okay, I will leave you here, but I must make one request.
Having failed twice, chances are they won't make a third attempt
on your life until they can be sure they won't fail again. I think
they will wait until they find you alone. Therefore, don't move
alone. Stay with somebody."

"I will try."

"Fine. Now close your eyes."

"Why? Why should I close my eyes?"

"Holy Dwarka!" He glanced around and saw the half-open
broom closet. Entering it, he closed the door behind him.

Sonal waited for him to come out.

Time passed. But the door remained closed.

When she could not wait any longer, she got up and opened the
closet. It held only a bucket, a vacuum cleaner, and small bottles of
cleaning fluids. He was not there.

The closet was the smallest one possible. It had no window and
no other door.

SPACE TAKE ME! Sonal Neera took a deep breath and started
hitting the walls with her palm. No panel got pushed! No hidden
door opened! How did he leave?

She did not believe in ghosts. There must be a hidden door here,
she thought fiercely. I am going to get out and ask one of the
NOPE members.

She moved towards the door. Walking past the wash basin, she
happened to look into the mirror and noticed her hair was a mess.
Her clothes were rumpled and a seam had split her silk stockings.
Look at you! she scolded herself—no wonder that strange, blue
monkey, that . . . that self-deluded, gift-giving jester wanted you to
check in the mirror. You are a sight! Better freshen up before you
show your face to anyone.

Also, ask someone's help to remove this piece of junk from
around your neck. As soon as possible.

The necessities enclosure contained a small sonic shower. It is
not a bubble bath, she thought, but something is better than
nothing. At least I will look neat and clean.

Locking the door from inside, she removed her clothes and
dumped them in the washer-presser. As she was kicking out her
shoes, her heel slipped and she started falling down.

Clutching at the slippery walls, her mind slipped back in time, and she remembered: When she was about four, one day while trying to climb Star Seeder, her favorite baby horse, her foot had slipped. She had fallen down and bruised both her legs.

Frightened that she would be scolded, she had hidden the injury under her stockings and not mentioned it to anyone. By the time her robo-mother discovered it, the wounds had turned septic and she was running a high fever.

Despite the best care they could give her, the illness had gotten worse. One night, lying alone and in pain, unable to take it anymore, she had started crying. She was wishing she could go to the other-land, where her robo-mother said her pet rabbit had gone—where no one ever got hurt, no one ever got sick. Where there was always day, and never any frightening night. And she had felt her head getting lifted and pulled against someone's chest that didn't feel at all like her robo-mother's.

"Angel," a soft voice crooned. "Angel, please don't cry."

Surprised, she had tried to look up at that face in the thick darkness of her room. "I'm not an angel." Despite her pain, she had tried to correct that ignorant being's mistake. "Angels are mythical beings in fairy tales. I'm my robo-mother's Sentinel-One."

"Yes, you are. But you are *also* my angel. My precious baby angel," the figure had crooned and hugged her.

She had felt like snuggling against that comforting chest and never moving from there. "You feel so different! Who are you? An other-land person?"

"Other-land?" the melodious voice had sounded a little frightened. "What other land?"

"The land where no one ever gets hurt. No one ever gets sick. Where there is always sunshine. Where Skippy, my rabbit, has gone."

"No, I'm not from that land." The fright in that voice was gone. Hands that did not feel like her robo-mother's hugged her. "I came because you are hurting so much."

"Doctor says I'm getting better."

"Of course you are. Much better. And tomorrow morning, you will be able to run around again."

"Tomorrow morning? But my wounds are still sore."

"Hush, my little angel. You talk too much! Try to sleep now. Close your eyes. I'll sing you a song."

Cradled in the warmth of those strange arms, lulled by the soft music wafting over her, she had fallen asleep. In the morning, when she woke up, there was a new pillow under her head, her fever was gone, and her wounds had disappeared as if she never had them.

If someone commented on her miraculous recovery, she did not know about it. But later, when the memory of that night came back, she had dismissed it as a figment of her wishful imagination, as a hallucinatory dream caused by her fever's delirium.

Now, however, she wondered. Is it possible that it was not a dream? Is it possible that learning about her near-fatal illness, her birth-mother had visited her that night? If it was her, was it her love that had cured her so miraculously? Or had she brought some other-world medication that she had given her while she was sleeping?

If that blue face joker is not an actor, if he is for real, would he know? Should she test the necklace, call him, and ask him? But he had said the necklace was for emergencies, when she was in some trouble of some kind.

Fine! The question could wait. Right now she had lots of other things to do.

Getting ready quickly, without giving the matter a second thought, she opened the door and stepped out of the small, solitary powder room.

The contrast was too much. The conference room was choking with the alien odor of fear, fury, and frustration. It seemed unfamiliar, enormous, and crowded.

Before she could blink her eyes, several voices rose to greet her. *There she is—you know how much trouble you gave us? . . . We were worried sick. . . . We looked everywhere!*

"Not everywhere!" Smiling, she moved towards them. Two of them detached themselves from the crowd, and moved towards her.

She recognized the poker-face Admiral, and her heart's desire, JR—relief written large all over his face. A few paces behind them was a third person, a memory-hidden face, with a parakeet perched upon his shoulder.

"Shirakoo!" Astonished and delighted, she quickly moved towards him.

JR seemed startled. "You know him?"

Sonal did not hear him. Making her way through the crowd of people parting for her, she grabbed both his proffered hands. "What are you doing here?"

"Just passing through. How's Ringaroo?"

"Getting too clever. You need to redo his circuits." Her tinkling laughter, tripping Shirakoo's boisterous one, brought smiles to the bystanders' faces.

Grabbing him by his elbow, she dragged him forward. "You met my boss? Chief, this is Shirakoo, my college chum. He is the one who gave me Ringaroo. Made it himself."

JR scrutinized the stranger with unreadable curiosity. Twenty-two or twenty-three. Chiseled, challenging nose. Full lips made for smiling. And large blue-gray eyes under arched thick eye lashes.

He looks more handsome than he is, he thought. Perhaps because the raw effect of his sharp features is enhanced by his unbound chestnut hair. Long and swinging loose, often touching his cheeks, his hair seem to intensify the pale translucence of his unblemished skin. His journeyman's plain clothes don't say much about his origins. But that swinging hair, touching his shoulders, did chant volumes about his unconventional tastes. If one could ignore that, he decided, and also ignore the sharp-eyed bird on his shoulder, one could consider him likeable.

"Nice meeting you," offering Shirakoo his hand, JR smiled pleasantly. In answer, the stranger's hand touched his right away. JR liked the young man's firm grip. The smile flashing in the young man's eyes suddenly seemed to sparkle with an inner strength, revealing entrenched, deeply ingrained, fire-kindling confidence.

"Well?" the Admiral's electrifying voice cut short the introductions. "Since Sonal's been found, we must move on. She can return to Space News and brief us when we return from Shady Point."

"Shady Point?" Sonal looked surprised. "Aren't we forbidden entry there?"

"Normally yes. But there's been some kind of accident there. We won't be touching down. We are just going to give it a look-see from up above."

"May I come with you, Admiral?" Sonal asked, her aquamarine eyes filling with hope. "You told me I need field training."

JR had found his ridiculous glasses and was pushing them up his nose. "Admiral, today they will be needing extra hands down there. As long as we are going, why don't I drop down for a few secs? I feel sure no one would object."

"Admiral, Sir," Shirakoo added his voice to the clamor. "I

haven't talked with Sonal for a very long time. Can she come with me? On my way, I will drop her at the Space News."

Admiral Shostakovich heard the pleas hanging in their hopeful voices and understood them. But this was not the time to indulge their fancies. "Shirakoo, you need to brief the Program Director here. You don't want to get Aacharya hopping mad, do you?"

"No, sir. Certainly not."

"Good. No need for Sonal to rush back. She can come with me and write up an eyewitness report of the blowout. It will be good experience for you, R-Seven. It will be splashed on the first page of New Space News and you will get a byline. JR, since your Sun Eagle is a two-seater, can you let us have it? You can take Sonal's skyrover. Sonal, you don't mind, do you?"

"Of course not, sir."

"Good." The Admiral turned towards the Peace Guards waiting behind him. "Lieutenant, I expect your report within an hour."

"Aye, aye, sir." The rock-faced Lieutenant saluted and snapped to attention. So did his stern looking guards. Returning their salute and glancing towards JR to signal they needed to talk, the Admiral moved towards the exit.

Sonal fell behind a few steps to walk with Shirakoo. She stroked the parakeet's head. "Kitty-Kat, Kitty-Kat, hello. Howdy. Remember me?"

The parakeet cocked her head and blinked an eye. Her silvery chirrup seemed to say, "Sooonal."

A talking parrot? JR thought, moving with the Admiral half-heartedly, *no wonder she seems so fascinated by him.* Falling back a few paces, he asked, "Where are you headed, Shirakoo? What kind of work interests you?"

"All kinds," Sonal's laughter tinkled like crystal bells. "But his first love is robotics. He forgets to eat and sleep when he is onto something new," she claimed, swinging his arm.

"That's where I'm headed." He made no effort to loosen her friendly grip. "To make an army of robots."

"No kidding!" JR's high eyebrows arched higher.

"What do they say—*Make the best of a bad bargain?* That's my motto, sir."

"Remember *that,*" the Admiral said, shaking an admonishing finger at him. Again he beckoned JR to join him.

Shirakoo parked a farewell kiss on Sonal's left ear. "Don't work too hard."

"Never," she laughed and tickled the parakeet's neck. "Come and visit me."

"Sooonal," the bird cooed, rubbing her head against her hand.

"I love you," Sonal said giving the parakeet a parting kiss. Moving to JR's Sun Eagle, she turned to wave good-bye.

JR stood for a few seconds watching the young man walk to his hovercraft. He moved at a quick pace, shoulders erect, head held high, as if any second he would spring, take a leap and touch the stars.

When she is with me, JR remembered: Sonal never laughs so freely, so naturally.

Is that because she thinks I am her *boss?* because of our age difference? Or because she is free of her teenage fascination and does not know it?

This star-aspiring Don Quixote, this striking specimen of our New Age adolescence, is perhaps only a few years older than her, and his first love is robotics—a profession that many of today's young ones adore. Where do I stand compared to that? JR squared his shoulders and walked to Sonal's waiting skyrover.

But stepping in the sky-rover, feeling her presence in her personal objects ornamenting her cockpit, his confidence returned. No. I've no reason to be jealous, he assured himself. Sonal is only mine. When I was removed from the teaching position, any moonstruck teenager would have forgotten her hero-teacher. She did not.

A smile lit up his hazel eyes. He believed he had reason to feel confident. He had never encouraged her. When they learned about her infatuation, they had pulled him away. She had every reason to believe she would never, ever, see him again. But she had waited for him. When she came into his arms, she had made it clear how she had continued feeling about him during all that lost time.

Feeling himself again, he was settling in her seat when the intercom beeped. "JR, if you'll open your channel, I'll feed the directions."

"Okay, just gimme a few secs." He looked at the programming panel. Was it similar to his own? Finding the switches, he soon got ready. "Okay, Daniel. Go ahead."

"Good. And JR?"

"Yes, Admiral?"

"Going down is your idea. When you do so, there is need to communicate it to me."

"Noted, Admiral."

"You may lead. We will follow closely."

"Not too close," he laughed and heard Sonal's delightful giggling. That brought another quick smile to his confidence-brimming eyes. I can make her laugh, he thought. I'll see her soon and I'll say things that'll make her laugh.

Unaware of the turmoil Shirakoo had triggered in JR's mind, Sonal was digesting the levels of communication, what was just said, and what was left unsaid. What was left was perhaps more important than what was said. If I'm going to work with them, she told herself, this I must start learning.

The admiral asked me to come with him. It must mean he likes me. Would he teach me? Guide me? Can I ask questions, or would they reveal to him how inexperienced I am? Should I keep my mouth shut? Speak only when I'm asked something?

They watched JR take off in her skyrover, quickly gain altitude.

Daniel switched on his engines. As he reached for the controls, the sky above seemed to catch fire. It was Sonal's skyrover. Their unbelieving, horrified eyes saw it flaring up like a space fireball. Flaring and disappearing, leaving no debris.

"Parachute!" Sonal shrieked, "Why didn't he parachute?"

Daniel sat staring with unbelieving eyes. JR was the best pilot he had ever come across. During the Seven-Day War, he had bailed out innumerable times, from various types of air vehicles, without a scratch or a burn on his body. Today, if he went away with the shuttle, it could mean only one thing.

Sonal felt hollow, empty, numb. As the reality of what had just happened hit her, her breath faltered. She slumped.

"Sonal . . . Sonal . . . SOONAAL . . ." Daniel gently shook her.

"The shuttle was serviced only yesterday," she choked. "I got it totally checked only yesterday."

"That was not due to any shuttle defect, Sonal."

"That means . . . that means that bomb was meant for me. I should have been there. If I was, JR would be alive." She shivered and started to sob uncontrollably.

Daniel's mind was smoldering like a nuclear chamber. Considering the questions tormenting him, he sat unmoving, unable to console her. Why was it that every murder made him wonder who was the targeted victim? Were they aiming for JR and got him? Or was that thunderbolt for Sonal?

The spacelink crackled. "Admiral, was that Sonal's shuttle?"

Daniel tried to focus his eyes. He glanced towards the spot where the ill-fated shuttle should have been. The void sent a convulsion sparkling through his body and mind.

"Admiral?" The voice was urging him to hold on. To focus. To speak. It was Shirakoo. "Admiral, are you there?"

"Yes, son. I think I must go to visit Aacharya right away. We may have to change our plans."

"You know, Thought-Admiral, Aacharya Shree must have witnessed it. Don't you think, sir, we should wait until he calls us?"

"If we do, next time . . ." Daniel stopped. He could not speak the words—*Sonal may not be so lucky.* Biting his lower lip, he glanced at the young girl sitting next to him, slumped in her seat. Her body still heaving with life-wrecking sobs.

"Next time we will try to be lucky, Admiral," Shirakoo's soothing voice came over the airwaves. "We will try. That's all we can do."

"No. Trying is not enough. We must do better." Looking at crumbling Sonal, the Admiral made an effort and straightened up. "We *will* do better." His voice returned to normal. It was again decisive. Authoritative. "Proceed as planned, Shirakoo."

He scanned the list on his audio and selected an old-time song. As he punched it on, soft music wafted towards them from the rear.

Beware of love.
Only love can catch you.
Only love can break your heart.
Beware of love.
Beware of love . . .

Sonal moved. He gently touched her shoulder. "Revenge is a deceiving, double-edge sword, Sonal. I never recommend it. But sometimes that's all that we have. Let's get going. There's a lot we must do in a very short time."

He offered her a tissue.

She accepted it, wiped her eyes, and blew her nose.

"Yes, Admiral," she replied, her voice heavy but not clogged. "Seems Shirakoo knows! He was not just my college-mate. He was doing JR's job! Wasn't he? Why? What's the big secret? Is it something that our parents did and SpacePol is afraid we may have inherited their dangerous traits. Is that it? Who were our parents? Who are we? Why does someone want to kill us?"

The Admiral was impressed by her ability to control herself.

"It's time for you to know," he replied evenly. "Let's get going. As soon as we are up, I'll tell you what I know. First, you need to learn about JALANGA and the blueprints its caretaker, Jal-O, has been preparing to trap our planet's future."

***

Jal-O sat slumped in his chair staring at the blueprints scattered around him. How could his immaculately drawn plans foul up so horribly?

Kato, his coming future's key, the best robo any mind could have conceived, was gone! Murdered by that vicious, conniving human, Falcon, who had disappeared destroying his precious LDM.

Falcon must be found and killed. Until then Operation Earth Shield must be shelved.

That would mean incurring Lord Kito's galaxy-spanning anger and delaying his own secret project, installing himself as the supreme ruler of this glorious water planet!

My biggest weakness, he was thinking, is that I care too much for others. I listen too much to others. If I had not listened to the stupid Board members . . . had not cared for them . . .

I was under the impression that analyzing my past failures, I had learned how to handle my weaknesses. This perfidious weakness I overlooked. That's why Falcon was able to benefit at my expense, just like that sorceress Drupatti had, more than once.

Was she behind this debacle, he wondered? Was it her spies who wormed into Falcon's mind and corrupted him? That must be it, because he did not have the knowledge or intelligence to engineer such a coup all by himself.

If he had not been merciful, if he had destroyed that Lokan Medusa, this would not have happened! Not again!

Lamenting, cursing himself, he again remembered that never-forgotten nightmare—that eligibility test in that snare-infested test arena. That stupid trickery, when protecting Ketki he was forced to surrender to that vicious hooliganism that no living being should be exposed to under any circumstances. Ever.

On that second day, it was still early morning, when trying to find the slowpoke Blackguards, they had reached those—now familiar—shoulder high, thick, sweet-smelling, blue and velvet bushes, and heard rustling sounds. Welcome sounds. Finally it was there—his best chance to kill the hiding cowards. This time he must teach Ketki how to toe the line and obey. He should not let her drag him to bite humiliation and defeat, he decided.

Looking around, he had tried to find her and had noticed she was well-hidden. But would she be able to protect herself?

The question was worth meditating. That, however, would mean diverting his attention. A no-no that he taught his students every day: that one must focus single-mindedly upon one's target. It was the only talisman one needed for success. A teacher must believe in his words. Therefore, he had immediately brought his mind back to those reckless, noisy feet that were trying to find him.

It was now or never. Remembering that, gritting his teeth, hidden amidst the tall, thick foliage, keeping his finger ready on his mock-gun, he started furrowing in the direction of the sounds. His progress was slow because he did not want to make noise. His legs were aching and barbed vines, drooping from tall trees, were snaring and pulling his hair. But untangling them, he kept bravely moving in the direction where dry undergrowth crackled under those steadily advancing, menacing feet.

As he moved closer, he heard voices coming from a clump of bushes on the opposite side. Holding his breath, he tried to pinpoint their location. The crunching leaves said they were moving away. That could be a false signal, a crooked trick of the Blackguards, devilish, conniving minds. They could not be trusted.

Soon he got proof it was good thinking. He heard soft twigs squelching nearby. Emitting a ferocious howl, he lunged from the safety of his bushes, aimed, and fired. His victim lunged at him and the ground came up to meet Jal-O as he found himself pinned under four round feet firmly planted against his waist and shoulders.

True to her character, Ketki came slithering right away to savor his humiliation. "Lokopokito," she hissed, "can't you distinguish between Lokan and animal feet?"

He felt revolted. It was her job to protect him. Neglecting it, without offering an apology, she was talking like *that!* "Get this thing off me," he had hissed. "Before it wolfs my neck."

"It's just a robo-hound. Programmed to act. It won't hurt you." Bending, she got hold of the hound's ear and turned it off. The light in its eyes instantly died, indicating that it was depowered.

Lifting it up effortlessly, she dunked it to one side. "Next time, do listen," she admonished and moved.

Cursing her silently, thinking about the humiliation—and because of it, having forgotten the nearby lurking Blackguards—he moved away from her, not realizing he was blindly pushing himself out of his bushes. It was only when the disaster suddenly loomed upon him that he realized he was standing in an open area, exposed to attack from three sides.

Once again Ketki had distracted him to the most deadly dead-stop brink that could exist in any universe. Thinking how to make her behave, as he was emerging from his secret shelter, a dye bullet came swishing towards his face.

Trying to dodge it, his foot got tangled in something and he plummeted. His palms got scratched, but the dye bullet missed. As he fell, hitting the twisted roots and heart shaped leaves, the mocking blood began to trickle down towards him. Before it could touch him, he rolled away and scrambled up. As always, after the tragedy had already happened, Ketki came running. Pushing him behind her back, she stood curtaining him as if she were capable of protecting him.

That was OK. What was truly atrocious was that her misplaced insolence got the better of her again. Not giving him time to get organized, without waiting for his orders, she started firing. Rapidly! Recklessly!

One's opponent's response in war, just like in love, always works like a rubber ball. It bounces back explosively. That's what happened. The Blackguards responded defiantly. They leaped out of their bushes, firing haphazardly. Their aimless bullets flew—whizzing, swishing, careening—splattering red dye on the swaying thistles all around them.

Following the time-honored battle tactic of backing one's troops' initiative, he decided to allow Ketki to win the glory of pushing back this assault, and kept himself behind her back.

She moved this way and that. Moving with her, maneuvering to maintain his position behind her, his foot got caught in vicious cobwebbing vines.

When he was yanking it out to get free, the lecherous vines tripped the leeching branches, and instantly, a flock of huge birds rose towards the blazing sky, cackling, flapping their enormous wings. That spontaneously triggered the Blackguard's cruel response. They drew knives from their belts and flung them up at the balloon-birds' lungs with all the force in their pitiless arms.

The balloon-birds exploded right away, not one by one, but all together.

From those scores of splitting, popping birds, foul, filthy liquid poured down upon them with such brute force that they reeled and doubled, drenched and suffocating, clawing for air.

To hide their stinking trick, to prove they had not set up that gutter-crawling trap, the Blackguard checkmaters started hurling foul curses upon him. "For this," coughing and spitting they shouted, "black holes will get you, freeze you in naked space."

"You chiliko-spits!" Coughing and wheezing, trying to recover his breath, he shouted back, "Your curses will roborang and blind you! Gobble every drop of your foul blood!"

They had been drenched in that foul smelling black liquid that only a vicious kid could have concocted in his secret lab. The only thing they could do was dash away from each other as fast as their feet, getting tangled in their wet uniforms, would allow them.

Soon Ketki slowed down. "Lokopokito, stop! Running like this draws attention. In this open area, anyone can pounce upon us."

"Let them. I don't care," he gasped, trying to breath.

"Yes, you do. Please listen . . ."

"For this," he shouted, stamping his feet, "space will gobble them alive. Their kids will stagnate in black holes."

"Stop such blasphemy! They were not responsible."

"Of course they were. They threw up their knives and ripped their bellies apart, didn't they? If they had not . . ."

"They were trying to save you. The robo-birds were right above your head. If they had not bursted their bellies, the birds would have swooped down, clutched you in their beaks or talons, and flown away. They spotted the danger planned in that trap and . . ."

"I'm suffocating with filth that won't clean for eons and you're laughing it away as if . . ."

"Who is laughing?" she retorted angrily. "I'm only saying you should not demean yourself cursing those who meant well."

"Why shouldn't I curse them?" he snarled. "Anyone would whose opponents checkmate him by setting up such a filthy trap."

"They did not set up that trap. It was an exam, to test our reflex action, and our presence of mind."

"How do you know that?"

"Just think. If it was their doing, they would have kept away. They also got drenched. Just like us. Second point: if they had set it up to checkmate you, they would not have risked dying by your bullets. They would not have tried to protect you from getting hoisted up atop the highest tree, to dangle in thin air, until the Rescue Shuttle could reach you."

That day, if he had not listened to Ketki's honey voice, he would have kept his anger alive and not shown any mercy to that treacherous Drupatti for designing that deadly, defeating trap.

If he had done so, she would not have been able to hypnotize Falcon, and subvert his life's most glorious mission.

If he had remembered his weakness of caring so much for the others, he would not have let the JALANGA Board members entrust such a secret, time-shattering job to a human. He would have allowed only Kato to handle it. Then all his plans would have worked perfectly.

When Drupatti hears about it . . .

Well, he wouldn't let her have the satisfaction. He would solve the problem and salvage the mission before she got a chance to learn about it.

Lord Kito is an experienced commander. He knows that one small setback does not mean one has lost a battle. No human exists in this whole galaxy who can checkmate a mind like Jal-O's. The LDM was his brain-child. He will make another. By using Falcon as his unwitting tool, Drupatti has only achieved a delay in the completion of his project.

A few weeks. That's all he would need to issue his second ultimatum. This time he would win because he would not depend upon any treacherous human. He would take care of everything himself. He would prove to Drupatti she could never match the expertise of a unicorn-blessed Lokan. He was capable of wresting control of a whole galaxy with only the help of his unparalleled creation, his alter-ego robot.

As soon as he had Kato-Two . . .

He must start designing him right away.

For that, Pashka's help would be needed.

Her vacation had to be canceled four times already this year. Last time he had agreed, there wouldn't be a fifth time. Would she rebel if he canceled it again?

Why would she? She is a logical person. She has a mind as good as his robos.

She knows how proud he was of Kato. She will understand how his Kato's untimely, undeserved death, would haunt him . . . tear him apart. If he presented the facts properly, hinted at Speedy Eyes' prompt, sudden, untimely demise . . .

That was it . . . that would do it.

Properly dressed in mourning clothes . . . presenting a mournful face . . . after a long, deep meditation session, and a relaxing bath. A bubble bath—something he never had on his home planet. Yes, that should put him in the mood to persuade dear Pashka.

She is only a human. Despite possessing a brain so logical that it seems more like a Lokan brain than a human hooter, she is a weak, maneuverable, emotional being. She will respond.

Feeling better, he pinned Kato's blueprint on the wall and strode towards his therapeutic bathroom to enjoy a long, healing bubble bath.

15

. . . To Keep the Earth

The world that is and the world to come are enemies. . . . We cannot be the friends of both; but must bid farewell to this world to consort with that to come.
                —St. Clement, *Second Epistle to the Corinthians,* c.150

                    .   .   .

O! pardon me,
thou bleeding piece of earth,
That I am meek and gentle
with these butchers;
Thou art the ruins of the
noblest man
That ever lived in the
tide of times.
                        —Shakespeare, *Julius Caesar*

                    .   .   .

*R*elaxing in his bathtub, he was playing chess. A new kind of game that he had invented—his pawns versus Kito's pawns.

His translink bleeped. Hoping it was the call for which he had been waiting, he quickly accepted it, "Yes?"

"Mano Bali, my orders just came," she sounded excited. "To catch the scheduled starflight, I must take the 2:00 P.M. shuttle."

Her excitement was catching. He had worked very hard to rescue the Earth Shield Project. Despite all his misgivings, he had succeeded. The truant Lokopokito had been checkmated. All that remained now was to tie up the loose ends.

It was obvious to everyone. Their culpable Lokopokito would not obey their orders and return. Someone needed to be sent to Earth to pick him up.

He was glad the Council had accepted his recommendation.

"Good," he said. "I'm glad. I know you will do a good job."

"I need your orders. I know they take precedence over all others. Do you have time now? Or should I call back."

He glanced at the chronometer on his wall. "Do you need time for last minute chores? How about Neha?"

She was touched. Despite all the worries and problems that must be crowding his mind, he remembered her unicorn! Feeling overwhelmed, she said, "Neha is in good hands. I am ready."

"Good. Meet me at the Unicorn Prairie in forty minutes."

"Thank you, Mano Bali. I will be there."

As he selected his traveling clothes, images of the recent past flickered in his mind. He saw Earth celebrating the twenty-third anniversary of its stepping into adulthood; Bakul's understudy bleeding on the stage; the holocaust at Shady point; Kato lying inert near the sabotaged LDM and Falcon flying away . . . the Lokopokito brooding over charts and blueprints to design Kato Two.

He flicked on the blue wheel, and turned its spokes until the central one rested on that last image. "Ah! my misbegotten Lokopokito, I can see how your third eye will behave when you would learn who I am sending to take care of you. You have become so fond of Earth literature. Hearing the news, would you still sing:

Tell me not here, it needs not saying,
What tune the enchantress plays
In aftermaths of soft September
Or under blanching Mays,

For she and I were long acquainted
And, I knew all her ways.

Switching off the wheel, he hastened to get ready. He needed to be careful because he had to make sure no one would be able to recognize him. It would have been easier to tell her to come to his Lokan Council office. But that was the best way to advertise that he had seen her. He had learned that from his father. The best way to keep his activities unnoticed was to conduct them in areas where anyone could walk in any time.

Camouflaged in his toe-length hooded robe, with the deep cowl that hid his face, he was satisfied that she wouldn't be able to figure out what he looked like. As an added precaution—just in case she caught a glimpse of his face—he browsed through his face masks and selected one that looked like an old Lokan's. It was a perfect disguise.

***

She was waiting for him.

As he energized near her, she smiled and handed him a disk containing her orders. He knew it was a copy she had made for him. Slipping it in his pocket, he asked, "I had suggested they should give you the rank of Kopokito. Did they?"

She nodded, "That was such a big surprise. I wasn't expecting it. What will our Lokopokito do when he learns about it?"

"That you are two ranks above him?" he grinned. "He should feel proud that such a senior-ranking officer came all the way to escort him home."

He has a good sense of humor, she thought. *He trusts me enough to let me handle the most sensitive jobs. Why doesn't he trust me enough to let me see his face?*

Misreading the quest on her face, he asked, "Are you feeling afraid? Worried?"

"No, why should I? This is the first time you have given me such an easy job. All I have to do is pick up our Lokopokito and bring him back. Shouldn't take more than a couple of days."

He looked at her excited face and wondered how to tell her what he had brought her here to tell. How would she react?

Just then two baby unicorns came running, as if racing who would reach them first. They nuzzled against his robe trying to find his legs. He scratched their foreheads and necks. "We will play later," he told them. "Right now, I am busy."

Nodding, they ran back.

"Why don't we sit down for a few minutes," he said, indicating the benches lying under a nearby tree and walking to them.

She followed quietly and pulled a low stool to sit near him. But as soon as she sat down, instead of saying anything, he got up and started pacing, his cowled head and shoulders drooping, weighted down by some unseen weight.

That surprised her. His visits were always short. Orders, brief and precise. Since she had known him, he had never behaved in such a brooding, indecisive manner. Was it the question of the seven youngsters that was tormenting him so much?

To help him, she said softly, "My orders say if the humans ask, I can tell them the seven are LAB-Lokans."

"That's right," he nodded absent-mindedly.

"If they ask why were they sent to Earth?"

He stopped, "The reason given to you in your briefings should be sufficient. The Lokan mothers hid them there to protect them from their LAB fathers."

Looking at her face, suddenly he realized he was creating in her mind needless anxieties. Returning to his bench, he sat down, "You are not going to catch Lokopokito and bring him back."

She was startled. So, that was it. Her orders had been canceled. She was being replaced by someone more capable. Hiding her disappointment, she asked, "Who is going to do it?"

"Sorry," he said. "I should begin from the beginning. You will go to Earth as scheduled. You will follow all your orders, except one. You will not capture Lokopokito."

"But that is the only reason for my trip. When the new LDM is ready, Prince Kadamb will himself head the Earth security delegation. The Council is sending me only to bring him back."

"True," he nodded. "The Council is sending you only to bring him back here. I'm sending you to make sure he stays on Earth."

He got up, paced a few steps, and came back, "You are entitled to an explanation. Last night, I checked Vishnu's Earth *Chakra,* the blue wheel. It requires Lokopokito to remain on Earth at least six months' Earth time. Perhaps, even more."

She looked appalled, "I would have to stay there that long?"

"If you prefer not to go, I will back you up," he said affectionately. "I will find an explanation for the Council."

"May I ask the reason?"

"Why he is required there? Sure," he sat down beside her. "I can only guess. The *Chakra* does not specify, it only displays. My logic says Earth's life force is gearing itself to take a critical turn. Perhaps, he is the cataclysm required to trigger it."

He touched her shoulder, gently, briefly, "You must forget it, as if you have never heard it. It is a secret between the two of us, that you cannot reveal to anyone. *Anyone.*"

She did not say anything, so he quietly added, "You have proved yourself several times. On Mandal Loka, there is no one else whom I can trust so implicitly. On Earth, you will be my only hands, eyes and ears. You have my personal code, Kopokito. Any problem you have, you call me directly."

"Oh, yes?" she looked up at him and smiled. "Call only if it is a matter of life and death. Not mine, but the planet's. That's what you told me the last time when you gave me the code."

The way she said it, he started laughing. "Good you reminded me. That was last time. This time the rules are different. This time you call me if you feel someone is getting close to catching him."

Would the surprises he was inflicting upon her never cease! "You mean ... "

"Exactly," he said, taking out his translink pad from his pocket, indicating he was ready to leave. "Without exposing yourself, making sure no one can guess you are doing it, you must make sure no one catches him, or harms him. I know you. You can do it."

She stared at him. *Easy for you to say,* she thought. *I will be alone there, on that primitive planet. My every breath will be dependent upon the whims of those blood-thirsty humans. If they find out about my duplicity, what will they do to me?*

Hiding her emotions, she merely asked, "What would happen when the Council starts asking why is it taking weeks and months to finish a five-day job?"

"Don't worry about that. You have a trump card—*Star Kahuna.*"

"The schooner he built for himself there?"

He nodded, "They did not tell you something. Perhaps hoping that if do not know about it, you may be able to overcome it."

"I have never known you to pose so many riddles. Overcome what?"

"No one knows why has he named it *Star Kahuna.* What is it capable of doing? So far, we have learned only one thing. Like that mythical Hansa Yan, it can change shape. The Council knows: they have given you the toughest job of your career; it will be almost impossible to find him. Forget months. If you take years, they won't question it."

"But . . . but, that means Operation Earth Shield is doomed."

"Why?" he sounded surprised.

"Our Lokopokito has a one-track mind. He loves the number four. In the privacy of his shape-shifting schooner, he can make four or forty, as many as he wants, and blow up the Earth to its moon."

"He won't."

"What makes you so sure?"

"Two reasons. First, he is craving to install himself as the first Lokani. He will inflict only so much damage as he thinks will bring the humans crawling to him on their knees. My logic, however, says that reason is not as important as the second one."

He stopped. Not able to bear the suspense, she said, "If you want me to guess it, the answer is *no*. I cannot guess it."

He heaved a big sigh, "I hate to say it, and would prefer not to believe it. But facts cannot be nullified just by not accepting them. Maybe . . . maybe, this would be the cataclysm the Vishnu Chakra is predicting."

"Space preserve me!"

"I will pray for that. Come back in good health. As long as you are there, may Mandal Loka's blessings protect you."

She smiled mischievously, "Not yours?"

"Mine you have had, Kopokito, since before you were born," he said cryptically, touched his translink, and disappeared.

She stood rooted staring at the spot where he had been standing. Often she had wondered. Today, again that suspicion whirled in her mind. "Are you an Upper One?" she whispered. "Is that why I cannot see your face?"

As if to answer her question, the baby unicorns came racing and stopped near her feet.

She put her arms around their necks, "Have you come to give me my home planet's blessings and bid me good-bye? I feel honored and privileged. To prove that, I will not use the translink to frizzle away. I will walk on my soil. I will take the boat to the shuttle waiting for me. If you will come with me, I will know—some day I will be taking that boat again to come back to you."

She got up and moved. The baby unicorns flanked her, one on each side, and moved with her at her pace. Not very far away, the lake shimmered. As she neared it, an automated boat came sailing and anchored itself to wait for her.

"*Star Kahuna,*" she whispered stepping into it, "here I come, riding upon the destiny of my unicorns. I bet our combined destiny that I will checkmate you at your own game."

Dr. Soma Vira

*T*his remarkable story, and the others in the series, come from a remarkable woman. Born in Lucknow, India, Soma Vira succeeded at writing at an early age, winning the *All-India Youth Festival* and *All-India Radio Play* awards.

Still in India, for a time she helped edit children's pages of the Bombay newspaper *Nava Bharat Times.*

Then Ms. Vira moved to the United States and earned a Masters Degree in journalism from the University of Colorado at Boulder. The University nominated her as one of the "Ten Outstanding American Women." In 1990, she was nominated for *Who's Who Worldwide.*

After her Colorado years, Ms. Vira gained a Ph.D. in political science and economic development from New York University. Simultaneously, she served as a lecturer with the Speaker Services division of the United Nations.

In addition to those duties and her continued writing, she has served in several ethnic organizations: as membership director and member of the Board of Trustees of the Association of Indians in Amerca, and as Founder-Organizer Committeee Member of the Global Organization of people of Indian Origin, Inc. She owns and operates Vira Insurance Protection Services in New York City.